D1244968

LATTER
END

LATTER END

A MISS SILVER MYSTERY

Patricia Wentworth

OPEN ROAD

INTEGRATED MEDIA

NEW YORK

All rights reserved, including without limitation the right to reproduce this book or any portion thereof in any form or by any means, whether electronic or mechanical, now known or hereinafter invented, without the express written permission of the publisher.

This is a work of fiction. Names, characters, places, events, and incidents either are the product of the author's imagination or are used fictitiously. Any resemblance to actual persons, living or dead, businesses, companies, events, or locales is entirely coincidental.

Copyright © 1949 by Patricia Wentworth

Cover design and illustration by Jeffrey Nguyen

ISBN: 978-1-5040-4792-0

This edition published in 2017 by Open Road Integrated Media, Inc.
180 Maiden Lane
New York, NY 10038
www.openroadmedia.com

LATTER
END

ONE

The room had seemed dark to Mrs Latter when she came in, but that was because everything in it was black. The carpet on the floor, the hangings covering the walls, the long straight curtains, were all of the same even velvety blackness. But it was not as dark as she had thought. Through the one unscreened window light shone in. She found herself facing this light, as she faced the man who called himself Memnon, across the table which stood between them. It was quite a small table, covered with a black velvet spread, and seeming smaller because the old man in the chair was so large.

As she took the seat he indicated she looked at him curiously. If he thought he could impress or frighten her by all this jiggery-pokery he could think again. She was a fool to have come. But when all your friends were doing something you did it too. If you didn't—well, what was there to talk about? Everybody was talking about Memnon. He told you the most thrilling things. He told the past, and he told the future. He managed to make the present seem important and interesting instead of rather flat and dull, with the war over and everyone too hard up for words.

She gazed across at him, and could see very little more than his shape, and the shape of the chair against the light. The chair stood symmetrically to the window, outlined against it—high arched back, strong spreading arms. Rising above the back, an old man's head covered with a velvet cap. She didn't know why she was sure that he was old. It wasn't his voice or anything she could see. It wasn't that anyone had spoken of him as old. It was just an impression. With the light in her eyes like this she couldn't distinguish his features, only a pale, blurred oval, so much higher up than one expected. He must be very tall to sit so high. And he must have very long arms. It was a long way to where two pale hands rested upon the jutting arms of the chair.

As these thoughts passed through her mind, she was settling herself, laying her bag across her knees, folding her hands upon it, leaning back, smiling easily. It wasn't every woman of her age who could face the light with so much equanimity. Thirty-seven years had taken nothing from the smooth brilliance of her skin. They had only refined tint, features, and outline, leaving her a good deal more attractive than she had been at twenty. Mistress of herself, of her thoughts, of her life. Very much mistress of Jimmy Latter, Jimmy Latter's thoughts, and Jimmy Latter's life.

The continuing silence gave her a slightly contemptuous feeling. It would take more than a dark room and an old man looking at her to disturb her poise. The situation or the circumstances which she could not dominate were as yet an unknown quantity. She had sailed easily through her life and her two marriages. James Doubleday had left her his money. The unpleasantness about his will had been triumphantly surmounted. She had chosen Jimmy Latter to succeed him, and she was prepared to maintain that she had chosen well. You can't have everything, and the will had been still in doubt. Antony was very charming—when he liked. But you don't take the poor cousin when you can have the rich one—not at thirty-five, when you are old enough to realise that if you are clever you can both eat your cake and have it.

Not that Jimmy was rich—he had far less than she had imagined. But fortunately James Doubleday's will had turned out all right, and Latter End was really the setting of her dreams—small and lovely, untouched by the war, needing only the money she would be able to spend on it now.

If it had only been Antony's . . . It might be yet . . . The thought passed through her mind like a breath. Antony—she was lunching with him when all this mumbo-jumbo was over. Her smile became a perfectly natural one.

All at once she saw Memnon looking at her. With her eyes more accustomed to the curious lighting, she could see that his were very deeply set. They looked at her from overarching caves of bone. She could see heavy eyebrows blurring the arch. And then she could only see his eyes. She thought they were dark. He said in a deep, whispering voice,

'Give me your hand—both hands.'

Lois Latter hesitated. The voice was a whispering bass. It set up curious reverberations in the room. There was a crystal ball on the table between them. The light from the window struck on one side of it, making it shine like a moon half full. Lois dropped her eyes to it.

'Don't you look in the crystal? I thought you did. That's what I came for.'

He put up a hand and took the crystal away. She didn't see what happened to it. The half-moon went out. When he moved she thought the drapery of a cloak moved too. The crystal ball had gone. He said in that whispering voice,

'Give me your hands.'

She put them out as if she were pushing something away, and he met them with his own, palm to palm, finger to finger, stiffly upright, like hands conjoined in prayer. His hands and hers. Two pairs of hands. There was a tingling contact. It ran up her arms and down through all her body to her feet. Her breathing quickened. She wanted to speak, to draw away. But for once in her life she didn't do what she wanted to do. She sat still and suffered the contact and the tingling. Her eyes were held by his. There was a sense of contact there too, a sense of being probed and searched.

Then all at once it was over. He dropped his lids, withdrew his hands, leaned back, and said,

'You will have to be very careful.'

Something startled her—something in the way he said it, the very deep voice muted to the verge of inaudibility. She lifted her hands from the table and folded them in her lap before she spoke.

'What have I got to be careful about?'

He said,

'Poison.'

The word came whispering into the air. Mrs Latter felt it vibrate somewhere deep in her mind. She waited for the vibration to die away. Then she said,

'What do you mean?'

'That you must be careful.'

'Of poison?'

'Yes.'

'Do you mean that someone is going to try and poison me? Is that what you mean?'

His voice was rather louder as he said, 'It might be—' There was a considering note in it.

She thought, 'He doesn't know anything really—he's guessing. It's nothing.' Aloud she asked,

'Is that all? What is the good of telling me to be careful if you don't tell me any more than that?'

He took a long time to answer.

'Each of us has to guard his own house of life. I cannot tell you how to guard yours. I can only tell you it is threatened.'

'By poison?'

'Yes.'

'What kind of poison?'

'That is more than I can say. There are many kinds. Some threaten the mind, and some the body. You just guard yourself. I can only warn you.'

Lois sat up straight. Her voice was tinged with contempt, but under the contempt something jerked. She kept her tone steady, but she could feel fear twitching at it under the control.

'You must tell me a little more, I think. Who is threatening me?'

'Someone very near.'

'Man, or woman?'

'Man—woman—I think—I am not sure. It might be you yourself. It is very near—you are mixed up in it.'

Lois laughed. Her laugh had always been admired. It rippled sweetly through the room now.

'I assure you I have no intention of poisoning myself.'

He said, so low that she could only just catch the words,

'There is more than one kind of poison.'

TWO

Anthony Latter stood against the pillar and watched Lois come in through the swing-door and make her way across the anteroom to the inner lounge of the Luxe. He was in no hurry to go and meet her. It was always a pleasure to see Lois come into a room—she walked so well, and she looked as if she had bought the earth. The earth and Jimmy Latter. His mouth tightened a little. Poor old Jimmy. What did it feel like to be thrown in as a make-weight? Not too good, but heaven doesn't help you unless you help yourself. Anyhow here was Lois, as fresh as paint in a slim black suit which showed off her figure and flattered her skin, the white camellia of a blameless life at the newest, smartest angle, and the latest bit of nonsense adorning the auburn waves of her hair. As he went to meet her he reflected that he had never seen her with one of those waves disturbed. Other women got hot and untidy, their hair straggled and their noses shone, but not Lois. Ben Jonson's verse flitted ironically through his mind:

> Still to be neat, still to be drest
> As you were going to a feast.
> Still to be powdered, still perfumed—

As he shook hands with her he wondered whether he dared quote the lines to Lois, and whether she would know how they ended if he did.

> Lady, it is to be presumed . . .
> All is not sweet, all is not sound.

In fact, Ben liked 'er untidy.

He laughed, and thought he had better be discreet. He and Lois had done some hard hitting in their time, but this was another time, and—she was Jimmy's wife.

As they moved towards the dining-room, one of the great mirrors reflected them side by side. Lois thought they made an excellent pair. Antony was distinguished—that tall, light figure, and the way he moved. He was better looking than he had been two years ago. He was twenty-nine—a man was at his best at twenty-nine. Eight years between them, but nobody would have guessed it. She was still at her best. No one would take her for more than twenty-seven. No one would dream that she was older than Antony.

She was still pleasurably occupied with these thoughts when they arrived at their table and sat down. They persisted under the light give-and-take of talk. Was he really quite fit again? What did it feel like being out of the army after five years? Was he going to like being in a publishing firm?

'You—and books? A bit dry-as-dust somehow!'

A dazzling smile made the words a compliment.

Antony said coolly, 'I happen to like books—a good deal.'

It went through his mind how eagerly he would have poured out all his plans two years ago. It seemed incredible now.

She was saying, still looking at him, still smiling,

'I'm sure you'll make the biggest success of it, darling.'

The word jarred. Common small change of her set though it was, it jarred. He said,

'I shall undoubtedly discover best-sellers right and left.'

She laughed.

'You haven't changed a bit!'

'Haven't I? Let me return the ball. You look marvellous. But then you always did.'

'Thank you, darling! But a little less of the always, don't you think? Rather dating, I'm afraid.'

'You don't need to mind about that.'

She said, 'Don't be stupid,' in quite a natural voice.

That was the worst of it—it was too easy to be natural with Antony. It always had been. However much she struggled against it, there was the temptation to let go, to relax, to stop being what she wanted people to think her and just be her-self—the self which she never allowed anyone to see—a self which Antony would probably not admire at all.

She laughed her pretty laugh.

'My dear, if I look like anything at all I'm a marvel. I've just had the most shattering experience.'

'Have you? Look here, I've ordered lunch—will you just take it as it comes?'

'Yes, please. You ought to know what I like—if you haven't forgotten. But really, darling, I meant it about the shattering experience. I've been to see Memnon.'

He gazed at her placidly.

'Memnon?'

Before she could answer, the waiter was bringing them fish. It was a curious moment to feel, as she did then suddenly feel, that she had been every kind of damned fool to let Antony go.

When the waiter had gone away she rushed into telling him about Memnon, because not for the world must there be one of those silences. Something in his look, in his dry, light tone, had got under her guard and shaken her as she had not been shaken for years. She must talk, make a good story of her visit, regain her cool direction of events.

When Antony said, 'That charlatan!' she was ready with a laugh.

'Perhaps. But, darling, such a thrill! It was worth every penny of what I paid him.'

Antony's brows lifted—odd crooked brows, black, in a dark sardonic face. Under them his eyes looked black too until the light struck them and showed them grey.

'And what did you pay him?'

'Ten pounds. Don't tell, will you. We're frightfully hard up and everything to do to the house, but everyone's going to him, and one might as well be dead as out of the swim.

Actually, I suppose, one's been dead for years—the war and all that. But now'—she let her eyes meet his—'I'm coming alive again.'

'Very interesting feeling. What did the magician say to you?'

She drew back. No good trying to rush him, he always hated it. Better go on talking about Memnon. She said with a catch in her voice,

'He was—rather creepy.'

'Part of the stock in trade.'

'No, but he really was. He very nearly rattled me.'

Antony looked politely surprised.

'He must be pretty good. What did he do—or say?'

He was looking at her with some attention. The clear, natural colour in her cheeks had ebbed. The women who refused to believe that it owed nothing to art would perforce have been converted.

Antony Latter made a mental note of the fact that the charlatan had really frightened Lois. He hadn't thought it could be done, but Memnon had evidently done it. It didn't occur to him then that her change of colour had anything to do with himself.

They were being served again. When their waiter had come and gone she said quite low,

'It was rather horrid.'

'Don't tell me he got fresh! But I'm sure you were more than equal to the occasion. Snubbing a magician would be a new experience—and what else does one live for? You're not going to tell me you lost your nerve?'

'It wasn't anything like that. And I'm serious—it was horrid.'

His eyebrows rose.

'Don't tell me he raised the ghosts of all the unfortunates whom you have stabbed with a glance or frozen with a frown!'

She said very low,

'I'm serious. I told you so.'

'And you expect me to encourage you, put straws in both our hairs—they'll spoil your wave—sit on the floor and moan to the appropriately barbaric strain which the orchestra is at present discoursing? We shall be in all the gossip notes, if that is what you want—"Major Antony Latter, who has just joined the publishing firm founded by his famous great-uncle Ezekiel—"'

She interrupted him in a gentle, hurt voice.

'I want to tell you about it. Won't you listen?'

She was pale and appealing. He hadn't ever seen her like that before.

'What on earth did the fellow say to you?'

She dropped her voice until he could only just hear the words.

'He said—I've got to be careful—about poison.'

Antony sat back in his chair.

'What an extraordinary thing to say!'

'Yes, wasn't it? Not very nice.'

'Not a bit. What made him say a thing like that?'

Her colour was coming back—the pure, bright colour which was her greatest beauty. Yet without it she had been younger.

Antony thought, 'That's curious.'

Lois felt an odd sense of relief. He was really looking at her, really listening to her now. She told him more than she had meant to tell—to him or to anyone.

'He said most extraordinary things. He said someone was trying to poison me—he really did.'

'The food here isn't really as bad as all that.'

'Don't joke about it. It was horrible. I'm not very easy to frighten—you know that. But he—almost—frightened me.'

'He was out to make your flesh creep, and apparently he succeeded.'

She shook her head.

'Not quite. But it isn't exactly pleasant to be told that some-one—very near—is trying to poison you.'

'He said that?'

'Yes, he did—someone very near me. But he wouldn't say whether it was a man or a woman. He said he didn't know. Why, he even said it might be I myself!' Her laugh was not quite steady. 'And I told him I was the last person in the world to take poison. I like my life a great deal too much to throw it away.'

'Yes—I think you do.'

She had taken out a cigarette, and leaned towards him now for a light. When the tip was glowing red and a little haze of smoke hung on the air between them, she said in a puzzled voice,

'He said such a very odd thing—he said there was more than one kind of poison.'

'How trite—how true!'

'It didn't sound trite—not when he said it.'

Antony laughed.

'The man has glamour, or women wouldn't be paying him tenners to turn it on.'

Those lightly sketched brows of hers drew together in distaste.

'He was quite old—there wasn't anything like that. Let's talk about something else.'

THREE

Antony came out of the Luxe and got on to a bus. Change of air was indicated. He was going in search of it.

When he got off the bus he made his way to one of those blocks of flats which were being built just before the war to accommodate office workers. This one had ridden out the storm, and with the exception of window-glass and paint it was as it had come from the builder's hands in 1938. There was an automatic lift, and Antony went up in it—right up to the fifth floor, where he pressed an electric buzzer and had the door opened to him by Julia Vane.

Julia and her sister Ellie Street were the daughters of Jimmy Latter's stepmother by a second marriage. Antony and Jimmy were first cousins on the Latter side. As the girls had grown up at Latter End and Antony had spent all his holidays there, they were on the sort of terms which admit of intimacy, affection, and a familiarity which may breed anything between contempt and love. In fact a very wide frame into which almost any picture could be fitted.

Antony may have had Julia in his mind when he contrasted Lois with the less fortunate women who got hot and untidy. Julia, opening the door to him, was hot and untidy. Her curly dark hair looked as if she had just run her hands through it, and there was ink on her nose. It would, of course, have been worse if the hair had been straight, but no girl looks her best when she is imitating a golliwog. Julia knew this for herself, and it was having a devastating effect on her temper. To expect the baker's boy, and to open the door all inky to Antony for whom she had broken her heart two years ago, was enough to set the mildest temper in a blaze, especially when he had been lunching with Lois. She had got over Antony of course—you do if you make up your mind to it. The whole thing was dead. She hadn't seen him for two years. She dared the dead thing to stir in its shroud.

Antony looked at her glowering at him across the threshold. He couldn't see that two years had changed her at all. One of her untidier moments, but the same Julia. Too much brow and too much chin, but the bones all good, and between brow and chin those dark, heavily lashed eyes which could be passionately glad or passionately unhappy. Julia never did anything by halves, just now they were passionately cross.

He put a hand on her shoulder, laughing, turned her about, and came in with her, shutting the door behind them.

There was no lobby, and only the one room—a big room, partitioned all down one side to make bathroom, dressing-room, kitchenette. There was a divan which obviously became a bed at night. There were two really comfortable chairs. There was a plain strong table littered with manuscript, but otherwise the room was surprisingly tidy, and the colours were good—deep, rich, and restful. There were a couple of Persian runners on the floor. He liked Julia's room, and was actually on the verge of telling her so, when he changed his mind.

'You've got ink on your nose, darling.'

She flamed at once. Quite the old Julia.

'If you *will* come when I'm working, you must take me as you find me! You've seen me with ink on my nose before!'

'I have. But, as I have invariably pointed out, you look better without it.'

'I don't care how I look!'

'Darling, that's only too painfully obvious. Comb the hair and wash the face, and then you can give me the low-down on the family.'

'I haven't really got time,' said Julia. But the flame died down. Quite suddenly the one thing she wanted on earth was to get away from Antony's teasing eyes.

She disappeared into one of the cubicles. When she came back the nose was inkless and the hair in not unattractive curls.

'As a matter of fact I didn't think you'd be here so soon. Lunch with Lois generally takes longer than that.'

'How do you know I was having lunch with Lois?'

'Didn't you tell me? No, she did—she would of course!'

'Darling, that sounds like womanly spite.'

'It is.'

A laughing look just lit her eyes, and then burned out. What was the use of talking to Antony about Lois? He'd been crazy about her two years ago, and even if he wasn't now, she would probably be one of those lingering memories. Men were more sentimental than women. And always, always, always they hated to hear a woman run another woman down.

She laughed, out loud this time. How furious Antony would be if anyone called him sentimental.

'What are you laughing at?'

Julia said, 'Us.'

'Why?'

'You might have been away two minutes instead of two years.'

'Because I told you about the ink? A nice homely touch, I thought.'

She nodded. When she wasn't in a rage with him, or breaking her heart, there was that quick give and take between them which uses words but hardly needs them. Just now she wasn't angry and her heart was behaving itself. She felt young and happy, as if not two years but a dozen had been rolled away, and Antony home for the holidays, coming up to schoolroom tea. You washed your face and hands and combed your hair, and as long as Miss Smithers was there you were on your best behaviour, but as soon as tea was over and they could escape to the garden—

They sat side by side on the divan, Antony in a beautiful new suit which must have cost the earth, and Julia, who wasn't a little girl any more but a struggling novelist, in an old red smock as inky as her nose had been.

Antony was saying, 'Well now, what about everything— and everyone?'

'You haven't seen Jimmy?'

'No. I rang him up. I shall be going down to Latter End in a day or two. I wondered if you would be there.'

Her black brows drew together.

'I may have to go down. I don't want to. Look here, what has Lois been telling you?' She reached sideways, rummaged behind a cushion, and produced a packet of cigarettes. 'Here—have one.'

'Thanks, I'll smoke my own.'

'Not good enough for you?'

'You've taken the words out of my mouth. Control the temper, darling, and have one of mine.'

If she had been going to be angry, it passed. She laughed instead. It was his old game of fishing for a rise. Just at the moment she didn't even want to.

He struck a match and lighted her cigarette. Their lips were very near. With sickening suddenness Julia's heart turned over. 'Oh, God, it's all going to begin again! How damnable to be a woman!'

She drew back, her face gone hard, all the muscles tightened, the brow heavy, the bones of the chin defined. Before he could speak she had repeated her question.

'What did Lois tell you?'

He drew at his cigarette.

'I gathered from her, and from Jimmy, that I should find a regular family party at Latter End. Ellie and Minnie are there, aren't they?'

'Oh, yes!'

'And what do you mean by that, and by *having* to go down?'

She blew out a little cloud of smoke.

'Did Lois tell you how she was running the house?'

'She gave me to understand that it was the perfect communist state—each for all and all for each.'

'Do you see Lois being communal?'

'Frankly, no. But she was quite lyrical over the beauty of the arrangement.'

Julia looked at him with frowning intensity.

'Did she tell you who did the work?'

'I gathered that Mrs Maniple was still in the kitchen, but practically single-handed.'

'There's a girl from the village, one of the Pells—quite a nice child. Even Lois couldn't expect Manny to scrub all those stone floors.'

'She did say Manny was getting past her work.'

'She cooks like an angel, but Lois will out her as soon as she can find anyone else. Manny hates her, and she knows it. Of course she's pretty old. She remembers Jimmy being christened.'

'Well, he's only—what is it—fifty-one?'

'She was kitchenmaid—that would make her about seventy. At the moment Jimmy is digging his toes in, but it's not much good with Lois. Well, that's the kitchen. Did she tell you who did all the rest of the work?'

Julia leaned forward with her eyes blazing.

'Mrs Huggins comes up from the village once a week and the garden boy fills the coal scuttles, and every other blessed bit of work in the house is done by Minnie and Ellie! Lois does damn-all!'

Antony murmured, 'Each for all, and all for each—'

'Each and all for Lois,' said Julia roundly. 'You've just been having lunch with her. Did her hands look as if she ever did any housework? Ellie used to have pretty hands—'

'Well, why do they stand it? Why don't they go off and get themselves decent jobs?'

Julia drew fiercely at her cigarette.

'What sort of job could Minnie Mercer get? She's never been trained for anything, and she's nearly fifty. She's always lived in Rayle, and ever since Dr Mercer died she's been at Latter End. She's a pet and an angel, but it's no good pretending she's got a backbone, because she hasn't. She's anybody's doormat. And as long as it was Jimmy and Mummy it didn't matter, because they loved her, and she was perfectly happy being their doormat. It's not so much fun when it's Lois.'

Her voice went down into its own depths and was lost, but her eyes went on speaking. They said furiously, 'Go on! Take up the cudgels and defend her! Say how delightful it would be to be Lois's doormat! Say how much you enjoyed it yourself two years ago!'

Antony said nothing. He allowed a slightly sarcastic smile to curve his lips and waited for the silence to suggest to Julia that she was making a fool of herself. When a betraying colour ran up into her cheeks he said,

'All right, I grant you Minnie—she wouldn't transplant. But Ellie could get herself a job, couldn't she?'

'She won't—because of Ronnie. I suppose they oughtn't to have married on nothing, but they were awfully in love, and everyone round them was doing it, so they did it too. He was training for estate management under old Colonel Fortescue's agent, and the job more or less promised to him when Mr Bunker retired. Well, now that Ronnie has lost a leg it isn't so easy. Colonel Fortescue has been awfully decent—he'll hold the job for any reasonable time. I believe he's doing the work himself, but it's too much for him. Old Bunker died just before the total surrender, and the bother is, Ronnie's not up to it—he still has a lot of pain, and they can't get him fitted with an artificial leg. Well, he's in hospital at Crampton, and Ellie can get over to see him two or three times a week. That's what keeps her at Rayle, but what with doing twice as much as she ought to do in the house, and those long bicycle rides, it's getting her down. She has just gone away to a shadow.'

The antagonism between them had died. She was talking and he was listening as if they were still part of one family, one household, with no Lois to disturb its peace or wrench its ties apart. He said,

'I see. And Ellie isn't much of a go-getter—she never was.'

'We can't all be go-getters. And I thought men didn't like them anyway.'

'They don't, unless it's very carefully concealed.'

Her eyes laughed scornfully back at him.

'That's it! I seem to remember your telling me I'd never get a husband if I didn't get a nice velvet glove to cover my iron hand. Well, I haven't got a husband.'

Antony smiled disarmingly.

'And you don't want one. You see, I know all the answers. You hate, loathe and despise my unfortunate sex, and you wouldn't dream of marrying one of them. But, my child, take it from me that the most ferocious man-eating female of the pack rather likes to feel that she could have had one of the despicable creatures if she had wanted to. It would, for instance, be a solace to your old age to remember how many of us you had refused. I suppose you would refuse us?'

'What do you think?'

'Well, I don't know, and I'd rather like to. Just as a matter of academic interest of course. Suppose I were to say, "Darling, I love you passionately," what would be your reaction?'

Julia was as honest as she was brave. Her courage stood up well to the stab, but her honesty took rather a bad fall. She was pleased and amazed to hear herself laugh and say,

'When you do love me passionately you'll find out.'

He said in rather an odd voice,

'The question is adjourned. Perhaps we'd better get back to Ellie. Street must have something?'

Julia felt as if she had been running hard. She took a long breath.

'They've got about three hundred pounds between them, and they're hanging on to it like mad to furnish their house if he gets Colonel Fortescue's job. There's a house, but nothing in it.'

'How soon is Street likely to be fit?'

'They don't know. That's really why I'm going down. Look here, you won't say anything, will you, but Ellie thinks they'd let Ronnie out of hospital if she had anywhere to take him. She says Matron told her so last time she went over. You see, he's rather got stuck. They think if he was at home with her, it would give him a lift. The question is, can it be managed?'

'Jimmy—'

'It isn't Jimmy, and you know it. It's Lois. Jimmy would say yes like a shot, but if Lois says no, it's no. You think I can't be fair about her, but I'm being as fair as I can. From Ellie's point of view and mine Jimmy is our brother, and Latter End has always been our home. From Jimmy's point of view Ellie and I are his sisters, he is very fond of us, and Latter End is still our home. But from Lois' point of view we don't count—we're not any relation at all. The way she looks at it, Jimmy's stepmother went off and married a man called Vane who got killed in a car smash, after which she came back to Latter End, had twins, and imposed on Jimmy's good nature by staying on and bringing them up there. Lois thinks Jimmy was lamentably weak over the whole business. At least when Mummy died he could have pushed us out to earn our living, instead of which he just went on pretending that we were his sisters, and that he liked having us there. You see, I'm being perfectly fair.'

Antony blew out a lazy curl of smoke.

'Oh, perfectly.'

'I do see her point, you know. She's married Jimmy, but she hasn't married his stepmother's twins. What gets me is that she tries to have it both ways—makes Jimmy think she's an angel to have Ellie there, and then treats her like a housemaid and works her to death. You know'—Julia's voice fairly throbbed—'if I weren't pretty strong-minded and a lot of other things which you think women oughtn't to be, I'd probably be doing scullerymaid at Latter End myself.'

Antony blew another cloud of smoke.

'A very nice womanly occupation, darling.'

His glance travelled to the hands which lay in the lap of Julia's old red smock. An ink-smudge not quite washed out made a blue shadow on the right forefinger. The nails, most beautifully shaped, were innocent of stain or varnish. The hands were innocent of rings. They were as nature had made them, and nature had made them well. They were not small, and they were not white, but they were very beautiful hands.

Antony said 'No!' with great suddenness and explosive force.

'No what?'

'I forgot about your hands. Let all the women with hideous magenta nails go and be scullions—it would do 'em good! You've got the second—no, the third—most beautiful hands in Europe. The other two are on statues. And if you don't take care of them, you'll find yourself in the special hell reserved for people who destroy works of art.'

Julia said what she had never thought of saying.

'What a pity my face doesn't match.' The words just came out of her mouth and left her feeling as if she had opened a door and let something escape.

Antony shook his head.

'You'd find it very inconvenient, darling—you'd probably get mobbed in the streets. Leave classic perfection to the museums. You wouldn't be comfortable on a cold white pedestal. Let's get back to business. When did you say you were going down to Latter End?'

'I didn't say. I haven't made up my mind.'

'What about going down with me on Friday?'

She was silent for a moment. Her cigarette ash dropped. She brushed it away with an impatient gesture and said,

'I suppose I could. I haven't broken it to Lois yet.'

'Will it need breaking?'

She nodded.

'Yes, it will. I don't generally stay there.' She was saying more than she meant to. 'As a matter of fact I haven't stayed there since Jimmy married her. We don't—she paused—'love each other very much.'

'You surprise me.'

He got a smouldering glance. She leaned forward and flung what was left of her cigarette into the fireplace, holding it like a dart and putting an extraordinary energy into the action.

'Do I? Very well then, you can have it straight! I hate her like poison!'

FOUR

Ellie Street was laying the table for dinner. Because Antony and Julia were coming down she had taken extra pains with everything. The flowers were lovely in that old glass épergne—much prettier than silver—and everything had been polished until it shone. The bother was that she couldn't polish herself. The Dutch mirror between Jimmy's great-grandfather in a stock and his great-grandmother in a primrose satin Empire dress with a turquoise fillet in her hair showed her a very unsparing reflection of Ellie Street—washed-out cotton frock; washed-out, pinched little face without a scrap of bloom or colour; fair hair gone flat and mousy; poking shoulders; a step without spring. No wonder Ronnie watched his pretty nurse.

She must hurry up and get finished here, change into something decent, and do things to her face before Julia came. The bother was that she was too tired to care. The ten miles into Crampton and back just about finished her, but the buses didn't fit, and she had to see Ronnie. Well, she had finished here now, and there would be time to sit quite still for twenty minutes before she need dress. She stood back for a last look at the table.

There was a step in the passage and Lois came in.

'Oh—have you finished? I hope you polished the silver. It hasn't been looking as it should.'

'Yes, I've polished it.' Ellie's voice dragged.

Two years ago she had been a pretty, fragile girl with the prettiness, the porcelain tints, and the fragility of a Dresden figure. It is not a type of looks to resist fatigue and strain indefinitely. If the Dutch mirror had not flattered her, neither had it borne false witness. She was just the ghost of Ellie Vane as she fixed her tired blue eyes on Lois's face and said,

'Yes, I've polished it.'

'Well, those spoons could do with another rub. And— oh, didn't I tell you to use the big silver bowl for the flowers? Jimmy likes it.'

Ellie went on looking at her. At last she said,

'Lois, do you mind very much about the bowl? I don't think I've got time to do the flowers again.' Her voice was like herself, gentle and very tired.

Lois's delicate dark eyebrows rose.

'I should have thought you would be glad to do something for Jimmy. After all'—the pretty laugh rippled out—'he's done a good deal for you and Julia. But of course if it's too much trouble—' She walked over to the table and stood there pulling Ellie's flowers about, spoiling them, scattering drops of water on the polished surface.

Julia would have given battle. Ellie only looked, and said in an extinguished voice,

'I'll do them again. Please, Lois—you're splashing the table.'

When she went through into the pantry to get the silver bowl Mrs Maniple was there.

'What is it, dearie? Aren't you through? What you want is a good lay-down for half an hour before they come. You've just about got time.' Kind old Manny. Ellie smiled at her gratefully. She must be quite old, because she remembered Jimmy being born, but she never looked any different or seemed any older than when Ellie and Julia used to slip into the kitchen for raisins and new hot jam, currant babies and sugar mice. Manny made the most enchanting sugar mice, pink and green, with chocolate eyes. At five years old a sugar mouse is heaven.

Mrs Maniple put a fat arm round her shoulders.

'You run along up, my dear, and get yourself off your feet.'

'I can't, Manny. Mrs Latter wants the flowers in the silver bowl, and it will have to be cleaned. It hasn't been used for months.'

The arm stiffened. Ellie stepped away.

'It's no good, Manny.'

Mrs Maniple held her tongue. If she couldn't do anything else for Miss Ellie she could do that. The red-apple colour in her large, firm cheeks deepened to plum. She jerked her head over a billowing shoulder and called sharply,

'Polly! You come here!'

Then she took the bowl out of Ellie's hands.

'Go on up with you, my dear. Polly'll see to this, and I'll see she does it proper. I'll put the flowers in myself, and if they're not right, you can coax 'em when you come down. And you take and put some colour in your cheeks, or Miss Julia'll have my life.' Her jolly laugh followed Ellie along the passage.

She went up the back stairs because it was quicker. Manny was an angel. Something like a laugh came and went. Because she had said that to Antony once, and he had drawn a wicked picture of Manny in a stained glass window with a voluminous nightgown bulging over her curves, and enormously strong wings just failing to hold her up.

She was going into her room, when Minnie called her. She had the room which had been Miss Smithers', and Ellie the one she had shared with Julia for as long as she could remember.

She pushed open the door and went in. Minnie Mercer was standing by the dressing-table doing up the brooch which had been her twenty-first birthday present from her parents nearly thirty years ago. It had a monogram of two Ms intertwined in seed pearls, and the pearls were not quite so white as they used to be. It was her best brooch, and she was wearing her best dress in honour of Julia and Antony. It wasn't quite as old as the brooch, and it had been very carefully preserved, but it had seen the war come in, and it had seen it go out. It could never have been what Minnie herself called 'stylish', and the rather bright blue colour was no kinder to the little thin face than was the skimpy make to the little thin body. But it was her best dress, and she took an innocent pride in it.

As she turned round, a thought like a long sharp pin ran into Ellie's mind '—That's what I'm going to look like. I'm getting to look like it now. Oh, Ronnie!' Because thirty years ago Minnie Mercer had been 'pretty Minnie Mercer', or, 'that pretty daughter of Dr Mercer's'. The features were still there, only so pinched and lined. The fair hair was still there, quite a lot of it. It would have been pretty still if it had been properly set and done. It wasn't grey even now, just limp and colourless. What neither the years nor anything else had taken or could take away was the sweetness of Minnie's smile and the kindness in her eyes. They had once been forget-me-not blue, and that was gone. But the kindness would never go. It was there, very quick and sweet, as she said,

'Ellie darling, how tired you look. Sit down and tell me about Ronnie. How did you find him?'

Ellie let herself down into the easy chair.

'He's about the same. He won't get any better there— Matron says so. I'm going to speak to Jimmy tomorrow.'

'He is so kind,' said Minnie, but she looked away. 'I wonder whether—you don't mind my saying this, do you, dear—I just wonder whether it wouldn't be better to speak to Mrs Latter first.'

Lois was Mrs Latter to Minnie Mercer, but Lois called her Minnie—a small matter but significant, setting them in their places as Jimmy's wife and Jimmy's humble dependent. It was one of those things for which Julia hated Lois. It left Minnie untouched on her own secure ground of humility.

Ellie wrinkled her brow. She was getting into the way of it. She was only twenty-four, but already a faint line marked the fair skin. She said,

'What's the use?'

'It might be better.'

There was a brief silence. Minnie turned back to the dressing-table and began to put things straight—the comb, the brush, the mirror, which had been presents from Mrs Vane.

From behind her Ellie's voice dragged wearily.

'She'd only say no. But if I got at Jimmy first, he might—he might—' The words petered out. No one who knew Jimmy Latter could really believe that he would hold out against Lois. He would say yes and mean it—it was always much easier for Jimmy to say yes than no. But that cut both ways, and he would find it quite impossible not to say yes to Lois, who would certainly produce a dozen excellent reasons for not giving house-room to Ronnie Street.

Minnie turned back.

'Don't worry about it now, dear. There's a little thing I wondered whether you would do for me—'

'Of course. What is it?'

Minnie was looking troubled.

'Well, dear—it was so stupid of me—but I came over a little faint when I was at the Vicarage work-party this afternoon . . . Oh, it was nothing—nothing at all, but Mrs Lethbridge—you know how kind she is—well, she did say something about ringing Mrs Latter up, and of course, dear, it wouldn't do at all. I did my very best, but you know how she is—so kind but not very tactful—and I'm really afraid—I wondered, dear, if you would ring her up and beg her not to. She was going over to see Miss Green, but she will be back by now. You could say I was quite myself again.'

'Yes, I'll do it at once. She mustn't ring up—it would make the worst sort of fuss.'

Ellie felt quite appalled at the prospect. She ran down the stairs, but as she approached the half-open study door she discovered with a sinking heart that she was already too late. Lois' sweet, high voice was plainly audible.

'She fainted right away? My dear Mrs Lethbridge—how trying for you! I'm so sorry . . . Yes, I know—she *will* do too much, and then she gets these nervous turns. Nothing to worry about of course, but—it's most kind of you to let me know . . . I'll do what I can—she's a very obstinate person.' A light laugh to soften this. 'I'm afraid you'll have to let her off these work-parties. I shall have to be strict about that. As you say, good people are scarce—we must take care of her. Thank you so much for letting me know.'

Ellie heard the click of the receiver. She gave a little start, turned round and ran upstairs again. She was panting when she came into Minnie's room.

'Ellie, darling!'

'Min, I was too late. Lois was there—talking—'

'To Mrs Lethbridge?'

Ellie nodded.

Minnie gave a very small sigh.

'Well, it can't be helped. My dear, you shouldn't have run—you are quite out of breath.'

'It's nothing—it doesn't matter. Min, you should have heard her! "Good people are scarce—we must take care of her"! What Julia calls her honey-snake voice. And—oh, Min, she said Mrs Lethbridge mustn't count on you for the work-parties any more. But you'll fight that, won't you? It's just the one pleasure you've got.'

Minnie stood quite still. After a moment she said,

'I'm not very good at fighting, my dear. And it upsets the house, and I wouldn't want to do that.'

Jimmy's name wasn't mentioned, but it was there in both their thoughts. It was Jimmy who mustn't be upset. Minnie would do anything and bear anything to prevent that. They both knew it, but today for the first time Ellie stopped finding it a matter of course. 'She feels like I do about Ronnie.' The idea just went through her mind and was gone. She didn't stop to think about it then, but it had changed something. She wouldn't ever quite take Minnie for granted again. She had been there for so long, they were all so used to her being devoted to them, that the quality of that devotion had never been questioned. Ellie had begun to question it.

She saw Minnie smile in her patient way.

'You must dress, my dear. I'll come and help you. We won't think of anything unpleasant tonight, with Antony and Julia coming. Such a pleasure! Why, we ought to be quite gay.'

As they crossed into Ellie's room, she went on talking.

'You can't think how pleased I am that Julia is coming here at last. It has been very, very kind of Mrs Lethbridge to put her up when she came down to see you, but it has made a good deal of talk—her not staying here, I mean. And I am sure it has distressed your brother and—and Mrs Latter. You'll wear your blue—won't you?'

Ellie said, 'Yes.'

She hung up the cotton frock and slipped into the blue crêpe de-chine. It went on only too easily.

'Fluff up your hair and put on a little colour, my dear. You don't want Julia to see you looking pale.'

Ellie was rubbing cream into her face with a towel round her shoulders. She ought to have done it first before she put on her dress. She couldn't bother to take it off now. That was the way it went—you scrambled into your clothes and scrambled out of them again. There was no time to do anything properly. This was the last of her face-cream. She took up the powder-puff and said,

'If Julia has a row with Lois—Min, I'm just terrified she will.'

'Oh, my dear, she wouldn't do that!'

Ellie said in a despairing voice, 'She might.'

'Oh, no!'

'She might want to have one.'

Minnie gave a little gasp.

'No one could *want* to have a quarrel!'

'Julia could.'

'Oh, my dear, why?'

'To blow things up. Julia's like that—you know she is. And she hates Lois like poison.'

In the mirror she could see Minnie standing there just behind her. She looked almost as if she might be going to faint again. She said in a low, shaken voice,

'Hating *is* poison.'

FIVE

The only one who really enjoyed the evening was Jimmy Latter. Everyone else was relieved when it was over, but Jimmy was as pleased as Punch. He was gregarious and sociable to the last degree. It was two years since he had had all his family round him, and it delighted him to see the table full again—Ellie on one side of him, Julia on the other, Antony next to Ellie, Minnie next to Julia, and his beautiful Lois smiling at him from the bottom of the table. It was the old family party, with Lois added. Lois—his wife—his beautiful, wonderful wife! He couldn't imagine why she had married him, when she might have had anyone, simply anyone. But there it was—she had. And here they all were together—Antony back from abroad, and Julia—he'd felt it very much when Julia wouldn't come and stay at Latter End, he'd felt it very much indeed. Jealousy over his marriage. Very wrong of her. But that was Julia all over—passionate, headstrong. She'd been like that from a child. But so warm-hearted, you couldn't help being fond of her. He was very fond of her, and Lois had been an angel about the whole thing. Lois *was* an angel, there was no doubt about that. She had been an angel about Julia—said they must just wait and she would come round. And she had. And here they were.

Julia in red—a nice dark red, like damask roses—a jolly sort of colour—very becoming. And Ellie in blue. She looked tired, poor girl. Fretting about Ronnie. A bad business, his losing a leg like that. What a blessing she had Lois to look after her.

Pity poor Marcia couldn't be here too. He looked past Lois to the portrait on the far wall—Marcia Vane in a red dress, very much like the one her daughter Julia was wearing. Julia was like her—oh, decidedly. But of course not beautiful like Marcia. Pity about that. And Ellie wasn't like her at all. Very good-looking woman Marcia—very nice woman. Didn't have much of a show, being left a widow twice and dying so young herself. He had been very fond of Marcia. She ought to have been here. Quite simply and regretfully he pictured Marcia and Lois living happily side by side at Latter End. And then, of course, Julia wouldn't have gone away, and they'd all have been one happy family. But of course they had a great deal to be thankful for. And he had Lois too. He beamed at her down the table and received a charming smile in return.

On the surface the party was quite a gay one. Lois and Antony saw to that. They kept the ball rolling, with Jimmy skipping lightly in and out of the game. Julia, if rather silent, was behaving very well. She neither frowned nor glowered, had a few things to say and said them, was polite to Lois, and affectionate to Jimmy.

It was not at all difficult to be affectionate to Jimmy. At fifteen he had been a light-hearted, curly-headed boy. At fifty-one the description would still do very well. He was no taller, no more important. The curly hair was receding a little on the temples, but it was as fair, and there was very little grey in it.

Mrs Maniple had cooked them an excellent dinner. When Ellie got up to change the plates Julia got up too. It was nice to be doing things with Ellie again, and if Lois got a kick out of it, for once Julia didn't care. She put a hand on Minnie's shoulder to keep her in her seat and shook her head laughingly at Antony across the table.

'No—please, everyone—I'd like to.'

It was like old times, only it should have been Mummy sitting there at the end of the table, warm and beautiful and kind, instead of Lois in that slinky white dress which showed just what her figure was like, and how much better it was than anyone else's. 'I'm a cat about her, and that's a fact. I don't mind how good her figure is. Oh yes, I do, I do, I *do*! And she might just as well be wearing a bathing-dress! If that's all Antony cares about, she can have him and welcome. No, she can't—not when she's Jimmy's wife—Antony wouldn't do that. He wouldn't come here if he hadn't got over her.' Her spirits rocketed up—a long dizzy swoop with a burst of rainbow lights at the end of it.

Mrs Maniple, handing her a dish of eggs and mushrooms, looked at her with admiration.

'Well, my dear, you've a nice colour and no mistake. Any-one 'ud think Miss Ellie was the town mouse and you was the country one. And it's all your own too—I can see that. If those that puts it on knew half the truth there's few that's taken in by it. Now, Miss Ellie my dear, mind these plates, for they're piping hot.'

When they got back into the dining-room Jimmy was off on one of his interminable stories.

'So I said to Haversham—not the Haversham you remember, Antony—he died, poor chap—this is a nephew, son of the brother who went up north. Now what did he go in for—blest if I can remember. It couldn't have been engineering, because he wasn't any good at figures. I think it must have been a shipping-office or—well, it doesn't matter, but this Haversham is his son. Not a bad young fellow, but of course he don't know the first thing about farming. Started to tell me about olive crops in Italy—he was there with the 8th Army—and what he had to say about the climate! And I said to him, "Well, you know, Haversham, olives are olives, and all very well for the Eyeries, but they won't grow here, and that's that . . ."' The story flowed along. It entertained Jimmy tremendously, and it never got anywhere.

Instead of being bored Antony found himself at his ease as he had not been for years. It was all so much the stuff of which he had been shaped and made—the family party, the girls coming and going, Jimmy so pleased that you couldn't help being pleased too. What did it matter if his stories never got anywhere? People who could tell a good story are three a penny. It was only among your own people that you didn't need to shine, because that wasn't what mattered. Your own people were your own people. You could take them for granted, and be taken for granted by them. The bosom of the family was an extraordinarily restful place.

In the middle of this he turned his head and caught a glance from Lois. It was as bright and hard as a diamond. It despised Jimmy. It beckoned Antony to despise him too. Suddenly and fiercely he hated her for an alien.

When dinner was over Lois trailed away to the drawing-room, taking the two men with her—Antony's attempt to stay behind and make himself useful receiving no encouragement from anyone, and Jimmy's 'No, no—the girls will see to it' being reinforced by Julia's 'Run away and play—you'll only be under our feet.'

Out in the pantry she turned to Ellie.

'How many take coffee? I don't, for one, so it's no use putting on a cup for me. Which are you using?'

'The old Worcester. Minnie and I don't take it either, and Jimmy has given it up, so it's only Lois and Antony, and Lois takes Turkish.'

'How like Lois! Well, Antony won't drink Turkish. And he likes milk.'

'Manny's got it all ready. Lois just has a cup. She has a drop of vanilla in it. And put the little bottle of cognac on the tray.'

Julia made a face.

'What muck!'

The others were out on the terrace. Beyond a grey retaining wall the level turf took the shadow of the cedar which was Jimmy's pride. It had cones on it this year, like flocks of little owls roosting on the great spreading branches. On the other side of the lawn a wide herbaceous border displayed a glowing pattern of every lovely tint, enriched by the evening sun. One of those perfect windless evenings when a

sky without a cloud has lost the heat which veiled its delicate blue.

They came in reluctantly, first one, and then another. Antony's mood of contentment deepened. His momentary anger
had passed. He felt at peace with all the world.

It was when Minnie Mercer was going out of the room
with the coffee-tray that Lois got up and went out too. She
hurried past Minnie in the hall, actually brushing against the
tray and bringing down Antony's cup with a clatter.

Minnie went on to the pantry, where she washed up the cups
and put them away. Polly Pell was busy with the dinner things,
wiping the glasses very slowly and carefully as Mrs Maniple
had taught her—a thin child of seventeen with a sensitive look.
Minnie talked to her for a minute or two about a married sister
whose first baby had just been christened, thought the name
they had chosen very pretty, and then turned to go back to the
drawing-room. She had to pass the downstairs cloakroom—
but she did not pass it. Such a distressing choking sound met
her ear that after a moment of alarmed hesitation she tried the
door, found it unlatched, and went in. Lois Latter, gasping and
retching, was bent forward over the lavatory basin.

Shocked and distressed beyond measure, Minnie did all
the kind offices that were possible, and when the spasm had
passed, tidied up in her quiet, methodical way. Lois sat where
Minnie had guided her, on the small hard chair which was all
that the place could offer. She was as white as her dress, her features sharp, the fine skin drenched with sweat, but as Minnie
turned round from the basin, she drew a long breath and said,

'I'm all right now.'

'Shall I help you upstairs?'

Lois took another of those breaths, moved a little, and said, 'No, I don't need help. I'm all right now. Just wait a minute.'

'Can I get you anything?'

'A little water—' She took two or three sips, and straightened up. 'I'm all right—that's going to stay. I can't think what came over me.' Her brows drew together in a frown. 'It must have been the mushrooms. Mrs Maniple must have been careless. The fact is, she's getting past her work. I'll have to speak to Jimmy.'

Minnie Mercer knew better than to make any comment, but she couldn't help looking grieved, and it needed no more than that. Lois let her temper go.

'Of course you'll stand up for her! Even if she poisons me! But it mightn't have been me, you know—it might have been Jimmy! You wouldn't be quite so calm about it then, or quite so sorry for Mrs Maniple!'

'Mrs Latter—' Minnie's gentle protest got no farther than that.

Lois got up, steadying herself by the chair.

'I really don't feel fit to have an argument. I'm going up to my room . . . No, I shan't need you. You'd better go back to the drawing-room. And you're not to say a word to anyone—do you hear? Not one single word. If I don't come down in ten minutes, you can come up. But it's over—I'm sure about that. Only I can't go back looking like this.'

It was really no more than ten minutes before she opened the drawing-room door and came in, her white dress trailing, a faint clear colour in her cheeks. To Jimmy and to Ellie Street she looked just as she had looked at dinner. Even to Minnie there was very little trace of what had passed. Julia thought, 'Damn it all—she's lovely!'

Antony gave her a hard scrutinising look as she went past him. If that was her own colour, he'd eat his hat. But in the dining-room it had been her own—he was quite positive on that score. He allowed himself to wonder—

SIX

Julia put out the light, waited for the darkness round her to clear, and went surefooted through it to the window. She drew the curtains back across the bay and stood there looking out. The three windows were open, casements wide and the night air coming in like a soft enchanting tide. The room looked to the side of the house. There was a clear sky, but no moon yet. Beyond a small formal garden there were the black mysterious shapes of trees. There was no wind. Nothing moved under that clear sky.

She came to the bed beside Ellie's and got in, humping the pillows at her back, because this was what they had both been waiting for—Ellie to talk and she to listen. As she settled down, Ellie's hand came out and clutched hers.

'Oh, Julia—' It was a sigh of utter relief. And then without any warning Ellie began to cry.

All day long, and for many days, the tears had lain cold and heavy at her heart, and at night she had kept them frozen there because she did not dare to let them fall. It would be like letting go, and she didn't dare to let go, because she mightn't be able to take hold again. Only now that Julia was here it was different. She could cry, and Julia would stop her when she had cried enough.

Julia let her cry, not touching her except that she left her hand in Ellie's—not speaking, but just being there. All their life Julia had been there. That meant security for Ellie. It was always Julia who led and Ellie who followed, Julia who dragged her into scrapes and then miraculously got her out of them again. Somehow deeply, despairingly, Ellie clung to the idea that Julia could get her out of this, which wasn't a scrape but the threatening of everything she cared for. Even as the tears ran down and soaked her pillow, she began to feel warm waves of comfort coming from Julia.

Presently Julia's voice came to her, warm too, and deep.

'Ellie, you've cried enough.'

'I expect—I have—'

'Then stop! Have you got a handkerchief?'

Ellie said, 'Yes', on a sob. She let go of Julia, felt under her pillow, and blew her nose.

'Now don't cry any more! You'd better tell me what it's all about.'

There was another sob, and a big one.

'It's Ronnie!'

'He might be dead, and he isn't,' said Julia. 'Suppose you think about that and stop crying.'

'I know—it's wicked of me, isn't it?'

'Idiotic!' said Julia.

Ellie began to feel better. There is something extraordinarily reassuring about being told that your fears are idiotic. She felt for Julia's hand again, and found it comforting and strong.

'I expect I am. But Matron says he'll never get better where he is, and I'm so frightened Lois won't have him here.'

'She won't if you're frightened. The more you're frightened of people like Lois, the more they trample.'

Ellie caught her breath.

'I know. But I can't help it—I *am* frightened.'

'It's fatal,' said Julia.

Ellie clung to her hand.

'It's no good saying things like that. I can't help it—it's the way I'm made. She's a trampler, and I'm a doormat, and she'll go on wiping her feet on me until I end up like Minnie, only not half so good.'

'She will if you let her,' said Julia.

'I can't stop her. But I'm going to speak to Jimmy tomorrow—not that it will do any good—'

'I don't know—it might. I could speak to him too, and—perhaps Antony. Between us we might get him to the point of remembering that it's his house, and that if he wants to have Ronnie here it's his business.'

Ellie said in an extinguished voice,

'You don't know Lois—she'd get round him somehow—she always does.'

'Well, I think we'll have a go at it.'

She felt rather than knew that Ellie was trembling.

'It won't be any good—she gets her own way. You know old Mrs Marsh—'

'What has she got to do with it?'

'I'm telling you. When her son came home from India she just didn't know how to be happy enough, and he was quite good to her in his stupid fat way.'

'Oh, he wasn't as bad as that. I rather liked Joe Marsh.'

Ellie pulled at her hand.

'He's got fatter and stupider. And he's married an odious girl from Crampton—as hard as nails—she really is. Lois has her up here to sew. Honestly, she's a most frightful girl. You should hear Manny on the subject.'

'I probably shall.'

'Well, this horrible Gladys had made up her mind from the beginning that she was going to get rid of Mrs Marsh, and she's done it. With her stiff leg, she can't take a regular job, but she did things like minding babies while the mothers went to the cinema, and she liked doing it. And it was her cottage, where she'd lived ever since she married Joe's father, and that beast of a girl just pushed her out of it and got her taken away to the Institute.'

There was a little pause before Julia said,

'What has that got to do with Lois?'

The answer came in a breathless hurry.

'Lois put it into her head, and backed her up. Manny's raging. The Marshes are some sort of cousins—'

'Does Jimmy know?'

'I don't know—not how it was done anyhow. He thinks she's had to go to the infirmary because of her leg.'

Julia said in a surprised voice,

'Why didn't you tell him?'

'It wouldn't do any good. It's the sort of thing that's happening all the time, only Jimmy can't see it. Lois puts it her way, and he can't see anything else. She wants old Hodson's cottage for some friends of hers, and you see, she'll get it.'

'Jimmy wouldn't do that.'

'She'll make him. You don't know Lois like I do. She'll persuade him that it's much better for old Hodson to go and live with his widowed daughter-in-law in London, where he'll hate every minute of it and go right down the drain. But of course that doesn't matter to Lois. She'll get her way, and her friends will get their week-end cottage.'

There was a silence. There were a great many things which Julia could have said. She thought perhaps she had better not say them. Soothing down was what Ellie wanted, not raking up. She held her tongue because she couldn't think of anything soothing to say.

After a moment Ellie burst out again,

'It will be just the same about Ronnie—you see if it isn't! Jimmy will say yes to me, and to you, and to Antony, and then Lois will get hold of him and he'll say no, because she'll make him believe that it's much better for Ronnie to be in a hospital or a convalescent home, just as it's much better for Mrs Marsh to be in the Institute, and for poor old Hodson to be in London with a daughter-in-law who doesn't want him. I wouldn't mind so much if she was honest about it. She isn't. She's got to pretend that it's what's best for everyone, instead of saying bang out that it's just what she wants.'

Julia said in her deep voice,

'Stop shaking, Ellie. And stop working yourself into a state over Lois. It doesn't do any good, and it wears you out. She's poison all right—I always knew she was. But she's here, and she's Jimmy's wife. Something can be done about Ronnie. That's why I'm here. Now the first thing that suggests itself is a job where they would let you have him with you.'

Ellie caught her breath.

'It isn't any good. I've tried. I put in an advertisement, with a box number. There were only two answers, and they were both from slave-drivers. All the work of a house—cooking and everything. I couldn't have done it and looked after Ronnie too.'

'What did you say in the advertisement?'

'I tried to make it stand out—there were such a lot of people wanting things. So I put, "I want a domestic job where I can have my husband with me. He has lost a leg".'

'And you only got two answers?'

'That's all.'

Julia lay frowning in the half light. The moon had risen. She could see the foot-rail of her bed and of Ellie's bed. She could see the black mass of the old-fashioned wardrobe against the wall beyond. The three bright windows showed the illumined sky. She said slowly,

'Ellie—'

'Yes?'

'If Ronnie could go to a really nice convalescent home, mightn't it be better for him than having rows with Lois here?'

She felt Ellie's hand jerk and pull away.

'I shouldn't see him—'

'But if it made him well? He would be able to take up his job, and you would be together all the time.'

Ellie said in a muffled voice,

'I didn't think you'd be against me too.'

'I'm not.'

It was like Julia not to make protestations.

'You don't understand.'

'Then hadn't you better explain?'

Ellie's hand crept back, catching at hers.

'We're not getting a chance. We had a month together, and after that two week-ends, and since then he's been in hospital. It isn't giving us a chance. I go over there, and I'm tired before I start. I haven't got any go or any colour, and half the time I can't think of anything to say. I can't be amusing, or gay, or any of the things he needs.' She burst into tears all over again. 'Oh, Julia, he's got such a pretty nurse!'

SEVEN

Julia got Jimmy Latter alone after breakfast next morning. He was smoking a pipe on the terrace, and she dragged him into the study and shut the door. Lois had altered the drawing-room almost beyond recognition—new covers, new curtains, new carpets, new ornaments, and all the furniture moved around and changed. But she hadn't started on the study yet. There were the old shabby rugs on the floor, the old brown curtains at the windows, the old shabby books on the shelves. Of course no one ever studied here or ever had, but it was Jimmy's room, and it had been his father's before him, and Julia felt a lot better when she had got him there and the door was shut. She would have locked it if she could, but the key had been lost a long time ago, nobody knew how or when.

She sat on the arm of one of the big chairs and said, 'Jimmy, I want to talk to you about Ronnie.' Antony had always told her she hadn't any tact, and when she flung back, 'But what's the good of beating about the bush? If I'm going to say a thing I say it,' he usually laughed and said, 'You're telling me!'

Well, she had said what she had come to say, and Jimmy was frowning, his pipe in his hand and the smoke going up between them. Even before he spoke she knew that Lois had got in first.

'You know, Julia, it won't do—having him here, I mean. It simply won't do. Of course it's natural Ellie should want it, and I'd be pleased enough to have him, poor chap—you know that. But, as Lois says, Ellie would kill herself looking after him. You've only to look at her to see she's not fit for it. Why, the poor chap's a cripple—she couldn't possibly manage. I tell you I'm very worried about her as it is. Here she is, at home, with every comfort, and Lois to look after her, and she looks like a ghost—no colour, no spirits. And you want her to take on a heavy nursing job like that. I won't hear of it!'

Julia's cheeks flew two red flags. She had very seldom been so angry. She had just sense enough to know that if she wanted to play Ellie's game she mustn't let her temper go. If it had been a game of her own, she would have thrown the cards on the table with a will and counted it well for the pleasure of saying what she thought about Lois. But it was Ellie's game.

Her cheeks flamed and her eyes smouldered, but she controlled her tongue. Jimmy, looking at her a little uneasily, was struck by her likeness to Marcia. And he had not only been very fond of Marcia, but he had respected her judgment. This, and the likeness, began insensibly to colour his thoughts. Julia's silence gave them time. When she spoke at last, her voice was pitched quite low.

'Jimmy—do you remember what staff you had here before the war?'

He said, 'That's a long time ago. Everything's different now.'

'I know. But all the same, do you remember? There was Mrs Maniple, with a kitchenmaid under her, and the between-maid after twelve o'clock, and Mrs Huggins to scrub the floors. That's on the kitchen side. For the rest of the house there was a butler, house-parlour maid, housemaid, the between-maid till twelve o'clock, and Mrs Huggins any time there was extra work—people staying, or spring-cleaning—all that kind of thing.'

He took an angry pull at his pipe.

'What's the good of talking like that? Everyone's had to cut down.'

'I know they have. But just think for a minute, Jimmy, and you'll see why Ellie looks tired. She and Minnie are doing what it used to take a man and three maids to do.'

'You're leaving Lois out.'

Julia looked at him.

'Yes—I'm leaving Lois out.'

He turned away, went off to the writing-table, and stood there with his back to her, picking up first one thing and then another from a crowded pen-tray—picking them up and dropping them again with flustered, jerky fingers. When he turned round his face was red. He said angrily,

'What do you mean by that?'

Julia's right hand lay clenched in her lap. She drove the nails into her palm. She mustn't let Jimmy see that she was angry too. She couldn't manage him that way. Mummy never got angry with him or with anyone. That was why everyone listened to her. If only things didn't boil inside you until you felt you didn't care—

She'd got to care about Ellie. She managed such a temperate, reasonable voice that it surprised her.

'Look here, Jimmy, I don't want to have a row—I want to talk. I just want you to listen, that's all. Lois does the flowers—that's all she does in the house. It isn't anything to be angry about—it's a fact. It's her house, and there isn't any reason why she should do more than she wants to. She hasn't ever lived in the country before. She's been so much in hotels that perhaps she just doesn't know what a lot there is to do.'

She began to feel pleased with herself. She was letting Jimmy down lightly, and who said she hadn't any tact? She went on, warming to it.

'I've got a really good plan, and it wouldn't cost very much—it really wouldn't. If you would have Mrs Huggins here every day instead of just once a week for Manny, it would make all the difference. You see, neither Minnie nor Ellie are what you'd call strong. They haven't the muscle for the heavy jobs, and they get awfully tired doing them. But Mrs Huggins is as strong as a horse—she'd just gallop through the work. And Minnie and Ellie could do the lighter things.'

Jimmy had stopped being angry. He looked puzzled.

'But Mrs Huggins does come. I've seen her.'

'She comes on Saturdays, and she scrubs Manny's floors. She doesn't do anything else.'

He said in a worried voice,

'I thought she did. And there's a girl—Joe Marsh's wife—I've seen her about.'

'She does sewing for Lois.'

'Are you sure she doesn't help in the house?'

'Quite sure.'

She left that to sink in.

'Jimmy—about Ronnie—I do want you just to listen. If Ellie hadn't the hard work, and those bicycle rides to Crampton which are much too much for her, I do think she could manage Ronnie. It would make her happy, and you can do a lot when you're happy . . . No, please listen. He gets about on a crutch now. If you let them have the old schoolroom, he wouldn't need to go upstairs at all. The beds could come down from our old room, and there's the cloakroom just opposite. It would all be quite easy, and—oh, Jimmy, it would make Ellie frightfully happy! You've always been so kind to us.'

She wasn't angry any more. She was remembering all the times that Jimmy had been kind—a long procession of them, stretching back, and back, and back until they were out of mind. This warm remembrance filled the room. The look she gave him was a lovely smiling one.

He came over to her and put his arm about her shoulders.

'Well, well, my dear—I'll see. Very nice of you to put it like that. Very nice to have you here again. I've missed you very much. Haven't given me much opportunity of doing anything for you the last two years, have you? But we'll see what we can do about Ellie. She's fretting, is she?'

'She's breaking her heart.'

'Well, well, we can't have that. I'll do what I can.'

EIGHT

Jimmy—*darling*!'

Jimmy Latter rumpled his fair hair.

'Well, it seems quite a good plan. Julia says—'

Lois came up to him laughing and put her hand against his lips.

'Oh, my dear, if it's Julia! No, Jimmy, really—I do call it the limit! She doesn't come near us for two years, and then she comes sailing in and wants to turn the house upside down. After all, you know, it is *our* house.'

'Well, it is—'

She was still laughing.

'I'm glad you'll admit that! But it wouldn't be if you were to let Julia loose on it. She's one of those energetic, upheaving sort of people, and I don't honestly think we should care about being upheaved.'

Jimmy was frowning.

'She says Ellie's breaking her heart.'

Lois sighed.

'She's fretting about her husband. I don't see how we can help that. She must try and pull herself together and not give way. She gets rather hysterical about it.'

Jimmy continued to frown.

'She oughtn't to do too much. Julia says Mrs Huggins only comes once a week. Couldn't we have her every day?'

Those delicate brows of hers went up.

'I suppose we could—if Julia thinks we ought to. Is there anything else she would like to suggest? If there is, of course she has only got to mention it.'

Jimmy said rather shortly,

'I don't think you ought to take it that way. It wasn't meant like that.'

Lois laughed again.

'Oh wasn't it? I wonder how it was meant.'

She put her hands on Jimmy's shoulders and kissed him on the chin.

'Now, darling, I want you to listen to me. Julia's been down here for not quite twenty-four hours, and she proposes to rearrange everything and set us all to rights. It isn't sense, you know. If I wasn't a very sweet-tempered woman I should be angry. As it is, I can see she is one of those impulsive people who mean well. She's very fond of Ellie, and she's very fond of her own way. But really, darling, I can't have her butting in like this. It's beyond a joke.'

He put his arms round her.

'Look here, Lois, couldn't we have Ronnie here—just for a bit?'

She drew away from him, her laughter gone.

'Oh, yes—if you want to break Ellie down. I suppose Julia thinks she is fit for that heavy nursing. I don't. I think she wants rest and a change. As a matter of fact I've been going to speak to you about a plan of my own. We can't really go on in this hugger-mugger way. I want to be able to ask people to stay, and to do some entertaining. It's not quite settled yet, but I've heard of a really good butler and a couple of maids. They'll cost the earth of course, but I think it's time we got back to civilisation. If Ellie likes to stay here, of course she can, but I think she'd be the better for a change. Ronnie can be transferred to a convalescent home, and she can take a room near him. I'd really rather not have extra people in the house whilst the new staff are settling down. By the way, I've heard of just the thing for Minnie Mercer. Brenda Grey's aunt wants a companion. Minnie is the born companion—isn't she?'

Jimmy stepped back.

'Wait a minute, Lois—what's all this? About Minnie, I mean. She's not going? There's no reason for her to go.'

Lois was smiling.

'Darling, there's no reason for her to stay. You could hardly expect her to work under the butler.'

'There would be no question of that. Minnie—why she's been here for twenty-five years. She was Marcia's friend. Why should she want to leave us?'

Lois shrugged, making a graceful movement of it.

'Don't ask me. But I think she's very wise. It saves me the trouble of giving her notice.'

'Notice?' Jimmy was gazing at her in a bewildered manner.

'Darling, quite frankly, she wouldn't fit in. If she has the sense to realise it, we shall all be saved a lot of bother.' She smiled again and blew him a kiss. 'Bear up, darling! You've no idea how nice it's going to be to have the house running properly again.'

They were in the small sitting-room opening upon the formal garden. For more than two hundred years it had belonged to the lady of the house. So far Lois had left it as it had been when Marcia inherited it from her predecessor, Jimmy Latter's mother, who had died at his birth. The pale brocaded curtains had been hung for her, the faded carpet had been laid for her girlish feet to tread upon, but most of the furniture was older than that. Lois planned to bring it up-to-date. Even as she blew that kiss to Jimmy she was mentally replacing the Empire couch by a well sprung sofa and relegating a number of watercolour sketches to the attics. Jimmy had a sentimental attachment to them because they had been painted by his mother, but when the room was decorated they would have to come down, and she meant to see to it that they didn't go up again.

Neither she nor Jimmy had heard the door open whilst they were talking. The hand which had opened it did not close it again. When Lois went out of the room she found it still ajar.

NINE

Antony ran into Minnie Mercer in the passage just outside his room—or rather it was she who ran into him, and he who avoided what might have been quite a collision by stepping back just in time. As it was, she blundered against his arm, and he had to catch and steady her, or she would have fallen. It was then that the light from his open door showed him her face, quite white, quite rigid, the eyes fixed and almost colourless. He had not been through five years of war without knowing shock when he saw it. He kept his arm about her, took her into his room, shut the door, and put her into a chair. She did not seem to know what he was doing, but when he said, 'What is it, Minnie?' her hands began to tremble. She sat stiffly upright and tried to keep them quiet in her lap, but they shook and went on shaking. Looking past him with her eyes on some distant point, she said,

'I shall have—to go.'

'Minnie dear!'

'She wants me to.'

'My dear, I don't know what you're talking about.'

She said very slowly and stiffly,

'I've been here twenty-five years—but it's no use—she'll turn me out.'

Antony began to distinguish a pattern. He put a hand on her shoulder.

'Minnie, you look all in. Lean back and rest whilst I get you something. Then if you like, you can tell me about it.'

She shook her head. Two slow tears overflowed and began to creep down towards her chin. She said,

'You can't do anything—no one can do anything. If she has made up her mind to send me away, I shall have to go.'

He pulled up another chair and sat down beside her.

'How do you know she wants to send you away?'

The two slow tears dripped down upon her shaking hands. Others took their place, as pitiful and as unheeded. She didn't turn her head, or look at him, or vary the tone of her voice.

'I went to the morning-room to ask her something—I forget what it was. When I opened the door I heard her say my name. She said, "I've heard of the very thing for Minnie. Brenda Grey's aunt wants a companion. Minnie is the born companion".'

Antony's face had set hard and dark.

'Who was she talking to?'

'Jimmy.' For the first time the stiff voice shook.

'What did he say?'

'He didn't seem to understand.'

'Well?'

'She told him. She said I was going, and he wanted to know why. She made him think I wanted to go. She said what a good thing it was, because it would save her the trouble of giving me notice. There's going to be a butler again, and she said I wouldn't fit in. I know she has heard of two maids.'

'But, Minnie, you were here for years when there was a full staff.'

She said, 'Twenty-five years—it's a long time. But I helped Marcia, and when she died there were the girls. There won't be any place for me now.'

He said, 'Jimmy wouldn't let her turn you out,' and hoped, without any certainty, that what he said was true.

She turned her face to him. The tears were still running down. The eyes had lost that fixed look. They were gentle and very sorrowful, and so was her voice.

'We mustn't bring him into it, my dear. It wouldn't do, you know. It doesn't do to come between husband and wife. It isn't right, and it only makes trouble. If she wants me to go, there isn't anything I can do—except go.' Her hands were still shaking. She got up. 'You have been very kind, Antony. I am sorry I gave way. I shouldn't have done so if I had had time to collect myself. It was just the shock, and running into you like that, and—and your kindness.'

She went quickly out of the room, leaving a very angry young man behind her. It was all very well to say nobody could do anything, but he certainly wasn't going to let it go at that. He thought probably the best chance lay in tackling Lois herself. You could work Jimmy up to the sticking point, but you couldn't keep him there—not unless you got on to one of his half dozen inhibitions. This business of turning Minnie out—well, would it stir one of them up, or would it not? It might. Very difficult to tell with Jimmy. He'd give in, and give in, and give in, and then quite suddenly you'd come up against something that wouldn't budge an inch. He had seen it happen a dozen times—sometimes about the merest trifle, sometimes about a thing that really mattered. But small or big, all the incidents had something to do with Latter End . . .

The hospitality of his house—that might be ground on which Jimmy would stand and fight. Antony was tolerably certain that Lois would never get him to turn either Ellie or Julia from his door, charm she never so wisely. Whether this went for Minnie too was what he didn't know. It might, but then again it mightn't. Jimmy was incalculable. He thought he had better try Lois, and if it came to a row, he was going to get a good deal of satisfaction out of speaking his mind. Of course he would have to see Jimmy first, because he couldn't give Minnie away. His knowledge of Lois' plans must be acquired from Jimmy. Nothing easier of course, because Jimmy would be only too ready to pour the whole thing out to a sympathetic ear.

From his window he could see Lois on her way to the rose-garden with a basket on her arm. Ten minutes with Jimmy and he could follow her there. If there was going to be a row, the rose-garden would be an admirable place for it—well away from the house, and no interruptions.

Jimmy actually took a quarter of an hour, because he was so very much distressed that he had to be placated. He tramped up and down the study, rumpling his hair and demanding why Minnie should want to leave them after all these years.

'I thought she was fond of us all—I thought she was happy here. But Lois says she wants to leave—I can't understand it.'

'Perhaps Lois could persuade her to stay.'

Jimmy brightened.

'Yes, yes—she can't really want to go—Lois must persuade her!'

'I think she might. She may have some idea that she isn't wanted.'

This was as far as he dared go, but it had a very good effect. Jimmy fairly snatched at it.

'Oh, if that's all! Women get these ideas into their heads. Minnie has never been one to put any value on herself. Very unselfish sort of girl—always was—ready to do anything for anyone. She might think she wasn't going to be wanted. Now how can we put that right?'

'Would you think I was butting in if I talked to Lois about it?'

Jimmy brightened still more.

'No, of course not—why should I? A very good idea. You know, it upset me so much that I don't feel I really got to the bottom of it. I don't know when anything has upset me so much. I don't like it, Antony—I don't like it at all. Why—let me see—Minnie is three years younger than I am, and I'm fifty-one. She's been here twenty-five years. Twenty-three—that's what she was when she came, and a very pretty girl too. And she's been like one of the family ever since. I can't understand it at all. Go along and talk to Lois and see if you can get to the bottom of it.'

He found her in the most romantic setting. The beautiful Mrs Latter in her rose-garden, the late summer sunshine bright on her auburn hair and the cool, flawless skin which never tanned or freckled. Her dress of honey-coloured linen blended pleasantly with the flowers in their September bloom. The basket on her arm was brimmed with roses in all the shades of coppery pink.

Antony's sense of humour, stirred angrily. A row would be a most glaring incongruity. Well, perhaps it wouldn't be necessary to have one. After all, Lois had a brain if she chose to use it. There really wasn't any sense in upsetting Jimmy and stirring up all this fuss.

Lois smiled delightfully as he came up.

'How nice of you! I was just wanting someone to carry the basket.'

He took it.

'You like being waited on—don't you?'

'Very much.'

'Jimmy tells me that you are arranging for quite a lot of it—butler and maids again.'

She snipped off another rose as she said carelessly,

'Yes—won't it be a relief!'

Instead of dropping the rose into the basket she held it up for him to smell.

'Well? Won't it?'

'Probably. At the moment Jimmy is considerably upset.'

She gave her rippling laugh.

'That's because of Minnie. He'll get over it. I hope you didn't encourage him.'

'He didn't need any encouragement. Look here, Lois, we've been pretty good friends, and we've never gone in for beating about the bush. Why are you outing Minnie? I know you told Jimmy that she wanted to go, but that won't go down with me.'

'Darling, how fierce!'

'I want to know why you are doing it.'

She was snipping quite idly now, a leaf here, a dead bloom there. She threw him a smiling look.

'Well, you see, I think she's been here long enough.'

'Why?'

'My dear Antony, she's the born old lady's companion. I'm not an old lady, and I don't want a companion. To be perfectly frank, I don't want Minnie. I don't want her at meals, I don't want to meet her about the house—she gets on my nerves. She can go and be a treasure to old Miss Grey.'

'And be eaten up alive like all the other companions she's had for the last fifteen years or so!'

She laughed.

'Oh, Minnie won't mind that. She just asks to be trodden on.'

Antony was silent for a moment. Then he said,

'Do you know, Lois, I wouldn't push Jimmy too far over this. I've known him all my life, and he can be—unexpected. I've got an idea that this is one of the things it would be better—' He hesitated for a word, and she took him up.

'Better for whom, darling?'

He said,

'You.'

'Really, Antony!'

'Lois, listen! Jimmy thinks the sun rises and sets by you—you've got him eating out of your hand. You think you know him. You think he's easy, and so he is—up to a point. I'm telling you you'd better not drive him past that point. If you do, he may be—incalculable.'

She gave a scornful laugh.

'All this fuss about Minnie Mercer! As if she mattered twopence!'

His eyes dwelt on her with a curious appraising look.

'Don't be stupid. You're not a stupid woman, so don't pretend you are. Jimmy's got his loyalties. I'm telling you that you'd better respect them. If you don't you may find you have smashed something you can't put together again. If you don't want Minnie to meals, give her a sitting-room of her own—she'd love it. She wouldn't want to meddle with your parties—she'd be only too pleased to keep out of the way. And she'd make herself useful. I know she did all the mending for Marcia and the house.'

'Thank you—Gladys Marsh does all the sewing I want. And she amuses me. You should hear her on the village. No, it's no use, Antony. And you had better not go on, or you'll make me angry. I don't want to be angry.' She looked at him sweetly and broke into a laugh. 'I'd have been raging if it had been anyone else, but you mustn't take advantage of my having a soft corner somewhere for you.' She came closer. 'I have, you know.'

He said in a hard, even tone,

'Minnie has been here a long time.'

The clear, natural colour brightened in Lois' cheeks. She kept her voice silky.

'And she's in love with Jimmy. Why don't you say it, darling? She's been in love with him for all that long time you keep harping on. I don't find it exactly a recommendation, you know.'

Antony was smiling. If Julia had been there she would have known just how angry he was when he smiled like that.

'My dear Lois, are you asking me to believe that you are jealous of Minnie? I really would like you to be serious, if you don't mind. We in this family have been Minnie's family for twenty-five years. We are the only family she has got. We rather take her for granted, and we all impose on her a good deal, but we are very fond of her. She loves us all a great deal better than we deserve. She adores Jimmy. It is all on such a simple, humble plane that the most jealous person in the world couldn't take exception to it. Be generous and leave the poor little thing alone. It's going to pretty well kill her if you tear her up by the roots. Jimmy has never thought of her except as part of the family. Let her alone there, and he never will.' The smile had gone. The dark face was earnest.

Lois put up the rose she held and flicked him lightly on the cheek.

'You ought to have been called to the Bar, darling. I feel exactly like a jury. And now I've got to consider my verdict.'

'Reconsider it, Lois.'

She said,

'We'll see. Come and help me do the flowers.'

TEN

It was about a fortnight after this that Miss Maud Silver received a visitor. As he did not come by appointment, she was not expecting him. Her mind was, in fact, pleasantly occupied with family affairs. Her niece Ethel, whose husband was a bank manager in the Midlands, had written her a most gratifying account of the way her son Johnny was settling down at school. Very pleasant—very pleasant indeed. One did not like to think of a child being homesick. But Johnny was so sensible—a good steady lad and likely to do well.

Altogether, she felt deep cause for gratitude. Not only had she herself been preserved without injury throughout the war, but her flat in Montague Mansions had suffered no damage, for one really could not count a few broken windows. The curtains had suffered, it is true, but they had done long and honourable service, and she had now been able to replace them in just the right shade of blue to go with her carpet—that rather bright shade which she still called peacock, but which now went by the name of petrol. A rose by any other name would smell as sweet, but a colour by such an ugly name as petrol lost half its charm, to the ear at any rate. Miss Silver continued to speak of her curtains as peacock blue.

The worn edge of the carpet was now very well hidden by the bookcase, and the carpet itself would do for another two or three years, but she was contemplating new coverings for the waisted Victorian chairs with their wide laps, their bow legs, and their carved walnut edges. She would have had them this summer if it had not been for Johnny going to school, but it had been a real pleasure to help Ethel with his outfit.

She sat very upright in one of the chairs that was going to be re-covered, precise and old-fashioned from the hair with its tightly curled fringe in front and its neat coils behind, to the small feet placed primly side by side. The hair was rigidly controlled by a net, and the feet enclosed in black thread stockings—in winter they would have been wool—and black beaded slippers. Where she procured the latter was a mystery as deep as any she had been called upon to solve in her professional career. Detective Sergeant Abbot of Scotland Yard, who was her devoted slave, declared it to be insoluble. For the rest, she wore a dress of artificial silk in a hard shade of brown with dreadful little orange and green dots and dashes disposed in aimless groups upon its surface. It had been new two years ago, and it was not wearing very well. Frank Abbott hoped for its early decease. It was fastened at the neck by a bog-oak brooch in the form of a rose with a pearl at the centre. She also wore a thin gold chain supporting a pince-nez. As she only used glasses for fine print, the chain was looped to the left side of her bodice and fastened there with a gold bar brooch. Except for the fact that her skirt cleared the floor by several inches, she might have stepped directly out of a photograph-album of the late nineteenth century. That this was still her spiritual home was made abundantly clear by furniture of the middle fifties, and by the pictures which hung upon her patterned walls, these being reproductions of some of the most famous paintings of the Victorian age. From time to time she shifted them round, exchanging them with those which decorated her bedroom. At the moment *Bubbles* hung above the fireplace, with *The Black Brunswicker* and *The Monarch of the Glen* on either side, whilst *Hope, The Soul's Awakening,* and *The Huguenot* decorated the other walls. The mantel-shelf, the top of the bookcase, and various occasional tables were thronged with photographs in plush and silver frames. Sometimes the two were combined— silver filigree on plush. But the photographs were of the young—for the most part the very young. There were babies of all ages—the babies who might never have been born if Miss Silver had not intervened to bring some hidden cause of evil to light and deliver the innocent. The fathers and mothers of the babies were there too—strong young men and pretty girls, all owing some debt of gratitude to the little dowdy spinster with the neat features and the mouse-coloured hair. It was her portrait-gallery and the record of her cases, and it grew fuller every year.

Miss Silver read the postscript to Ethel Burkett's letter again:

'I can't thank you enough for everything. Johnny shouldn't need any more stockings this year, but if you have any of the grey wool left, I shall be so grateful for some for Derek. He is growing so fast.'

She smiled as she put the letter back into its envelope. The wool for Derek's stockings was already wound, and half an inch of ribbing on the needles.

As she got up to put Ethel's letter away, the door opened and her invaluable Emma announced,

'Mr Latter—'

She saw a slight, fresh-complexioned man with a worried air. That was her first impression of Jimmy Latter—his slightness, his fresh colour, and his worry. By the time she had him sitting opposite to her and her fingers were busy with her knitting-needles, she had placed him as a country gentleman who didn't spend very much of his time in London. His clothes had come from a good tailor, but they were not new—oh, by no means. They were pre-war. Material as good as that had only become available quite recently.

If the clothes were old, and her visitor middle-aged, she judged the worry to be new. Anxiety of long standing leaves unmistakable marks. Mr Latter's fresh skin showed no lines that were not pleasant ones. There were the puckers which laughter leaves about the eyes, and the moulding which it gives to the lips. Whatever the trouble was, it was quite recent. She smiled and said,

'What can I do for you?'

Jimmy Latter was wondering why he had come, and how he could get away. The smile changed the direction of his thoughts. Nice little woman, friendly little woman. Comfortable. Nice comfortable room. Rather jolly pictures. He remembered that one over the mantelpiece, hanging in Mrs Mercer's drawing-room as far back as when he and Minnie were children. Something about this little woman that reminded him of Minnie. Nice quiet way with her—didn't rush you. Only of course older. He said,

'Well, I don't know—I mean, I don't know that there's anything you can do. I don't know that there's anything to be done.'

'But you have come to see me, Mr Latter.'

He rubbed the bridge of his nose.

'Yes—I know—one does things like that, and then when you get there you feel that you are making a fool of yourself.'

The smile came again.

'Does that matter very much? I shall not think so.'

He said, 'Oh, well—' and began to fidget with a bunch of keys he had fished out of his pocket. 'You see, I heard about you last year from Stella Dundas—she's a kind of cousin of mine. She couldn't say enough about you.'

Miss Silver's needles clicked. Derek's sock revolved. She held her hands low, knitting with great rapidity in the continental manner.

'I was very glad to be able to help Mrs Dundas. It was quite a trifling matter.'

'Not to her, it wasn't—she thought a lot of those pearls. She said it was marvellous the way you spotted the thief.'

Miss Silver inclined her head.

'Have you had something stolen, Mr Latter?'

'Well, no, I haven't.' He jingled the keys. 'As a matter of fact it's something a good bit more serious than that. Look here, if I tell you about it, it will be all in confidence, won't it?'

Miss Silver gave her slight cough.

'Naturally, Mr Latter. That is understood.'

He hesitated, swinging the key-ring to and fro.

'I suppose you get told some pretty queer things?'

She smiled again.

'You must not ask me what my other clients say.'

'Oh, no, of course not—I didn't mean that. But this isn't a thing to be talked about. The fact is, I don't believe it myself, and it worries me. It's about Lois—my wife. She thinks someone is trying to poison her.'

Miss Silver said, 'Dear me!' And then, 'What makes her think so?'

Jimmy Latter rumpled his hair.

'Well, it all began with her going to that fellow Memnon. I expect you've heard of him.'

Miss Silver coughed disapprovingly and said, 'Oh, yes.'

'Well, he told her to beware of poison. But she didn't think anything about it, you know—not until she began to have these queer attacks.'

'What kind of attacks?'

He looked very worried indeed, and he sounded worried too.

'Nausea and retching. She's never had anything like them before, and they come on just for nothing at all.'

'Has she seen a doctor?'

'No—she won't do that.'

'Why not?'

'She says what's the use? If there is someone trying to poison her, he can't stop them—there isn't anything one can do—well, is there? That's what she says.'

'I cannot agree as to that. I should like to hear a little more about these attacks. When did she have the first one?'

'About a fortnight ago. She'd been up in town, and she went to see this fellow Memnon, and he warned her like I told you. She came back home—we were having a family party. After dinner, when we were all sitting in the drawing-room, she suddenly ran out of the room. She came back again presently, and I didn't know what had happened until afterwards, but it seems she had been very sick. That was the first time.'

Miss Silver coughed.

'How long was she away from the room?'

Jimmy dropped the keys and bent to pick them up.

'About a quarter of an hour—not more.'

'You noticed that particularly?'

'I always notice when she isn't there.'

'And how did she seem when she returned?'

He said with complete simplicity,

'I thought how beautiful she looked.'

Miss Silver knitted for a moment in silence. Then she enquired,

'Did anyone see her during the attack?'

'Oh, yes, Minnie Mercer did—Miss Mercer.'

'I will ask you to explain your household presently. You say that you were a family party.

Just now I would like to know whether Mrs Latter had anything to eat or drink which the rest of the family did not.'

'Only the coffee,' said Jimmy Latter.

ELEVEN

When Miss Silver had elicited that Mrs Latter was the only one of the household who took Turkish coffee, and that in fact only one other person had taken coffee at all—that the Turkish coffee was prepared by the cook in the kitchen, a drop of vanilla added, and the cup placed together with a sugar-basin and a miniature decanter of cognac upon a salver in the pantry where every member of the household could have had access to it, she shook her head slowly and said,

'A very confusing incident. When was the next attack?'

'On the following day, after lunch.'

'Was it more severe, or less?'

'About the same.'

'Did you witness the attack?'

'Yes, I did. She was very sick, poor girl.'

Miss Silver was knitting rapidly.

'But she was all right a little while afterwards? There were no ill effects?'

'No, thank God.'

'Now, Mr Latter—what did your wife eat at lunch that the rest of the party did not?'

Jimmy rumpled his hair again.

'That's what's so puzzling—she didn't have anything.'

'No coffee?'

'No.'

'Nothing to drink?'

'She doesn't drink at meals. Slimming, you know—but she's got a lovely figure—she doesn't need to.'

The ribbing on Derek's stocking was more than an inch deep. The needles twinkled briskly.

'Mr Latter, will you tell me just what you had to eat?'

Jimmy rubbed his nose.

'Well now, let me see if I can remember. I ought to be able to, because I went over it with Minnie to see if there was anything which would account for Lois being upset, but there wasn't. There was cold lamb and salad—lettuce, beetroot and tomato, and potatoes in their jackets. Then there was a cheese savoury, but Lois didn't have any of that—and custard-glasses of fruit salad in syrup. She had one of those and so did I, and so did Ellie, and Antony, and Julia.'

'They were separate custard-glasses?'

'Yes.'

'Who served them?'

'Lois had them in front of her. She took one, and helped the others.'

'She helped herself?'

'Oh, yes, definitely.'

'Was there any reason why she should have taken one glass rather than another?'

He dropped the keys again. This time he let them lie.

'Yes, there was,' he said. 'There was only one without cream. I never thought about that—she doesn't take cream.'

Miss Silver stopped knitting for a moment. She looked at him gravely.

'Who would have access to these glasses of fruit after the cook had prepared them?'

He plunged into explanations.

'Antony—my cousin Antony Latter—he collected the meat-plates and took them out. We haven't a proper staff at present, so we wait on ourselves . . . Julia and Ellie, my step-sisters—Mrs Street—and Miss Vane—they were in and out . . . And so was Minnie. I didn't want her to do anything, because there were plenty without her, but she would go. I think Julia brought in the savoury, and Minnie the custard-glasses. She will always be doing something—she's so unselfish.'

Miss Silver laid her knitting down on the arm of her chair and rose to her feet.

'I think, Mr Latter, that you had better give me the particulars of your household before we go any farther. I find there is a tendency to confusion.'

As he picked up his keys and followed her to the writing-table he had a guilty conviction that the confusion could be nobody's fault but his own. If he had not had a step-mother who had remarried, it would all be so much easier to explain, but still there would have been Minnie who was no relation at all—

At this point he became hopelessly fogged, because it occurred to him that if it hadn't been for Marcia and her twins, Minnie never would have been imported into his household. He found himself quite unable to think of the last twenty-five years without her, and quite bewildered at the prospect of having to face a future in which she had no part. He watched gloomily whilst Miss Silver took out a bright red copybook, wrote a heading, and waited, pencil poised, for the particulars she desired.

It cannot be said that the manner in which he produced them was calculated to clarify the situation. But Miss Silver was experienced and firm. When he digressed she brought him back, when he became involved she picked up a thread and disentangled it. In the end she had everyone written down neatly in her red copybook:

Mr James Latter—51—of Latter End, Rayle.

Mrs Latter—37—formerly Mrs Doubleday—two years married.

Antony Latter—29—first cousin—recently demobilised—about to enter family publishing business as a junior partner.

Miss Julia Vane and Mrs Street—24—twin daughters of Mr Latter's stepmother. Mrs Street has a husband in hospital at Crampton. Miss Vane is engaged in literary work in London, but has been a frequent visitor during the past fortnight. Before that there was a breach.

Miss Minnie Mercer—48—daughter of the late Dr John Mercer, family physician to the Latter household, which she entered on her father's death, just after Mrs Vane returned to Latter End as a widow for the second time. The twins were born a few months later.

Mrs Maniple—70—cook-housekeeper—in her fifty-fourth year of service at Latter End.

Polly Pell—17—kitchenmaid.

Mrs Huggins—occasional daily help.

Not a very long list, and not so very many particulars, but it had taken some time to get them.

Miss Silver sat up straight with the pencil in her hand and gave a slight preliminary cough.

'And now, Mr Latter, will you tell me if any of these people have a grudge against your wife?'

'How could they have?'

'That is for you to say. You mention, for instance, that Miss Vane, who is now a frequent visitor, had not been so for some time past—that strained relations had in fact existed. With whom had the quarrel been? With your wife?'

'Well, there wasn't exactly a quarrel. I must have given you a wrong impression. I hope you didn't write it down. It was just they didn't hit it off—at least Julia didn't. Lois was an angel about it—never bore any malice—always said Julia would come round. And she has.'

'There was no quarrel?'

He shook his head.

'Nothing to quarrel about. I'm very fond of Julia—always have been—but she flies off the handle. Very warm-hearted girl, but impulsive—doesn't stop to think. Ellie's quite differ-ent—gentle, you know. Bad luck for her, her husband losing a leg like that . . .' He wandered off into a life-history of Ronnie Street, from which Miss Silver presently recalled him.

'Quite so, Mr Latter. I hope that he will soon be sufficiently restored to take up the appointment of which you speak. Now about Miss Mercer. You say she is leaving your household after twenty-five years in it. Is that in consequence of any breach with your wife?'

Jimmy showed considerable distress.

'Oh, no—of course not. She wants to go.'

Miss Silver coughed.

'That is not an answer to my question, Mr Latter. Why does she want to go?'

He ran a hand through his hair.

'I don't know. And that's what's worrying me—it's not only the time she's been with us, but all the time before. You see, my mother died when I was born, and my father couldn't bear it. He went off abroad—travelling about, you know. Well, Mrs Mercer took me on. She'd just lost a child. Minnie was born three years later. My father didn't marry again till I was fifteen. I was with the Mercers till I went to school, and for the holidays after that. Minnie is all the same as my sister.'

Miss Silver's small nondescript eyes regarded him intelligently.

'Sisters and wives do not always agree, Mr Latter.'

Jimmy rubbed his nose.

'No—no. Can't think why women don't hit it off. Not that Lois—besides you couldn't quarrel with Minnie—nobody could. She's one of those quiet, gentle girls—always doing things for other people—never thinking about herself. But

Lois says she gets on her nerves.' He rubbed in a most scarifying manner. 'Why should she?'

'I do not know, Mr Latter. It is quite possible that Mrs Latter does not know either. But you have said quite enough to account for Miss Mercer's decision to go elsewhere.'

He looked wretched.

'I asked her point-blank why she wanted to go, and I couldn't get to the bottom of it. You've only to look at her to see how unhappy she is. Why, I begged her to stay, and she only turned as white as a sheet and went out of the room.'

Miss Silver coughed.

'Well, Mr Latter, there are two members of your household who are not on very good terms with your wife. What about Mrs Street?'

It took Jimmy Latter about a quarter of an hour to explain how angelic Lois had been to Ellie—'Looked after her like a mother. And of course, as she says, it would never do to have that poor chap Ronnie Street in the house—Ellie would only wear herself out.'

Miss Silver mentally added Ellie Street to the list of those who had no great reason to love Mrs Latter. Her enquiry as to the attitude of Mr Antony Latter also provided some grounds for speculation.

'Oh, he was quite a pal of Lois'—knew her before I did. In fact I don't mind saying I got the wind up about him. Of course he's a bit younger, but she doesn't look her age—not anything like. And there they were, always about together—well, I give you my word, I didn't think I'd got a chance. Antony's one of those clever chaps. I never thought she'd look at me, but she did—I can't think why. Anyhow he's been off abroad for the last two years—just got demobilised. I told you about that.'

Miss Silver had one more question.

'Your cook, Mrs Maniple—has she any reason to dislike your wife?'

'Oh, no.'

'She is not under notice to leave?'

Jimmy looked quite horrified.

'Of course not! Why, she saw me christened.'

Miss Silver wrote a few more lines in the red copybook. Then, closing it, she looked up and said,

'I would like you to tell me a little more about your wife and these attacks she has been having. The two you have described occurred about a fortnight ago. I imagine that you would not have come to see me unless something had occurred since then. Now that I am clear as to your household, I should like you to tell me of these more recent happenings. When, for instance, did Mrs Latter begin to think that someone was trying to poison her?'

'After the second attack. She told me then about going to see this chap Memnon—said he'd warned her about poison.'

Miss Silver coughed.

'When was the next incident, Mr Latter?'

Jimmy rubbed his nose.

'Well, I don't know. I've been away—had to go down to Devonshire to settle up the affairs of an old cousin of mine. Lois didn't say anything when I came back, but now she says she didn't feel at all well once or twice whilst I was away. To tell you the honest truth, I didn't take a great deal of notice—I mean, I thought something had just happened to upset her. People do get upset—don't they? That first time, for instance, we had had a very good sort of dish with mushrooms in it—well, you know there might have been a bad one. And the second time there was the fruit salad—all dodged up with kümmel—I mean, it might have upset her. And when I came home, there she was, looking the picture of health, so I thought perhaps she'd just got it a bit on her mind because of what this Memnon chap had said to her.'

'Very natural, Mr Latter.'

'But the day after I came back she was very bad again, after drinking her coffee.'

'The Turkish coffee which was made specially for her?'

'Yes. She was sipping it, and we were talking, when all at once she said, "There's something wrong with this coffee," and she put down the cup and ran out of the room. I went after her, and she was very sick, poor girl. When I could leave her I went back to get hold of the coffee-cup. It had been taken through into the pantry, but the dregs were there. I took it over to Crampton in the morning to a big chemist's shop. There was plenty left at the bottom of the cup, and they got it analysed.'

'Well, Mr Latter?'

He looked at her with puzzled eyes.

'They didn't find anything.'

Miss Silver coughed.

'Is your wife imaginative—neurotic?'

'I shouldn't have said so.'

'There are two possibilities in this case. One is that Mrs Latter has induced these attacks by becoming obsessed with the idea of poison. The other—' She paused for a moment. 'Mr

Latter, has it occurred to you that the dregs in the coffee-cup might have been tampered with?'

He appeared to be very much startled.

'How do you mean—tampered with?'

She replied with gravity.

'If a noxious drug had been introduced into the coffee, the dregs might have been thrown away, the cup washed out, and a little more coffee poured in.'

He stared at her.

'That's what Lois said when I came back and told her about the chemist. She said the cup might have been washed, and anyone might have done it.'

'Who were present, Mr Latter?'

'Antony, Julia, Ellie, Minnie, Lois, and myself.'

'And Mrs Maniple and the girl Polly in the kitchen?'

'Yes.'

'Who took the cup out to the pantry?'

'Minnie did.'

'Could any of the others have had the opportunity of washing it?'

He looked wretchedly unhappy.

'Minnie didn't wash it—I asked her. I asked them all, because Lois said that one of them must have washed it. But they all said they hadn't.'

'What did your wife say to that?'

'She said that any of them could have done it.'

'Was that the case?'

'I suppose it was. Ellie went out to speak to Mrs Maniple, and Julia went to look for her. Antony went with her.'

'And were they together all the time?'

He rubbed his nose.

'No, they weren't. There was a lot of coming and going. As a matter of fact it's all very worrying and uncomfortable, because Lois has got it into her head that someone is trying to poison her, and it means she thinks it's someone in the family.'

Miss Silver closed her eyes for a moment. She had seen photographs in the picture papers of the beautiful Mrs Latter. She was trying to recall those photographs. She looked at Jimmy and said,

'I have seen pictures of your wife. I should like to refresh my memory. Have you by any chance a photograph?'

He took a folding case out of his breast pocket and handed it to her with a look of anxious pride. The portrait inside was a miniature on ivory. He said as he watched her scrutiny,

'It's exactly like.'

Miss Silver looked at the miniature for quite a long time. During that time the idea of Lois Latter as the subject of an hysterical fancy faded from her mind. This was the portrait of a resolute and strong-willed woman. The line of cheek and jaw, the moulding of the chin, the curve of the lips, were eloquent of this. The beautiful red mouth was hard. The eyes, for all their beauty and their brightness, were hard. This was a woman who knew what she wanted and knew how to get it.

The case was handed back across the table with the remark that it appeared to be a speaking likeness. Then, while Jimmy was agreeing, she fixed her serious gaze upon him and said,

'Would you like me to tell you what I really think, Mr Latter?'

'Yes, yes—of course I would.'

Miss Silver coughed.

'Before I do so, will you tell me if there were any ill effects from this last attack? For instance, did your wife rejoin the party in the drawing-room as she did on a previous occasion?'

'Yes, she did,' said Jimmy. 'She seemed to be quite all right again, I'm thankful to say.'

Miss Silver spoke with authority.

'Then I do not believe that an attempt has been made to poison her. I think that someone has been playing a trick. A very wrong and spiteful trick of course, but not, I think, intended to have any serious consequences. The symptoms you have described could be produced by a harmless emetic such as ipecacuanha, a drug which is to be found in most households, and whose sweetish, not unpleasant taste would be readily disguised by fruit-salad or coffee—especially if, as in this instance, sugar and a liqueur were added.'

She saw his face revert so suddenly to its natural boyishness as to suggest a ludicrous comparison with one of those rubber masks which can be drawn out to look lugubrious or compressed into jollity. Miss Silver dismissed this irrelevancy from her thought, and answered his smile with one of her own.

He said, 'That's marvelous—' and then broke off. 'But there isn't anyone who would play a trick like that. I mean, who would?'

Miss Silver coughed.

'Do you really wish me to answer that question, Mr Latter?'

He stared.

'Why, yes—of course.'

'Then I should have to come down and stay in the house.'

'Would you?'

She inclined her head.

'If you wish me to take up the case professionally.'

He pushed back his chair, appeared to be about to get up, but changed his mind.

'Well, I don't know—' he said in a doubtful tone. 'No—I don't know at all. I can't believe that anyone in the family would do a thing like that—I can't really. I don't feel I can bring a detective in on them—I mean, it would upset the whole bag of tricks.'

'It would not be necessary for them to know that I was a detective.'

The colour came up into his face.

'Oh, I couldn't do that,' he said quickly. He got to his feet. 'It's been very good of you to let me come and see you. It's relieved my mind no end—it really has.' His voice became tinged with embarrassment. 'Will you tell me what I—I mean I owe you something—besides being awfully grateful—don't I?'

Her smile had the effect of making him feel about ten years old.

'Not unless you decide to employ me, Mr Latter.' She got up and put out her hand. 'May I give you a word of advice?'

'I should be very grateful.'

He took her hand for a moment, and found it cool and small in his. She withdrew it and said,

'Do not try to combine in one household people who are not really congenial to one another. Until your marriage, Miss Mercer was to all intents and purposes the mistress of the

house. She is now in a different, and possibly difficult, position. I think her decision to go elsewhere is wise. Pray do not
attempt to dissuade her. In the same way with your two young
stepsisters, Mrs Street and Miss Vane—until you married, Latter End was their home. It is unwise for them to continue to
look upon it in that light. Encourage them in every way you
can, even if possible financially, to make homes and centres of
interest for themselves—' She paused, and added, 'You might,
I think, consider pensioning your old housekeeper, if it could
be kindly done. So old a servant does not always fit in with a
new mistress, and after more than fifty years of service she has
earned a rest. There is one thing more. I should strongly advise
Mrs Latter to avoid eating or drinking anything which is separately or especially prepared for herself. Good-bye, Mr Latter.'

TWELVE

It was a couple of days later that Antony Latter rang Julia up at her flat.

'Can I come round and see you?'

'If you don't mind an awful mess. I've brought a lot of my things up from Latter End—books chiefly—and I'm unpacking them. They're all over the floor.'

When he walked in twenty minutes later he discovered this to be an understatement. They were not only all over the floor, but stacked on every chair and piled in sliding strata upon the table and the couch which was Julia's bed. Julia herself in the red smock, which appeared to have been washed since he saw it last but which was rapidly acquiring a good deal of dust, looked up at him with a frown.

'It's grim—isn't it? I don't know what happens to books when you get them out—there always seem to be about ten times as many of them. I've got a man coming to put up some

LATTER END   93

shelves all round the window there, and I don't know how I'm going to eat or sleep until he's done it. I thought perhaps a big pile on each side of the door.'

'All right, we'll each do one. No, I'll bring you the books, and you can build the stacks. Your clothes won't hurt, and mine will.'

She said, 'Your precious trouser knees! All right.'

They began to build. After a minute or two he said,

'Well—how's everything?' To which Julia replied,

'Hellish!'

He raised an eyebrow.

'In what particular way?'

She thumped a heavy book down on to the stack and said,

'In every way you can possibly think of! Lois swears some-one's trying to poison her. Jimmy has been practically tearing his hair out, Ellie's worrying herself into an illness, and Minnie looks as if she was having one. I don't know how I've stuck it out. I wouldn't have if it hadn't been for Ellie, but I can't leave her down there alone. I had to come up on business, so I brought these wretched books, but I shall go down again tomorrow. I suppose you couldn't come too?'

'I could, darling—but you make it sound almost too alluring.'

He found her eyes fixed on him with an appeal which it was difficult to resist.

'Antony, do come! It's quite awful—it really is. I don't think I can tackle it alone, and I think it ought to be tackled. I've got an idea—'

'What sort of idea?'

She hesitated.

'This poison business—it's beastly, and it might be serious. Lois has had about five of these attacks. They're not serious in themselves—she's just sick, and then she's all right again. Well, either she's playing a trick on us, or somebody's playing a trick on her. She won't see a doctor, and she swears someone's trying to poison her.' She gave a short scornful laugh. 'Poisoners aren't as inefficient as all that. No—she's doing it herself, or someone else is doing it to frighten—or punish her.'

Antony shook his head.

'She isn't doing it herself—you can wash that right out.'

'Yes, I think so. Too unbecoming. Well then, it's somebody else. Who?'

'I don't know. You said you had an idea. Are you going to tell me what it is?'

'Yes—I must. I've got a horrible feeling that it might be Manny.'

He looked first startled, and then relieved.

'Manny?'

'Who else is there? Ellie—Minnie—me—you—Jimmy? You see? But Manny—well, I'm not so sure. She was frightfully angry about Mrs Marsh going to the Institute. She said—and it's perfectly true—that Gladys Marsh wouldn't have dared if Lois hadn't backed her up. She's seething about Hodson's cottage too, and about Lois not wanting to have Ronnie at Latter End, and—oh, heaps of things. Poor Minnie is the last straw. Manny knows she's going, and of course she knows that Lois is at the bottom of it. And she's got a nice bottle of ipecac sitting in the corner of the kitchen cupboard, with every opportunity

of putting a teaspoonful in here and there when Lois has anything that the rest of us don't.'

'Darling, what a lurid imagination you've got!'

She shook her head.

'I wish I had. I mean, I wish I didn't think it was true,
but—well, I'm practically sure. And—it isn't safe, Antony.'

He said soberly, 'There's no proof. What are you going to
do about it?'

He was sitting on the arm of a book-laden chair. She
frowned up at him.

'I don't know—tackle her, I suppose.'

His mouth drew awry.

'And what will you do if she bursts into tears on your shoulder and owns up?'

Julia turned a shade paler.

'I suppose I should have to tell Jimmy, and get him to pen-
sion her.'

He murmured, 'Pensions for old age poisoners—Darling, I
must say you've got a nerve! But suppose she denies it—where
do we go from there?'

Julia's eyes widened. The slanting light from the window
behind Antony slid down into them, making them look like
peaty water with the sun on it. She said slowly,

'I—don't—know. I don't know what there is to be done.
It keeps me awake at night. You see, Lois makes everyone
hate her, and when you get a lot of people all hating, things
happen—horrid sorts of things. It's like having a lot of elec-
tricity about—you don't know where the lightning is going
to strike.'

He said coolly, 'Keep the drama for the great works, darling.'

The angry colour ran up into her face.

'You can laugh, but you don't know what it feels like! I'm not dramatising, I'm telling you about facts! Lois—well, she's either got the wind up, or—I don't know what. You know what it is when a person doesn't show anything, but you can feel them being all worked up underneath—she's like that. And Jimmy won't let her take anything that's made separately. He wanted her to knock off her beastly Turkish coffee, but she wouldn't, so now he takes it too, poor darling, and you can see him hating every minute of it. Of course he knows perfectly well that no one will play tricks if he's taking it.'

'So there have been no more attacks?'

'Not since you left. I say, that sounds rather incriminating, doesn't it?' Her lips widened in the beginning of a smile, but it never got anywhere. She reached out for a small pile of books, dumped them on the stack, and said in a careful voice, 'But it wouldn't be you, naturally.'

He sat there swinging his foot and watching her.

'Is that intended for a compliment—a kindly tribute to my law-abiding character?'

'No, it isn't. You're out of it because—' She bit her lip and stopped suddenly. What an absolute damned fool jealousy made of you. Only when it was goading at you all the time something suddenly gave way and you came out with the very last thing you meant to say.

He looked at her quizzically.

'Gratifying, but inconclusive. I should like to know why you are not considering me as a possible poisoner.'

She spoke then, quite gravely and simply.

'Because you are fond of Lois. You used to be very fond of her.'

He shook his head.

'The answer is in the negative, darling.'

She blazed up suddenly.

'You were in love with her!'

'Quite a different thing, my child.

'Yesterday's fires are clean gone out, yesterday's hearth is cold;

No one can either bargain or buy with last year's gold.'

Julia felt her heart leap up. He was telling her what she would have given almost anything in the world to be sure about. It leapt up, and it sank down again. Because what else could he say? He wouldn't tell her or anyone else if he was still in love with Jimmy's wife. She said in her deepest, gloomiest voice,

'I've got to go back there tomorrow, and it's going to be absolute hell. Lois hasn't got her new staff coming in for another fortnight, so we've all got to hang on till then. Ellie and Minnie are doing the work, so they can't clear out. As a matter of fact neither of them has anywhere to go. Minnie won't go to that awful old Miss Grey, I'm thankful to say, and Ellie hasn't managed to find a room yet—they're sending Ronnie to Brighton, and it's packed. I shall have to stand by as long as they are there. I only hope I get through without having a final row with Lois.'

He gave a short dry laugh.

'Feeling optimistic about it?'

She said vehemently, 'I mustn't have one—because of Ellie. I keep telling myself that. You know, Antony, I'm not letting myself really hate her, but I could.'

'You're putting over a pretty good imitation, darling.'

She looked at him, her eyes sombre, all the light gone out of them, her brows a black straight line.

'I've thought about it a lot. You can hate in such a lot of different ways. I think it's all right to hate with your mind. Because what your mind hates isn't people—it's the things which are really hateful—the things everybody ought to hate. That's all right, but when you begin to hate with your emotions it's dangerous, because they swing you off your balance and the hating carries you away. You don't know where it's going to take you, or what it's going to make you do. I'm trying very hard only to hate the things that Lois does, but sometimes—I'm afraid.'

Antony got up. She had moved him more deeply than he cared to show. He brought her half a dozen books, and when she had taken them he put both hands on her shoulders and shook her a little.

'You're a stupid child, but you mean well. Stick to it! It won't do Ellie any particular good if you pour oil on the troubled embers.'

She laughed, releasing the happiness she always felt when he touched her. Far below the words they used the current ran between them smooth and strong. She said in a young voice,

'I don't want to have a row.'

THIRTEEN

Antony went down to Latter End next day. He didn't want to go—his every instinct warned him against going. But he went. It wasn't Julia's asking that took him there. He had found it hard to say no to her, but he had said it. He hoped he would have stuck to his no, but he was to have no means of telling, for that evening Jimmy rang him up. No to Julia was possible, if difficult. No to Jimmy became quite impossible during the three minutes of that country call.

'I've a very particular reason for wanting you to come. The fact is I want to talk to you—about the girls. They'll have to have some money. Old Eliza Raven left me a little—you know I went down to settle her affairs. Well, I want the girls to have it. Thought perhaps you'd be trustee. And then there's Minnie—I'm very unhappy about Minnie—I don't mind saying so. I've got to talk to you.'

Not possible to go on saying no. Afterwards he was to wonder what difference it would have made if he had. It might have made a very dreadful difference, or it might have made no difference at all. The part which depended upon a guilty premeditation may have been already fixed. The part which depended upon the turn of a chance might still have turned the way it did. Or there might have been no chance at all, in which case the tragedy would have been so much the deeper. Just how much Antony's presence at Latter End contributed to the event, he never found it possible to decide. The only thing certain was that had he known what lay ahead he would, even at the last moment, even in the village of Rayle itself, have turned his car about and gone back to town.

He took Julia down with him. As far as she was concerned, the barometer had risen, the sky was clear, and the sun shone. The fact that it was one of those unseasonable weeping September days made no difference. She carried her weather with her, and when Antony and she were together there were no dull days. There might be a storm, there had been one or two earthquakes and an occasional conflagration, but there were also floods of sunshine and quite enchanting rainbows. Today it didn't matter to her in the least that the rain fell, and that when they emerged into the country their view was bounded by dripping hedgerows and curtains of white mist. You could always talk. Julia talked.

'Lois has had one in the eye anyhow.'

'Darling—your English style!'

She laughed.

'I know! But you've got to take a holiday sometimes. If you don't you get all clamped up and stiff. I'm frightfully particular on paper.'

'*Dulce est desipere in loco!* All right—who's been giving Lois one in the eye?'

'Jimmy. He met old Hodson down the lane, and Hodson let him have it—really good stuff on the lines of "It wouldn't have happened in your father's day, nor yet in your grandfather's—taking the roof from over a poor man's head to let foreigners in!" All that sort of thing. And all Jimmy could do was to stand there and gawp. And when he said, "But I thought you wanted to go to your daughter-in-law," Hodson came back at him with "And who told you a dirty lie like that, Mr Jimmy?"'

Antony whistled.

'What happened after that? By the way, how do you know all this?'

'I was there. I don't know when I've enjoyed myself so much. Jimmy told Hodson there had been a misunderstanding, and that the cottage was his for as long as he wanted it. Then he went home and blew right up. I got out of the way, but not before I heard him tell Lois that she must leave the management of the place to him. I hope it will do her good.'

'A pious hope can do no harm,' said Antony drily. 'When did all this happen?'

'Just before I came up. Antony, it's Minnie I'm miserable about. I think Ellie will be all right if we can get her through the next six months. Jimmy is going to give her an allowance, and if she can get a room at Brighton she'll be able to see Ronnie every day, and she won't have all this housework which is wearing her out. I think she'll be all right—I've got to think she will, or I shall blow right up. But Minnie—she's proud, you know, though she's so gentle. She won't take money from Jimmy—I believe she'd rather die. That's what frightens me— she hasn't got anything to live for. And she looks desperate— Jimmy's awfully unhappy about it. The only person who can do anything is Lois. I suppose you couldn't say something?'

Antony frowned at the long, wet road running on into the mist.

'I did.'

'Any good?'

'I thought so at the time. At least I thought there was a possibility. Now I don't. The fact is, Minnie has got on Lois's nerves, and when that happens it's the end—no good arguing about it. There'll be a clean sweep, and we'll all start fresh. I don't suppose Latter End will see very much of any of us after this.'

Julia was silent for a long time. Then she said,

'It's rather an—amputation, isn't it? I oughtn't to feel it, because I haven't been down there so much, but it hurts all right. It's stupid of me, but one of the things I mind most about is Mummy's picture hanging there on the wall behind that woman's chair. It hurts like hell.'

'Jimmy would give you the portrait if you asked him for it.'

The dark colour rushed into her face.

'I couldn't do that! It would be like turning Mummy out— for *her*!'

They drove in silence for a while, the mist closing them in. It was like being together in a room with white walls, a room so small that they could not move away from one another. He was aware of her thoughts—the colour and rhythm of them coming up out of warm depths. What Julia was aware of she kept to herself. Presently she said,

'I wish we were going anywhere else.'

He gave her a light answer.

'Wishes are cheap. Where would you like to go?'

'To Latter End ten years ago.'

Antony laughed.

'I've just left school, and you and Ellie are fourteen.'

'And there isn't any Lois. It would be heaven, wouldn't it?' Then, with sudden energy, 'Do you know what she has done now? She's got that odious Gladys Marsh in the house.'

'What's happened to Joe?'

'Gone down to a sister in Devonshire. There's supposed to be some idea of his going into his brother-in-law's business. The fact is, he's up against it in the village—everyone's crying shame on him about his mother. And Gladys hates Rayle—they'd like to get out. The sooner the better, I should say. But meanwhile there's Gladys at Latter End, putting on the most awful side you ever saw.'

'What is she supposed to be doing there?'

'Odds and ends of sewing, maiding Lois—and whether she's supposed to or not, she listens at doors. Ellie did dig her toes in and say she must do her own room, but there was some head-tossing over it—"I don't know, I'm sure. Housework is so bad for the hands, and not at all what I'm accustomed to".' Julia gave an angry laugh. 'I told Ellie I'd scream the house down if she gave in, so she stuck it out. Gladys now gives a perfect imitation of gentility with a mop and a duster—little finicky dabs and flicks, as if she'd never done a room in her life.'

Antony put out his left hand and let it rest for a moment on Julia's knee.

'Darling, do turn off the gas and simmer down! If you go on boiling up like this you'll boil over, and then the fat is going to be in the fire, which none of us particularly want. Suppose you tell me about the new book instead.'

She gave him a look, half angry, half melting.

'There isn't any new book.'

'There seemed to be a lot of well inked paper lying about on your table.'

'It's not a book—it's a mess. I can't write when things are happening.'

But she began to tell him about it all the same.

FOURTEEN

Antony had hardly set foot in Latter End before he was convinced that, Jimmy or no Jimmy, business or no business, he would have done better to have stayed in town. It had not been a happy household when he had said goodbye to it ten days ago, but it was a paradise compared with how he found it now. Minnie Mercer's looks fairly horrified him. She had the air of a sleepwalker set apart from those around her in some miserable dream. It reminded him of a picture which he had once seen and been unable to forget. The artist had painted a girl who was just about to be shot as a spy. Before his colours were dry she was dead. In the picture she scarcely looked alive. Every time he looked at Minnie the picture came into his mind. No wonder poor old Jimmy was worried about her.

By the time he was half-way through his talk with Jimmy in the study he was worried about Jimmy too. There was something wrong, and he had only to see him and Lois together at the evening meal to realise that this something lay between husband and wife. Lois, in extreme good looks, lost no opportunity of making this clear. Her glance flicked over Jimmy with light contempt. She called him darling in a voice like splintered ice—a voice which melted charmingly to Antony a moment later. After which it sank to a murmur which Jimmy at the other end of the table was vainly trying to follow.

Antony was sitting next to her. You cannot turn your back upon your hostess. You cannot change your place at table. He kept his own voice audible, and presently endeavoured to make the conversation general. Only Julia responded. Ellie looked worn out. Minnie was in her dream, and Jimmy quite unmistakably in one of his rare queer fits of temper. Usually the most abstemious of men, he poured himself out so liberal an allowance of whisky that Lois raised her eyebrows, upon which he drank it off with the merest modicum of soda. And did it again.

When he looked back afterwards Antony was to wonder by what variation in his own conduct the issue might have been avoided. He was left with the hopeless feeling that too many other people were concerned. There was too strong an undertow. It would have taken more than any effort of his to stem the flow which was sweeping them to disaster.

If Jimmy hadn't asked Julia to sing, insisting until it would have been folly to refuse; if he himself had not gone out into the garden with Lois; if Jimmy hadn't tuned up his obstinacy, his hurt feelings, his vague suspicions, with all that whisky; if Gladys Marsh hadn't taken it into her head to have a bath . . . What was the good of all those ifs? There are states of the mind, and states of feeling, in which some mounting passion turns everything to its own ends, as a fire, once it has taken hold, will feed on what is meant to smother it, and turn all efforts to get it under into an added heat.

One of the changes which Lois had made in the drawing-room was the removal of the piano. It was supposed to be somewhere vaguely in store, but Julia said roundly that Lois had sold it. There was, however, an old piano in the schoolroom, and to the schoolroom they repaired, with Jimmy demanding that Julia should sing.

Lois lifted her eyebrows and gave a faint icy laugh.

'My dear Jimmy—how antediluvian! I thought "a little music after dinner" was dead and buried!'

He gave her a resentful look.

'I happen to like music after dinner. I happen to want to hear Julia sing. Haven't heard her sing for years. Sit down and begin. Perhaps it'll sweeten this revolting coffee.'

The eyebrows rose again.

'You needn't take it.'

'You know damn well why I take it.'

Lois laughed.

'That's Jimmy's latest!' she said to Antony. 'If I'm to be poisoned, he'll be poisoned too. Touching devotion—isn't it?' She picked up her cup off the tray and crossed over to the window where he stood half turned from the room. 'He's in a filthy temper, isn't he?' She hardly troubled to drop her voice. 'We had a row about Hodson's cottage. I wanted it for the Green-acres, you know. And it was all fixed up—the old man was going to a daughter-in-law in London, where he'd be properly looked after. But now Jimmy's come crashing in on my nice plan and says he won't have it. What do you think of that? I'm furious.'

He smiled at her.

'I think you'd better let the cottages alone.'

She leaned nearer.

'Come into the garden and soothe me down. You haven't any unnatural craving for the drawing-room ballad, have you?'

'I want to hear Julia sing.'

She threw him a bright, sarcastic glance, settled herself on the window-seat, and lighted a cigarette.

After a moment's hesitation Antony sat down too. He had drunk his coffee and left his cup on the tray. Jimmy was making faces over his and drinking it doggedly down. Lois's cup, with only the dregs left in it now, stood between them on the broad oak sill.

His eye travelled to Ellie sitting by herself in the corner. He wondered what she was thinking about. It would not have comforted him very much if he had known. She was going over and over what had happened at the hospital that afternoon. Well, what had happened? She kept on saying to herself 'Nothing—nothing—nothing.' But it wasn't any use saying that when you felt sick with misery. Nothing had happened— nothing at all. You had to keep on saying it. It was like being in a boat with the water coming in through a hole you couldn't see—you had to keep on baling. But if the hole was too big, it wasn't any use, the water would swamp you.

She saw Ronnie's face, all pleased and lighted up as she had seen it when she got to the hospital. The pleased look wasn't

for her. She had a bare half minute of thinking it was, and then
he was telling her about Nurse Blackwell being transferred to
Brighton, to the home he was going to. Nurse Blackwell was
the pretty girl who laughed. She always looked as fresh as if she
hadn't anything to do except look like that. Ronnie said, 'Isn't
it marvellous?' Ellie said, 'Marvellous—' Her voice sounded
like a tired echo. She felt like that too—just an echo fading
out. Something cold touched her heart.

Julia struck a chord or two and began to sing. She had
what Antony had once called a voice of cream and honey—
sweet and rich without being very large. Contraltos are apt
to be ponderous. Julia's voice flowed easily in the old country songs which Jimmy demanded—Barbara Allan—The Bai-
liff's Daughter. Lois's drawled 'Rather infant school, don't you
think?' was taken no notice of.

Jimmy was asking for 'the jolly tune you used to sing—the
one with all the animals. You know—we used to call it the
Zoo.'

Julia's laugh rang out quite naturally.

' "Love will find out the Way"? All right.'

She began a spirited prelude, and sang to an old and charming tune:

'Over the mountains,
And under the waves;
Under the fountains,
And under the graves;
Under floods that are deepest,
Which Neptune obey;

Over rocks that are steepest,
Love will find out the way.
Some think to lose him,
By having him confined;
And some do suppose him,
Poor thing, to be blind;
But if ne'er so close ye wall him,
Do the best that you may,
Blind love, if so ye call him,
Will find out the way.
You may train the eagle
To stoop to your fist;
Or you may inveigle
The phoenix of the east;
The lioness, ye may move her
To give o'er her prey;
But you'll ne'er stop a lover:
He will find out his way.'

On the last word Lois stood up, throwing her cigarette-end out of the window. Her voice cut clearly across Julia's closing chords.

'Well, we're going to leave you to wallow in folk song. It isn't my line. Antony and I are going into the garden.'

This was one of the times he thought about afterwards. If he had stayed where he was, imitating her frankness with a cool and quite truthful declaration that he liked the old songs and liked to hear Julia sing them, would it have made any difference? Lois would probably have stayed too, fidgeting with the things from the bag she always carried—cigarette-case, lighter, compact; talking without taking the trouble to lower her voice; rasping Jimmy's temper. It really seemed better to go off with her into the garden, leaving Julia to minister to Jimmy's mood.

He stepped out over the low sill and gave Lois his hand. The swish of her dress knocked her coffee-cup over. It fell and rolled, but did not break.

Minnie came out of her corner to retrieve it. She stood looking at it for a moment before she set it down with its saucer upon the tray.

It's not broken,' she said—'just the tiniest chip by the handle. Marcia was so fond of these cups, and there aren't a great many of them left. I'm glad it isn't broken.'

She spoke as if she were talking to herself—as if she were alone in the room, or alone in that dream of hers. Then she picked up the tray and went away.

In the garden Antony laid himself out to entertain his hostess. That, at least, was the part he had cast himself for, the entertaining guest. Unfortunately, it takes two to play a scene. Lois had her own idea of the scene she meant to play. A fine sunny evening; still, warm air; a bird or two calling; a glow of colour from the autumn border—these were the setting. And for characters, what could be more promising than a pretty woman who is bored, and the man who used to ask nothing better than to make love to her?

She began to show him that it would not be disagreeable to her if he were to do it again. If that had been all, it would not have been too bad. Antony could hold his own in a verbal cut-and-thrust. But with every passing moment he was made aware of something underneath the play. Some current, dangerously alive, ready to give off sparks.

He began to wish very heartily that he had remained in the bosom of the family. And then quite suddenly she changed her tone. The lightness went out of it. She said in a voice which sounded perfectly human and sincere,

'Antony. I'm bored to death.'

Relief brought a smile to his lips.

'What do I say—"Thank you for the compliment"?'

It was her turn to frown.

'I can't live here. I was a fool to try.'

He said, 'Why you're only just beginning. A week or two ago you were full of all the things you were going to do.'

She said in a curiously sombre manner,

'The bottom's dropped out of it. I can't live in the country. I shall take a flat in town.'

'I don't think you'll get Jimmy to live in town.'

'I could if I tried, but—I don't intend to try.'

He gave her a keen glance. This was a Lois he did not know. Her face seemed to have grown heavier. Her eyes looked past him with something fixed in their expression, pupils narrowing against the light. He said casually,

'And what do you mean by that? Or do you mean anything at all?'

She said in a low, obstinate tone,

'Yes, I mean something. I think you know what I mean.'

'I hope I don't.'

'It's no good hoping. I'm not going on like this.'

He kept the casual note.

'Because you and Jimmy have had a row?'

She said, 'No,' left time for that to sink in, and then went on with a warm change of expression, manner, everything. 'Antony, don't you see that I can't go on?'

'Frankly, I don't.'

'Don't you? Then try! Antony, won't you just try ? I was a fool two years ago. There—I've said it! If I'd known that those Doubleday relations would settle out of court . . . I can't do without money, you know—it's no use pretending that I can. I've always been quite honest about that, haven't I?'

'Perfectly.'

'I can't do without money, and I can't do without people. I've got to get back to town.'

He said quite seriously,

'Lois, I think you're being stupid. What have you been making all these changes for if you're not going to be here? You're clearing the house, you've got a new staff coming in. You're planning to entertain—to have people down here. Jimmy won't stop you—he likes having the house full.'

She laughed.

'No—Jimmy won't stop me.'

He would rather she had remained sullen, but he laughed too.

'Well then, what do you want?'

She turned her head and looked past him again, but this time she was smiling.

'I'll tell you if you like. Or perhaps you can guess. And when I want things I generally get them.'

'Do you?'

Their eyes met for a moment. Hers were full of a sparkling vitality. The current was dangerous again. Then she laughed.

'I shall have my flat in town. You'll come and see me there, won't you? We can have weekend parties down here, just to keep the staff up to the mark and give the village something to talk about.'

'It sounds marvellous. And now don't you think we'd better go in?'

'And join the community singing?' She dropped her voice a note. 'Afraid of being alone with me, darling?'

She got a black frown.

'Look here, Lois—'

'Saint Anthony?'

Under the frowning brows his look was cold.

'I suppose you know what you're playing at.'

'Don't you?'

'Oh, certainly. You've had a row with Jimmy, and you think it's a bright idea to annoy him by flirting with me. And I'm telling you quite seriously and frankly that there's nothing doing, and that you'd better watch your step! I won't be used to annoy Jimmy!'

She looked up at him with a provoking smile.

'You'd make an awfully good-looking parson. Have you ever thought of taking orders?'

'Lois, listen a moment! You're bored. You're angry with Jimmy—'

'And you've turned my head. Darling, do go on! This is thrilling!'

'Yes, I'm going on. I said you'd better watch your step, and I meant it. I've seen Jimmy in this mood before—not very often—perhaps three or four times. Well, there's no knowing what he might do. He got up against his father once—Marcia told me about it—when he was about twenty. And he just walked out of the house and off the map. They didn't know whether he was alive or dead for a year. Then he turned up again—walked in full of bonhomie as if nothing had happened. But he never told them where he had been, or what he had been doing. That's a new light on Jimmy, isn't it?'

'Oh, quite—very intriguing. Are you trying to warn me that Jimmy will vanish out of my life if I walk in the garden with you for half an hour in broad daylight? I've got a feeling I might be able to bear it, you know.'

He gave her a dark, hard look.

'I'm trying to warn you. You're getting what you want all along the line. The girls are clearing out—Minnie will be clearing out. We'll all be off on our own business, and you'll get the place to yourself. Well, that's all right—that's what you want. But Jimmy doesn't like it. He's clannish—he doesn't see any reason why the family shouldn't continue to lead the tribal life at Latter End. Quite out of date and flat in the face of human nature—families don't do that sort of thing any more. Well, just ride him easy whilst you're changing over. Most men hate changes. Jimmy loathes them. He's got you on a pedestal about a mile high. Don't choose this moment to come unstuck. It's a damned long way to fall.'

He had not cared whether she was angry or not. She showed no sign of anger, but stood there, her face lifted to his, her smiling eyes intent upon him.

'You say I'm getting what I want. I told you I generally did.'

'You'll be getting rid of us, won't you?'

'And you think I want to get rid of you?'

The final you was undoubtedly stressed. She made a movement which brought her very near. Not near enough to touch him, but there was a sense of being touched—a most disquieting sense.

Antony had often been glad to see Julia, but never so glad as he was at this moment when she came round the corner of the yew hedge a dozen feet away. She came directly up to them and said in an uncompromising tone,

'Jimmy wants to play bridge. Will you come in and make up a four?'

FIFTEEN

It was not a comfortable game of bridge, but at least it afforded no opportunity for a tête-à-tête. Jimmy was fuddled, touchy—the word suspicion presented itself, and was rejected—but he was, most undoubtedly, in every way the opposite of his usual self. He held magnificent cards, and played them with a lavish disregard for everything except the whim of the moment. Julia, who partnered him, had the air of being somewhere else. Her features seemed to have closed down over her thoughts. From start to finish she did not utter an unnecessary word. Lois looked merely bored. If she did not speak, it was because, very plainly, it wasn't worth the trouble. No, not a comfortable game, but vastly preferable to being alone with Lois.

'I'm afraid I'll have to be off rather early in the morning.' He addressed Jimmy. 'There's a man I want to catch. He's only passing through London—coming down on the night train from Scotland. It's rather important for me to see him. I think

I'd better try and catch him at breakfast. He's not going to have much spare time.'

Jimmy gave a sort of grunt.

'Rather sudden, isn't it?'

'Well, no—not really. It was my coming down here that was sudden. I had to fit it in, as you wanted to see me on business.'

Lois raised her eyebrows.

'Business?'

'My business,' said Jimmy Latter.

Julia looked suddenly and directly at Antony. Her face had come awake. She said nothing, and almost immediately took up the cards and began to deal.

Lois laughed.

'I hope you don't expect any of us to get up and see you off!'

At half past ten everyone was ready to say good night.

Antony went up to the room which had been his since he was ten years old. It was on the first floor, but separated from the principal bedrooms by a door giving upon the back stairs. The stairs went down steeply from a landing with, on the left, a small sewing-room where Marcia Vane's maid used to work in the days when people had maids to sew for them, and, on the right, the room which was still called 'Antony's room'. There was also a bathroom.

As he was going along to have a bath, a girl came up the back stairs. He slowed down to let her go to wherever it was she was going, and saw her pass along the passage to the old sewing-room. Just before she got to it she looked back at him over her shoulder. He saw extravagantly waved fair hair, extravagantly darkened lashes, a mouth like a scarlet gash, and peeping pale blue eyes.

He went into the bathroom and shut the door. If this was Gladys Marsh, he was not surprised that she didn't go down well with Julia and Ellie. As he turned on the taps and blessed Manny for having the water piping hot, he reflected that if Joe Marsh had been lacking in filial piety he would probably not go unrequited.

He lingered in the hot water. The worst was over. He would take the road before seven, and wild horses wouldn't get him back to Latter End until—he had a feeling that it might be the Greek kalends. Whether Lois was serious or not, it was extremely evident that she meant to precipitate a scene. Just why? He wondered then, and was to wonder more in the horrible days to come—and never to be quite sure that he had found the answer.

He put it away and switched his thoughts with determination to his business with Latimer. His book was extraordinarily good—there was no doubt about that. The firm took exception to the handling of certain incidents. They were getting him to tackle Latimer, who was notoriously touchy. Antony had served with him in the early part of the war. There was some degree of friendship. The middle-aged partners had patted the new boy on the back and told him to go to it. 'You'll have to exercise tact. We don't want to lose him, but we can't publish those chapters as they stand.' He wondered how prickly Latimer was going to be, and then found himself thinking that he owed him something for providing such a good excuse for an early start. Nobody but Julia was to know that Latimer and he were to have lunched together. For that matter, they would probably do so still. Breakfast after a night in the train wasn't perhaps the moment when a tactful approach would be appreciated, but as an excuse it served a useful turn.

He came back to his room, and to the realisation that it was probably the last night he would ever spend there. His books still filled the shelves of a huge ramshackle bookcase, the sort that runs up to the ceiling and down to the floor—the bottom shelf crammed with bound volumes of the *Boy's Own Paper,* school prizes in the next, the kind you never read; and so on through the idols of his teens to long rows of small leather-bound editions at the top. Some of them he would want to take. For the rest, what did one do with the relics of one's youth? They ought to have gone in salvage during the war, but he could just see Jimmy with his foot down and a peremptory 'None of Mr Antony's things!' If he couldn't think what to do with the books, the pictures were much worse—an endless collection of school groups, college groups—rows and rows of faces, blazers, jerseys. A bonfire was really the only solution. The years of the war made an impassable gulf between himself and the face, the blazer, the jersey, which had been his on the farther side of it.

He stood looking at one or two of the later groups, and found it melancholy work. Bill Rogers, killed at Alamein—Jervis at Hellfire Corner—Mapleton in the blitz—Anstey in Burma—Danvers in France—Macdonald just gone, nobody knew where. No use looking back. Good fellows with whom he had had a good time, but you have to go on . . . He reflected that there was another side to it. Thompson was a Brigadier. Amusing in its way, because Thompson hadn't really cut much ice with the crowd. Well, Antony Latter who had cut quite a lot of ice in his day was only a captain. It all depended on what you pulled out of the bag. He was lucky to be alive and sound after Alamein and the wound which had kept him on the shelf for two years. The thing he really resented was breaking his leg in France because he'd been given a lift in a jeep by a chap who had never driven one before and had got off himself without a scratch.

He switched onto a plan for asking Julia to clear up his room, and then thought perhaps better not, because it might hurt Jimmy's feelings. He had reached this point, when a very slight sound made him turn.

Besides the ordinary door of this room there was another. It wasn't one you would notice unless you happened to know it was there, because it was papered to match the rest of the room and there was no handle on this side. This room had once been a double room, and the slip beyond the papered door its attendant dressing-room, but ever since he could remember the dressing-room had been Marcia's dress-cupboard. It was strictly forbidden to use it when they played hide-and-seek, but they always did. It was too tempting. The cupboard had its own door on to the main landing. It didn't communicate with Marcia's room, which lay on its farther side, but you could nip out of her door into the cupboard, and so into this room, and on to the back stair landing, with a choice of going either up or down, or through the swing-door back to the main landing again. Very strategic.

All this was in Antony's mind as he turned, not very consciously, but as things are which you have always known. The paper-covered door was opening. In another moment it had opened and Lois came in.

She was a shock. He had been away back in the past—she wasn't in the picture. She hadn't any business in Marcia's cupboard. That was the first instinctive reaction, changing to 'Of course it's hers now' and obliterated by the crashing conclusion, she hadn't any business in his room.

It was midnight. Probably everyone else in the house was asleep—he hoped so at any rate. He was in his pyjamas, and she in the sort of negligée which the vamp wears in every bedroom scene, something transparent and flesh-coloured, slipping at the shoulder. There was an atmosphere of scent and emotion. He was so angry that he could hardly find words or get them out. She didn't wait for them, but said hurriedly,

'I must speak to you. Antony, please do listen.'

'Lois, are you mad? We can't talk here—like this. For God's sake go back to your room!'

She gave a muted version of her rippling laugh. 'Thinking of my reputation, darling?'

He said bluntly, 'I'm thinking about Jimmy. You'd better think about him too.'

She came up close and said,

'I'd so much rather think about you, darling.'

'Lois—'

'It's two years since you kissed me. Don't you want to kiss me now?'

'Lois—'

'You used not to be such an icicle, my sweet.'

'You used not to be Jimmy's wife. And I hate to remind you that two years ago is two years ago.'

'You were in love with me then.'

'I'm not the least in love with you now.'

She laughed and narrowed her eyes at him.

'Joseph!'

He was too angry to care what he said. If she asked for it she could have it.

'Are you really keen on being Potiphar's wife? Definitely repulsive, don't you think?'

The door moved again. The paper had a pattern of bunches of violets on a white ground. The bunches on the door were moving. He could see them over Lois' shoulder—the shoulder from which that damnable garment was slipping. The door opened quite wide and Jimmy came in.

It needed only this to plunge them all into tenth-rate farce, but even through his swirling rage he was aware that the farce had a sinister slant. Jimmy, in pale blue pyjamas with his light hair wildly on end, ought to have fitted the part of the comic husband, but he didn't. He was starkly tragic. He stood a yard inside the door and looked at them, his eyes pale and fixed between reddened lids, his face dead white and pouring with sweat.

For the moment even Lois had nothing to say. It was Jimmy who spoke.

'Go back to your room!'

'Really, Jimmy!'

He spoke again.

'I heard what you said.'

She gave a short laugh, shrugged her shoulders, and walked past him.

To Antony the last crooked twist was given by the fact that though she almost touched Jimmy, he did not move to avoid her. She might not have been there. In a moment she wasn't there. The door in the wall had shut behind her. But for Jimmy Latter she had been gone before that. There wasn't any Lois any more.

It was all over between one minute and the next. Antony got hold of himself, and prepared to save anything that could still be saved. He said, 'Jimmy, old chap—' and Jimmy turned those pale eyes upon him.

'I heard what she said.' And then, 'She said, "two years ago". I'd like to know—what happened—two years ago.'

There was no expression in his voice, no trace of his usual manner. The words came with dreadful pauses between them. Jimmy—whose words tumbled over one another because there were always too many of them to pack neatly into a sentence! And now this dreary monotone—'I want to know—what happened—two years ago.'

'Nothing for you to mind. You've got to believe me. I was in love with her, and I asked her to marry me. She said no, and she married you. That's all there ever was. I thought you knew.'

Jimmy nodded. He said, still in that difficult way,

'Not—your—fault—'

Antony came up and put a hand on his shoulder.

'Look here, Jimmy, don't make too much of this. There's no harm done. You really mustn't make too much of it. I'll tell you the bare truth. For God's sake try and believe it. Lois had had a row with you—about old Hodson's cottage—'

'She lied to me about it.'

The shoulder under Antony's hand was as cold and hard as ice. He went on insistently.

'Well, you had a row, and she was angry. She doesn't like not getting her own way. She wanted to score you off. The best way she could think of was to flirt with me. Well, we've known each other long enough to be blunt—I told her there was nothing doing. And just then Julia came to call us in. Women don't like leaving a row unfinished—they think of ways to get even with you and have the last word. I do honestly believe that's what brought Lois here tonight. It was damned silly of her, and you've every right to be angry, but don't think it was worse than it was. I'll be off at six in the morning, and I'll keep out of the way—you can trust me for that. Jimmy—for God's sake—'

It was no good. Jimmy Latter gave him a heartrending look and said so.

'It's no good. I heard what she said.'

He turned and went out through the door in the wall.

SIXTEEN

Antony left Latter End before anyone was up. His step rang as hollow in the hall as if the house were empty. When he drew back the bolts and turned the key in the lock it seemed as if someone must wake. He came out into the early morning—dew on the grass, and a light breeze blowing. He got out his car and took the road with a sense of escape.

During the next two days he was kept extremely busy. He lunched with Latimer, got on better than he expected, and was dragged off by him to his cottage on the Thames. Latimer would take no denial. His manuscript was there, they could go through it together—'Your partners are damned old women, but I can't be bothered to fight them.' And, most unexpected of all, 'It's no good saying no—you must come down and meet my wife.'

Latimer the married man! Antony could hardly stretch his mind to take it in. He felt the most lively curiosity as to Mrs Latimer. In the event he found her a comfortable, placid housewife, comely in a country fashion and an inspired cook. In fact just what Latimer ought to have married. Being Latimer, it was quite unbelievable that he should have done so. Yet there she was, and there was Latimer, very much the husband and as pleased as Punch.

Leave of absence having been granted with alacrity by the firm, it was six o'clock next evening before he returned to his hotel. Just time in hand to change and get out to Hampstead to dine with the Mathiesons, where he spent a very pleasant evening. In the back of his mind the sense of escape persisted.

He came back to the hotel after midnight to find a slip in his room—'Miss Vane has rung up twice. She says will you please ring her when you come in.' Antony stood frowning at the words. They forced the doors of his mind and brought a sense of catastrophe with them. Nonsense of course, utter ludicrous nonsense. She might have a dozen good reasons for ringing up . . . 'Miss Vane has rung up twice. She says will you please ring her when you come in.'

He sat down on the edge of the bed and lifted the receiver of the table instrument. When he had given the number he stayed there waiting. It was ten minutes past twelve. The only upstairs telephone extension at Latter End was in Lois' bedroom. If Julia was expecting a call from him she must be waiting for it in the study. He had the strangest, strongest impression of her waiting for him to call her up—the instrument on Jimmy's table—Julia in the writing-chair, waiting in a fixed silence which went on, and on, and on.

It was nearly half an hour before the call came through. At the first sound of the bell he lifted the receiver and heard her say,

'Antony?'

'Yes. What is it?'

'Something has happened.'

'What is it?'

She went on in French—the French she had learned in the schoolroom with Miss Smithers, its familiar British ring just making what she had to say incredible.

'It's something dreadful, Antony. It's Lois—she's dead.'

He made some exclamation, he didn't know what.

'How?'

'I don't know. It was something in her coffee.'

'Julia!'

He heard her take a shuddering breath.

'The police have been here. They'll be coming back in the morning.'

'When did it happen?'

'After dinner—as soon as she drank her coffee. Will you come down?'

'Of course.'

'Early?'

'I'll be down by eight.'

'Make it half past seven. I'll meet you at the first milestone beyond the village. I want to talk to you.'

Something ran like a taut string between them. He said, 'All right,' and hard on the last word there came a click and they were thirty miles apart.

He hung up at his end, and found his hand stiff and numb from the grip in which he had been holding the receiver.

SEVENTEEN

She was standing by the milestone, a bicycle leaning against the hedge behind her. When Antony drew up she went across to the car.

'We'd better get off the road. Turn up Hob Lane. I've got Ellie's bicycle—I'll be there as soon as you are.'

The car almost filled the lane. Not that it mattered, for nothing came this way more than once in a blue moon. Julia got in, leaned back into the corner, and said without any preliminaries,

'They think it's murder.'

'Why?'

She said, 'Everything.' And then, 'I'd better tell you.'

'Yes.'

She took one of those long breaths. She was bare-headed, her hair a little misted with the early morning damp, her face quite colourless and strongly set, her voice low and steady.

'It's been a dreadful two days—ever since you went. There must have been some frightful row. I expect you know what it was. Jimmy doesn't say. He was out nearly all the first day. Lois stayed in her room till lunch, then she came down. Jimmy wasn't there. They didn't speak at dinner, and afterwards he went off and shut himself in the study.'

'What about the coffee?'

'He came into the drawing-room for it—just tossed it off with a gulp as if it was medicine and went away. Next day—yesterday—it was the same thing. She had her breakfast in her room. Jimmy went out and didn't come home till the late afternoon. He looked awful. Nobody—*nobody* in the house could help knowing that there had been some awful row. Dinner was ghastly. Ellie and I washed up—Minnie looked so bad that we sent her away. I took the coffee-tray through. Manny put a drop of vanilla into each of the cups—she did it in front of me. The sugar and the cognac were on the tray. I took it into the drawing-room and put it down. There wasn't anyone there. I went out on to the terrace to see if Lois was there, but I didn't find her, so I went along to the study and called through the window to Jimmy to tell him the coffee was in the drawing-room. I didn't hurry back. It was all being pretty grim.' She paused, stiffening herself against a shudder. She had on a warm frieze coat, but nothing warmed her. The cold came from within. It was her mind and her heart that shuddered.

Antony said, 'Go on.'

'Yes—I will. After a bit I came up to the drawing-room window and looked in. They were all there. Jimmy was in his usual chair. His coffee was on the table beside him. He took

it up and drank it off the way he always does. Lois had hers
in her hand. She was going over to her chair by the window.
Minnie was by the fireplace. Ellie was near the window. I didn't
want to go in. I said to Ellie, "Get off to bed early, darling. I'm
going for a turn." I went down through the garden and across
the fields. It was a lovely evening and I just didn't want to go
in. I don't know if it would have made any difference if I had.'

The shudder came again.

'Go on, Julia.'

She fixed her eyes on his face.

'It was ten o'clock when I got back. The door from the
drawing-room on to the terrace was open. I went in that way.
There wasn't anyone there but Lois, and I thought she was
asleep. I didn't particularly want to wake her, so I turned back
and was going to go round by the side door. And then I wasn't
sure—I mean I wasn't sure about her being asleep. I mean she
doesn't—and she had slipped down in the chair—she didn't
look right. I went over and spoke to her, but she didn't wake
up. Then I touched her, and she slipped right down. I went
and got Jimmy. She wasn't dead yet, but we couldn't wake her.
I tried to get Dr Grange on the telephone, but he was out at a
baby case. Then I tried to get someone from Crampton. There
was a hospital concert on, and I tried three people before I got
a man called Hathaway. He said to give her strong coffee and
walk her about. I think we got a little of the coffee down, but
she was past anything like walking. She died just after he got
there.' The shudder which she had been holding back shook
her from head to foot.

Antony put a hand on her knee.

'Don't, my dear—'

Her hand came out ice-cold and caught his. She went on speaking.

'He said we must ring up the police, and nothing must be touched. I had to do the ringing up—Jimmy just sat with his head in his hands. And all in the middle of everything that awful Gladys Marsh had hysterics—her idea of getting any limelight that was going. Manny and I were trying to stop her, when Dr Hathaway came out of the drawing-room. He's the disagreeable, conscientious sort—good at his job—nasty suspicious mind. It only needed Gladys to set him off. She was screaming out, "You want to shut me up, but you can't! Murder—that's what it is—murder! And you're not going to be able to hush it up!" Well, this Hathaway man was on to it like a knife. He told her to control herself, and if she knew anything, to say what it was.'

He felt her hand jerk on his. She wasn't looking at him now. She took her hand away. He said sharply,

'What was it?'

'Worse than anything you can possibly imagine. Antony, she was outside your door that night—she was listening. I told you she listened at doors. She says Lois was in your room, and Jimmy found her there. She says there was a terrible row.'

Antony's face was as bleak as a north-east wind.

'That's not true. Lois came through Marcia's cupboard. I needn't say I wasn't expecting her. Jimmy must have followed her. There wasn't any row. He told her to go back to her room—that's all he said to her. There wasn't any row with me. He said it wasn't my fault, and I told him I'd clear out and keep out of the way.'

Julia's cold hands took hold of one another.

'Gladys says that Lois called you Joseph, and you called her Potiphar's wife, and that Jimmy kept saying, "I heard what she said". '

'Substantially correct. Is that all?'

'No, it isn't. She came out with the whole thing—how Lois had said someone was trying to poison her, how she'd had these sick attacks, and finished up with, "They've done it—somebody's done it! Poisoned her—that's what they have, among them! And trying to shut my mouth! But if there's any law in England, they shan't! " All that kind of thing.'

'Well?'

'The Inspector came—he's a new man. He saw the doctor, and he saw Gladys alone. He took statements from us. We were up most of the night. You see, it's either suicide or murder, and neither he nor Hathaway believe it's suicide—because of Gladys, and the previous attacks, and because she took it like that in her after-dinner coffee. They haven't analysed it yet of course, but they seem pretty sure it was the coffee. Hathaway says if she was going to commit suicide she wouldn't have done it like that—she'd have waited till she was in bed. He says sleeping-draught suicides always do.'

'Why are they so sure it was the coffee?'

Julia looked at him with tired, tragic eyes.

'There wasn't anything else. We had fish for dinner—baked haddock. Lois helped it, and we all had some. It couldn't have been in that. And a sweet omelette—she helped that too. We all had some of it. No—it must have been the coffee.'

'Julia—that idea you had about Manny—you thought she might be playing tricks. You said you were going to tackle her about it. Did you do it?'

'Yes, I did.'

'What did she say?'

Julia was silent. She looked down at her clasped hands, where the knuckles stood up white.

'What did she say?'

Of course it was no good—she couldn't keep it back. She said very low and distressed,

'I was right—she had been playing tricks.'

'Good God! *Manny!*'

'Not what happened last night. Antony, she didn't do that—she couldn't!'

'How do you know? You'd better tell me what happened.'

She was looking at him again.

'Yes, I will. I got her alone, and I went straight at it.'

'When?'

'The day you went. I said straight out, 'Manny, you've been playing tricks—it's no good your saying you haven't. And it's got to stop." She went absolutely purple and said, "I don't know what you mean, Miss Julia." So I said, "Oh, yes, you do, Manny—you know perfectly well. You've been putting ipecac or something in Mrs Latter's coffee to make her sick, and it's got to stop. You don't want to end up in jail, do you?" '

'What did she say?'

Julia's lips twitched into the ghost of a smile.

'She said, "You take and get out of my kitchen, Miss Julia— saying things like that!" But I could see I'd frightened her, so I put my arm as far round her as it would go, and I said, "You're a wicked old woman, Manny, and it's got to stop." '

'What did she say to that?'

'Tossed her head and went right through the roof. "What's a little sickness to what she's done to others? You tell me that, Miss Julia! Poor Mrs Marsh turned out of her home for that flashy piece Gladys! And no thanks to her poor Mr Hodson isn't turned out of his! You and Miss Ellie driven away out of your own home, and Miss Minnie that's a born saint turned out with nowhere to go! I'm sure it's heart-rendering to see her!" I kept my arm round her, and I said, "You'd better make a clean breast of it, Manny." And she burst out crying and said, "Lois did ought to be punished, and it wasn't no more than a spoonful of ipecac that wouldn't hurt a child." '

There was a strained pause. After which Antony said,

'Well, she doesn't seem to have stopped at a spoonful of ipecac.'

Julia cried out.

'No, no, it wasn't Manny—it couldn't have been Manny—not last night!'

'You'll have hard work to convince the police of that.'

She caught him by the arm.

'No, no—you mustn't tell them! Antony, you mustn't! She didn't do it—she couldn't have done it!'

'Why couldn't she? She made the coffee.'

'Yes. She made it—for Jimmy as well as for Lois. She knew—everyone in the house knew—that Jimmy was taking that horrible coffee, and why. Do you think she'd have put anything into it to hurt him?'

'Somebody did.'

'Then it was someone who knew which cup Lois was going to take.'

'The coffee was poured out?'

'Yes. There were the two cups, but Manny couldn't possibly have told which one of them Jimmy would take. She adores him—she'd let herself be cut in pieces before she would do anything that could possibly hurt him.'

She knew the moment when he accepted that, and the other moment when the thought rose up between them—'If it wasn't Manny, who was it?'

Neither of them was ready to deal with that. Antony put up his hand to the steering-wheel.

'We'd better be getting along, hadn't we?'

She said, 'No—wait! There's something I want to say. I was thinking it would be better, it would make things easier, if you don't mind saying you were engaged to me—just whilst all this is going on. We could break it off afterwards.'

He gave her a strange hard look. Courage—yes, she certainly had that. He said,

'A little sudden, isn't it? Are you, by any chance, protecting my reputation?'

Her eyes had a piteous simplicity.

'I don't know. Not if you don't want me to. I just thought it would be easier for Jimmy—and everyone. I thought if we said we were engaged, nobody could say you had come down because of Lois, and we could break it off whenever you liked—after it was all over.'

He was most deeply moved, but his face showed nothing. It remained dark and intent. His voice was quiet and ordinary.

'All right, my dear, if that's what you want. I think perhaps you're right—it will make it easier for Jimmy. And now let's go.'

EIGHTEEN

Miss Silver took up the telephone receiver. There was a considerable buzzing on the line. A high, young voice said, 'So I told him I'd never speak to him again—' and ceased abruptly. Miss Silver speculated with mild interest as to whether this was a sidelight on the love affairs of the rather spectacular young woman who had recently moved into the flat below her own. She had encountered her in the lift, but had never heard her voice, or she would not have had to speculate.

The buzzing continued. In the midst of it her own name sounded very faintly. She at once repeated it in a precise manner. Quite suddenly the line was clear. A man's voice said, dragging on the words,

'I want to speak to Miss Silver.'

'This is Miss Silver speaking.'

The drag became more evident.

'She's dead. You said it was a trick. But she's dead.'

Miss Silver's face assumed a grave expression.

'Is that Mr Latter?'

The voice said, 'She's dead.' It was like listening to a gramophone record which is running down.

She said, 'Dear me!' And then, 'I am very sorry indeed, Mr Latter. Is there anything I can do?'

'You said—you could—come down—'

Miss Silver coughed.

'Is that what you wish me to do?'

'You said—you would—' Jimmy Latter's voice faded out. A faraway click suggested that he had replaced the receiver—perhaps to plunge his head in his hands and sit there waiting.

It never took Miss Silver very long either to make up her mind or to complete her preparations for a journey. She would travel in her afternoon dress, with the black cloth coat which she had had for so many years that its waisted style had been in and out of fashion quite a number of times. Since the stuff showed no sign of wear, the idea of discarding it would have shocked her. In her shabby but serviceable suitcase she packed a silk daydress for wear in the evening—it was as a matter of fact her last summer's best—and a genuinely antique black velvet coatee as a provision against possible draughts. Country houses were sadly prone to draughts. In view of a possible change in the weather, she also packed a small fur tippet, rather pale with age but astonishingly well preserved.

It would be unbecoming to pry into a lady's underwear. Miss Silver's was sensible, warm, and hard-wearing—the stockings of black thread, the dressing-gown of crimson flannel trimmed with cream crochet lace of her own making. There

were also a pair of slippers, the beaded house-shoes, and, carefully wrapped in a white silk handkerchief, a worn and well
read Bible. None of these things took long to assemble, nor
did the invaluable Emma Meadows require any instructions.
After keeping house for Miss Silver for twenty years she took
everything just as it came with imperturbable calm.

Miss Silver caught her train comfortably. She had time to
send a telegram to announce the hour of its arrival. She had
time to settle herself in a corner seat with her suitcase in the
rack overhead. After which she removed her gloves, took her
knitting out of a shabby capacious handbag, and went on with
Derek's second stocking.

She had a very pleasant journey. A delightful middle-
aged lady who had recently returned from France gave her
an extremely interesting account of social conditions there,
and the agreeable gentleman in the opposite corner was able
to contribute a most informative description of the island of
Cyprus. Really quite an instructive afternoon.

The station for Rayle is Weston, a slightly larger place some
three miles away. When Miss Silver alighted a tall, dark young
man advanced to meet her, introducing himself as Antony
Latter.

'Jimmy is my cousin. He is too knocked over to come and
meet you himself.'

As he picked up her suitcase and led the way through
the booking-hall to where his car was waiting, Antony concluded that poor old Jimmy must have had a complete mental
breakdown. Nothing else would account for importing this
dowdy elderly spinster into his tragic affairs. She looked like a

composite portrait of the Victorian governess, and she talked like it too—if you could imagine a portrait endowed with speech. With the feeling that her arrival was just about the last straw, he bestowed her and her luggage and drove away.

Rather to his surprise, she chose to sit beside him in the front of the car. He was irritatingly aware of her, prim and upright in an impossible hat, a shabby black umbrella depending from her wrist, her hands in worn kid gloves clasped upon a bulging bag.

They had driven perhaps for half a mile, when she turned to him with a slight dry cough.

'Would it be possible for you to draw up for a little, Mr Latter? Your cousin was too agitated to give me any information. I know nothing except that Mrs Latter is dead, and that he wished me to come down. I should be glad to have a simple statement of what has occurred.'

They were in a lane with hedges on either side. The afternoon was fine though not warm. September had thinned the sunshine. There was already a breath of damp from the fields on either side, even a hint that the damp might turn to frost before the morning. The hips and haws in the hedgerows were ripening fast. As he stopped the car unwillingly he resented the parody on his conversation with Julia. They had talked in a lane this morning. She had sat where Miss Silver was sitting now. She had had the mist in her hair. She had looked at him with tragic eyes and asked him whether he would mind if they were engaged—'Just while this is going on.'

The travesty repelled him. He avoided looking at Miss Silver as he said,

'I'll tell you as much as I know. But it's secondhand—I wasn't here.'

'If you will be so good.'

She listened attentively while he repeated what Julia had told him. He did not go beyond the immediate facts surrounding Lois's death—the evening meal; the two cups of coffee; who were present in the drawing-room; Julia's absence after she had brought in the tray; her finding Lois unconscious at ten o'clock. When he had finished she said,

'Thank you.' And then, 'The police, of course, have been notified?'

'Yes.'

Miss Silver coughed.

'May I enquire, Mr Antony, whether they have been informed of Mrs Latter's previous attacks of sickness? Do they know she had declared that someone was attempting to poison her?'

'Yes.'

'Was it Mr Latter who informed them?'

'No, it wasn't.'

Why did she want to know that? It startled him. He turned, glanced at her, and met a look of such direct intelligence that he received something like an electric shock.

'Then who gave them this information, Mr Antony?'

'A girl called Gladys Marsh—Mrs Marsh. She's the wife of a man in the village, a tenant of my cousin's, but she was staying in the house and more or less acting as maid to Mrs Latter.'

The look of intelligence became quite piercing.

'Maid—and confidante?'

Antony said, 'Perhaps—I don't know. A persevering eaves-dropper at any rate.'

Miss Silver nodded.

'A dangerous person to have in the house.'

His 'Yes' was so heartfelt that she drew her own conclusions from it. It appeared to her to be very probable that he could have said a good deal more about Gladys Marsh if he had chosen to do so, and perhaps about some other things as well.

She preserved a short silence, during which Antony adjusted himself. The electric shock which he had received had left him with the need of adjustment. The little governess person whom he had met at the station was there before him in her dowdy clothes, but startlingly clear to his inner vision was quite a different Miss Silver. He was sufficiently intelligent himself to recognise and respect intelligence. The impression he had received was of an intelligence keener than his own, a controlled and ordered thought, a cool authority. It surprised him very much. He had for the moment a sense of double vision—of two Miss Silvers indefinitely linked, and then quite suddenly, as if by some focusing action of the mind, quite defi-nitely merged. There was only one Miss Silver, but she was not what he had taken her for. Unconsciously his manner changed.

Miss Silver, who had been watching him, produced an encouraging smile. Like a great many other people who had had dealings with her he had a flash-back to his schoolroom days—his very first schoolroom when he was a very small boy, everything frightfully new and desperately unknown. And the teacher, that awful, godlike being behind the desk, had looked at him and smiled—'Come, Latter—I'm sure you know that answer.' Absurd reminiscence. He had a smile for it himself.

Miss Silver was saying, 'Pray continue, Mr Latter. I shall be glad to know just how things stand.'

His face hardened.

'I came down early this morning. Miss Vane rang me up. By the way, do you know who we all are?'

'I think so. Mr Latter gave me a good deal of information when he came to see me. You mean Miss Julia Vane?'

His brows drew together.

'Yes—my fiancée.'

Miss Silver coughed.

'Mr Latter did not mention that.'

He said shortly, 'We were not engaged then.'

'I see. Miss Vane telephoned you, and you came down early.'

'Yes. My cousin is in a dreadful state.' He hesitated for a moment and then went on. 'There had been a—' He hesitated again.

'A quarrel?'

Something inside him said, 'How did you know?' He would have denied it if it had been any use. But it wasn't any use. Murder is like the day of judgment—the secrets of all hearts are opened. He frowned deeply and took another word.

'They had had a disagreement. It makes it much worse for him. He reproaches himself. And the police—'

'Yes, Mr Antony?'

He said gloomily,

'It puts ideas into their heads. That's why we thought it would be a good thing if you came down. That is to say, it was my cousin who thought about it. It's the only thing that has seemed to rouse him at all, and we agreed that he ought to have someone to advise him.'

Miss Silver coughed.

'You say that it puts ideas into their heads. What kind of ideas?'

'I expect you can guess.'

There was a shade of reproof in her look.

'What I require just now is facts, not guesswork, Mr Antony. I would like the answers to one or two questions. Has the post-mortem taken place? If it has, to what is Mrs Latter's death attributed?'

She got her answer to both questions in a single word.

'Morphia.' Then, after a moment, 'A considerable quantity.'

She said, 'Dear me! Was she known to have any in her possession?'

He shook his head.

'She never took drugs. She was boasting about it one of the last times I saw her. She had—a very good complexion. She was laughing and saying it was because she never took anything like that. I don't know how we got on to the subject, but that's what she said.'

'Morphia is not very easy to get hold of nowadays. It could be obtained abroad . . . Did anyone else in the house have any in their possession?'

'Not that I know of—I should think it most unlikely. I'm the only one who has been abroad. I certainly did not bring any morphia back with me.'

Miss Silver gave him a long look, deep, kind, and searching.

'Do you think that Mrs Latter committed suicide?'

'I should say it was most unlikely.'

He received an inclination of the head which appeared to express approval.

'That is honest of you. It will make my work very much easier if everyone will be as frank. It would interest me to hear your reasons for the opinion you have just expressed.'

Antony was not feeling particularly frank. The midnight scene in his room stuck in his mind. He didn't believe that Lois had taken her life. He told himself with emphasis that he didn't believe it. But she might have done. She had offered herself and been refused, and Jimmy had come in. Suppose it really was suicide . . . He felt a kind of horror at the thought, which was purely instinctive, since reason was prompt to suggest that any other solution must be more horrible still. He spoke quickly lest Miss Silver should read his thoughts.

'She was very fond of her life. She had most things she wanted—good looks, health, money. She was full of plans.'

Miss Silver considered that. She put the word 'most' away for future thought. She enquired,

'Do the police reject the idea of suicide?'

'I gather the local Inspector made it tolerably clear that he didn't think much of it. What the Yard people think, I don't know. They haven't been here very long.'

Miss Silver looked up brightly.

'Do you mean that Scotland Yard has been called in?'

'Yes. I take it that means they don't think it's suicide.' He gave a short hard laugh. 'Old Marsfield, the Chief Constable, is a family friend. My guess is he's dropping the case before it burns his fingers. He's a bit of an old woman anyway. The idea of encountering a criminal in his own walk of life has never occurred to him till now, and it's given him the jitters—he can't get rid of us fast enough. Hence Chief Inspector Lamb and Sergeant Abbott.'

Miss Silver coughed.

'Two excellent and intelligent officers,' she said.

NINETEEN

Chief Detective Inspector Lamb sat solidly in Jimmy Latter's heavy oak writing-chair, which he filled a good deal better than Jimmy did. On the table in front of him was a pile of papers. He had left his bowler hat in the hall and appeared, in his neat dark clothes, as a stout, strongly built figure, very upright and as solid as the oak which supported him. His strong black hair had receded a little at the temples, leaving the large square face rather more in evidence than it had been twenty years before. His round brown eyes, which Frank Abbott irreverently compared to peppermint bull's-eyes—the dark, strongly flavoured kind—were turned upon that young man, who in a beautiful suit of summer grey sat in an easy attitude on the farther side of the table. There could have been no greater contrast than that which the two men presented. Lamb, the old-time policeman, experienced in discipline and life, just, honest, intelligent. Frank Abbott, product of the public school and

Police College, much more educated, but under all his irreverence a loyal subordinate and a staunch admirer of his chief. To look at him, one would not suppose him to be given to loyalties and admirations. Rather an exquisite young man—rather blasé, very fair hair slicked back with unguents, pale blue eyes fixed in a meditative stare, the latest collar, the latest tie, hands noticeably well shaped and beautifully kept, slim elegant feet in slim elegant shoes.

The Chief Inspector tapped the table and said,

'Well, Frank, what do you make of it?'

'It's not for me to say, sir.'

Lamb made a sound which might have been described as a snort.

'Oh, it isn't, isn't it? Very proper and respectful all of a sudden, aren't you? Not feeling ill, I suppose?'

'No, thank you, sir.'

The table was banged.

'Then come off it! I asked you a question.'

Sergeant Abbott smiled negligently.

'I should like to hear your opinion first, sir.'

The Chief Inspector's colour had risen. Frank was an insubordinate young dog. There were times when he wanted taking down a peg or two. There were times when he got the taking down. This morning had been one of the times, and Lamb had dealt faithfully. Young men with swelled heads were what he never had tolerated and never would. Frank was a good boy, but none the worse for a setting down—too free by half with his opinions. And now he was getting his own back. Insubordination—that was what it was, and he'd got him in a cleft stick. You can't discipline a man for being respectful. He said rather loudly,

'It's too soon to be giving opinions, but if the locals hadn't thought it was murder they wouldn't have called us in.'

Frank Abbott gave a slight cool nod.

'As you say, sir.'

'The Chief Constable didn't want to be mixed up in it. I don't think his opinion's worth having. He's overdue for retirement. But that Inspector—what's his name, Smerdon?—he's a smart fellow, there's no doubt about what he thinks. And Dr Hathaway. The doctor's right, you know, about sleeping-draught suicides—they take the stuff in bed, every man jack of them. I suppose it's natural—what they call association of ideas. You go to bed and you go to sleep—especially the women. The only exceptions I can think of are the people who try and get off the map altogether—go off into a wood or something like that where they think they won't be found. Now this Mrs Latter, she's a smart, sophisticated woman—a good-looker too. She's had a row with her husband. He finds her in his cousin's room in the middle of the night. By Mrs Marsh's account she's chucked herself at his head, and he isn't having any. Then the husband comes in—says he's heard everything and sends her packing. Well, there's no denying that's a slap in the face for a woman— about the worst she could have. She might commit suicide.'

Frank Abbott nodded, but did not speak. Lamb went on.

'She might, but I can't see her doing it like that. To my way of thinking, the sort of woman she was would have made a better show of it—dressed it up a bit. Suicides do, you know. There's a lot of the old "They'll be sorry when I'm dead" about them, especially with women who kill themselves over love affairs. They want to make a good dramatic impression that'll give them plenty of limelight and leave the man in the case something to think about for the rest of his life. As I see it, by all accounts Mrs Latter wasn't the sort of person to want to slip away quietly and not give any trouble. No woman who's managed to get herself as much disliked as she had is going to think about other people's feelings. That sort of woman wants to make a splash. She makes up her face, she does her hair, she puts on her best nightgown, and she leaves a suicide note to harrow the man's feelings up.'

Frank's indifferent look had changed. He said,

'Yes—I think you're right.'

Lamb had talked himself into a good temper.

'Then I must be! Well, if it isn't suicide it's murder. And if it's murder, then it's one of the people in this house—one of seven people. Mr Antony Latter is out of it—he wasn't here. A bit of good luck for him. He'd no motive either as far as one can see. You don't poison a woman because she sets her cap at you. Well, that leaves Mr Jimmy Latter the husband, those two half-sisters who aren't really half-sisters at all—'

'His stepmother's daughters.'

'That's right. It leaves them, and that Miss Mercer, and the servants—the old cook who's been here donkey's years, the kitchen-maid, a girl of seventeen, and Mrs Gladys Marsh.' He repeated the last name in a very disapproving tone, 'Mrs Gladys Marsh. Well, I'm sorry for her husband, whoever he is. A thorough-going bad lot is how I'd put her down. Why, she'd the impudence to make eyes at me.'

With a perfectly straight face Sergeant Abbott said, 'Incredible, sir!'

The bull's-eyes bulged a little.

'Look here—how do you mean, incredible? You saw her, didn't you?'

He got a properly respectful reply.

'I mean it would have been incredible if I hadn't seen it.'

Lamb grunted.

'Well, bad lot or no, I think we can count her out. I can't see what motive she'd have. She was by way of being the spoilt favourite, I gather, and if she'd had any hand in the business, I shouldn't expect her to put herself forward the way she did. I don't suppose we'd have heard a word about Mrs Latter having those sick attacks and saying someone was trying to poison her if Mrs Gladys Marsh hadn't had her fit of hysterics and let it out. I don't see anyone else stumbling over themselves to tell us. They'll all stick together, the rest of them will. There's the family—that's natural. And there's that old woman in the kitchen—she's been here more than fifty years. Well, people like that, they'll stick even closer than the relations will.'

'*Plus royaliste que le roi,*' murmured Sergeant Abbott, adding hastily, 'You're quite right, sir.'

He got a glare.

'Oh, I am, am I? And let me tell you that my own language is good enough for me, and if it isn't good enough for you it ought to be! If you've got to put a thing into a foreign language, it's either because it's something to be ashamed of, or it's because you're showing off.'

Having waved the red rag, Frank made a strategic retirement.

'It was a quotation, Chief.'

'Then you can quote in English! There's the whole of Shakespeare, isn't there? Extraordinary what a lot of quotations there are in Shakespeare.'

'Quite true, sir.'

'Then stick to 'em! And don't go foreign on me—it puts me out! Where was I?'

'Mrs Maniple sticking closer than a relation.'

Lamb nodded.

'She's that sort. And she's got the girl Polly What's-her-name—'

Frank offered 'Pell.'

'Polly Pell. She's got her well under her thumb, I should say. Kitchenmaids were kitchenmaids when she went into service. She'll have gone through the mill herself, and she'll not be standing any nonsense. Things don't change so much as you'd think in a village. I was brought up in one, and I know. The world's been turned upside down, but there's a long way to go before you can stop a determined old woman having her own way with a girl like that. So we come back to where we started. If Gladys Marsh hadn't let the cat out of the bag, I don't suppose anyone else would have done it.'

'I don't suppose they would.'

'Well then, if we leave out Gladys Marsh we get the family and the old cook. I think we can leave the girl out of it too—she wouldn't have any motive. So then there's Mr Latter, Mrs Street, Miss Vane, Miss Mercer—I'm counting her as family—and Mrs Maniple. Well, Mr Latter has the strongest motive. He's been married two years, and by all accounts he's very devoted to his wife—thinks no end of her. And then all of a sudden he gets this frightful shock. He finds her in his cousin's room in the middle of the night in her nightgown, fairly throwing herself at him, and his cousin saying no. It's enough to throw a man off his balance. If he'd killed her then he'd have got off with a nominal sentence. Provocation—that's what he had. But he didn't kill her then. He takes the rest of the night, and all next day, and the best part of another twenty-four hours after that. And Mrs Latter dies of an overdose of morphia administered in her after-dinner coffee. He had the motive—there's no stronger motive than jealousy. He'd put her on a pedestal and she'd come down with a crash. He had the opportunity—he was alone in the room, with the coffee in those two cups on the tray. You may say that all the rest of the family had an equal opportunity, and that's true. Take their own statements. Miss Vane brings the tray in and puts it down, goes out on to the terrace and along to this study window, where she looks in and asks Mr Latter if he is coming into the drawing-room for his coffee. He says yes, and she wanders about for a bit. By the time she looks in to say she's going for a walk the rest of the family are in the drawing-room, Mr Latter is drinking his coffee, and Mrs Latter is going towards her chair with her cup in her hand. Miss Vane goes away, and doesn't come back till ten o'clock, when she finds Mrs Latter alone in the drawing-room in a state of collapse. That's Miss Julia Vane. She could have put morphia into either of the cups, but she had no means of knowing which one Mrs Latter would take.'

Frank Abbott had straightened up. His eyes were cool and keen. He said,

'Quite.'

Lamb went on.

'Miss Mercer comes next. She says she came into the drawing-room and found Mrs Latter there, standing by the coffee-table. She says she was putting sugar in her coffee. Mrs Latter said something about where were the others, and went out on to the terrace by way of looking for them. Miss Mercer says she followed her. If it ever comes to trial, I suppose the defence will say it wasn't sugar Mrs Latter was putting into her cup, it was the morphia powdered up to look like sugar. I suppose that's possible—but it don't seem likely. On her own showing Miss Mercer had the opportunity of doctoring one of the cups.'

'That would mean premeditation.'

Lamb nodded.

'That goes for all of them . . . Mrs Street comes next. She says she came into the drawing-room and found it empty. The coffee-tray was on the table. She hadn't been there more than a moment, when Mr Latter came in. He didn't come along the terrace and in through the window, but followed her through the door. Mrs Latter and Miss Mercer were on the terrace. She said she would call them, and went out by way of the window, leaving Mr Latter alone in the room. She had her opportunity, and she left him with his. That's all plain—each of them was alone with the coffee-tray. One of them must have poisoned the coffee which Mrs Latter drank. I don't think it's reasonable to suppose it was the cook. She is by all accounts devoted to Mr Latter, and if she poisoned one cup, it would be an absolute toss-up whether he got it or not. She could have no motive except general resentment, and she'd never have risked it. I think we'll cut her out. That leaves us with

Miss Vane, Mrs Street, Miss Mercer, and Mr Latter. They all had an equal opportunity of putting something into one of the cups. But Miss Vane, like the cook, had no control over who took which cup. They all agree that she didn't come back into the drawing-room. So she's in the same boat as the cook, and I'm going to leave her out too, at any rate for the present. Now we've got Mrs Street, Miss Mercer, and Mr Latter. And this is where they all go vague on us. I want to know who dished those cups out. When Miss Vane looked in Mr Latter was in a chair by the window drinking his coffee, and Mrs Latter was crossing the room with her cup in her hand. Mrs Street was sitting quite close to the open terrace door. Miss Mercer was picking up some rose leaves which had fallen from a vase on the mantelpiece. Mrs Street says she didn't touch the coffee-cups or notice who did—she was very tired, and she was only thinking about how soon she could get off to bed. Miss Mercer says she didn't go near the tray or touch the cups after she and Mrs Latter came in together from the terrace. She says Mrs Latter walked straight up to the tray and took her cup. Mr Latter says his cup was on the small table beside his chair. He says he didn't notice whether it was there when he first came into the room. Well, maybe he's lying. If he put morphia into one of the cups he wouldn't want to risk getting that cup himself—he'd make sure there wasn't any mistake by putting his own cup out of harm's way. Mrs Street says she can't remember whether both cups were on the tray when she went through. She'd been to see her husband that afternoon—he's being moved to a convalescent home at Brighton—and she says she was much too taken up with thinking about him and how tired she was to be bothering about coffee-cups. Miss Mercer says both cups were on the tray when she came into the drawing-room. Of course either she or Mrs Street could have put the morphia into one of the cups and shifted the other to the table by Mr Latter's chair. Or Mr Latter would have done it himself when he was alone in the room.'

'So where are we?' said Frank Abbott.

'Motive,' said Lamb. 'There's four of them with opportunity. But if we're to believe Miss Mercer, who says there were two cups on the tray when she came in, Miss Vane couldn't have moved Mr Latter's cup, as she couldn't have told who was going to take which. So she's much less likely than the other three. Let's take it that it lies between the three of them who could have put the harmless cup by Mr Latter's chair. We don't know which it was. Two of them mayn't know any more than we do. One of them must know, because one of them moved it, and the one who did is the one who knew what was in the other cup. That's as far as we're likely to get an opportunity, without direct evidence. So we come to motive. As I said to start with, Mr Latter has the motive which is one of the strongest a man can have—he had actually heard his wife making love to another man in very compromising circumstances. Now for Mrs Street. She's got a motive too. It don't seem so strong, but it's a motive all right. Remember that Gladys Marsh saying, "They all hated her—they'd all have liked to do her in. Mrs Street wanted to have her husband here, and Mrs Latter wouldn't have it—said she didn't want to be cluttered up with relations, and she didn't see turning the house into a hospital neither"? And then she tossed her head and said, "Mrs Street's been crying her eyes out about it. There's some good-looking nurses in that hospital. Afraid she'll lose her husband the way she's lost her looks, I shouldn't wonder." She's an unpleasant, spiteful young woman, but there's a motive there, you know.'

Frank's shoulder lifted in a slight shrug.

'Mrs Street hardly looks the type for murder.'

Lamb thumped his knee.

'There isn't any type for murder—how often am I to tell you that? People do it when what they want and what they think they ought to have gets to be so important that there's nothing else matters. They've lost their balance and come down on the side where there's only themselves and they can do what they like—all the things that keep people back from killing when they're angry don't count any more. It's liable to happen to anyone who doesn't keep a hold of himself. Do you know what's struck me most in what that Gladys Marsh said? It's the bit about their all hating Mrs Latter. She might be exaggerating, or she might not. But hate is a very dangerous thing to have knocking about—it's one of the things that takes people off their balance. And the woman's dead. I don't say I suspect Mrs Street—not on the evidence we've got so far—but I'd say she had a motive.'

'I suppose so—'

'Then there's Miss Mercer. She's got a motive too, but I'd say it's the weakest of the three. She's lived here for twenty-five years. She's leaving because Mrs Latter wanted to start fresh with a staff she's picked herself. Well, that's the sort of thing that's happening every day—a middle-aged man gets married, and the woman who's been running his house for him don't hit it off with the new wife. It may be a daughter, or a sister, or a housekeeper—it isn't often it answers. By all accounts, this Miss Mercer is a quiet, gentle little woman. Not the kind to make trouble, or it wouldn't have lasted two years as it has. I don't doubt she's got some sore feelings. Looks ill too. But, as I said, it's the sort of thing that's always happening, but not what you'd do murder for.'

Frank Abbott's colourless eyebrows rose. He gazed at an upper shelf of the book-lined walls where the Waverley Novels had stood unread these sixty years except by Julia Vane, and said,

'Doctor's daughter, wasn't she?'

Nothing could have been more casual, but Lamb looked at him hard.

'What do you mean by that?'

'Village doctor's daughter. Village doctors usually dispense their own drugs. I was wondering what happened to the late Mercer's stuff—the morphia, you know. Smerdon says he took away a medicine chest out of Miss Mercer's room—the police surgeon was going to go through it. I asked what about finger-prints, and he was inclined to be huffy—said of course they'd thought of that—been over everything before they turned it over to the surgeon. I asked what they'd found, and he said he hadn't had time to check up, but he'd let us have the results this evening.'

He got up as he spoke and wandered to the farther of the two windows. One looked upon the terrace, the other com-manded a view of the drive and its approach to the front of the house. It was from this window that Frank Abbott watched the progress of a car which was coming slowly up the winding drive—Antony Latter's car, with Antony Latter at the wheel. A clump of shrubs obscured the passenger beside him. The car emerged from the shrubs. Frank Abbott gave a long, low whistle. The car passed out of sight. He turned round with a gleam in his eye and said drily,

'Latter went to meet someone at Weston, but nobody told us who it was. Now we know.'

The Chief Inspector stared. His mind, which Frank had once irreverently compared with a tram, ran very efficiently upon its own lines but was not equipped for a rapid side-step. He was considering morphia in connection with Miss Mercer and a village dispensary. Antony Latter and the person he had been meeting at Weston constituted an intrusion. They broke the thread of his thoughts. He stared, took hold rather angrily of Frank's last words, and said,

'So now we know? What are you talking about?'

'Maudie,' said Sergeant Abbott.

The purple colour rose in Lamb's cheeks. His eyes bulged.

'Not Maud Silver!'

Frank smiled maliciously.

'The one and only Maudie,' he said.

TWENTY

Miss Silver heard the schoolroom door close behind her. That was Mr Antony going away, an action she very much approved. She always preferred to be alone with a client, and in a case like this it was more than usually desirable.

Jimmy Latter was sitting at the schoolroom table. He had lifted his head from his hands when his cousin opened the door and said her name, but he had made no attempt to rise. She came forward with her hand out, saying, 'How do you do, Mr Latter?' and after a moment's hesitation he took it. She was not prepared for a grip that was both painful and prolonged. She released herself at what she considered a suitable moment and took a chair on the other side of the table. He continued to stare at her with red-rimmed eyes which had a lost, bewildered look. His first words were those which he had used to her on the telephone.

'You said it was a trick—but she died. She's dead, you know—last night. It seems much longer ago than that. Why did you say it was a trick? She's dead.'

She looked at him kindly.

'Yes, Mr Latter. I am deeply sorry for you. Since you have asked me to come down here, it seems that you think I can help you.'

He shook his head.

'Nobody can help me,' he said.

'Then why did you send for me, Mr Latter?'

He put up a hand and rubbed his nose—the old gesture, but with something forlorn about it.

'I want it cleared up—I want to know how it happened. The police are here—from Scotland Yard. They seem to think—I don't know what they think—' His voice trailed away.

Miss Silver looked at him very directly. She said in a clear, firm voice which held his attention,

'Mr Latter, will you listen to me? I should like to help you. I will do so if I can. You say you want to know how this thing happened. That is, you desire to know the truth. Sometimes the truth is painful. It may be so in this case. Remember that there will be police officers in charge. If your wife did not die a natural death, I may be able to be of some assistance in discovering how it came about, but I can give no pledge that what I discover will not be painful to you, nor can I undertake to conceal any material evidence from the police. Do you really wish me to take the case?'

He said doggedly, 'I want it cleared up.' And then, 'It wasn't natural. They say it was morphia—an overdose of morphia.

She didn't take things like that—she never took them. If she took it herself, it was done on purpose. If someone else did it, then she was murdered. It's got to be cleared up.'

Those red-rimmed eyes had not moved from her face. They looked as if they had forgotten how to sleep. There were marks like bruises under them. All the rest of the skin had the ghastly pallor of a normally fair, freshly-coloured complexion from which the blood has withdrawn. He kept his eyes on her and said without any change of voice,

'You see, I've got to know whether I killed her.'

In her time Miss Silver had heard more than one startling confession. She appeared undisturbed, though the gravity of her expression deepened. She said in a quiet voice,

'Would you like to tell me just what you mean by that?'

He nodded.

'That's why I wanted you here. The police don't care about that part of it, but it's what matters to me. I've got to know whether I killed her.'

Miss Silver coughed.

'That has a strange sound, Mr Latter.'

He nodded again.

'Yes, I suppose it has. You see, we had quarrelled. It hadn't ever happened before. I don't suppose that many people who have been married two years can say that. But all I ever wanted was for her to be happy and have things the way she liked them.'

'What did you quarrel about?'

He ran a hand through his hair and said vaguely,

'It was about one of the cottages. It must have been a mis-understanding, because she told me old Hodson wanted to go and live with his daughter-in-law in London. But it seems he didn't, and of course I couldn't turn him out—his family has always lived there. Lois was vexed because she'd promised the cottage to some friends of hers—for week-ends. Of course it was just that she didn't understand. But she was angry with me—that's how it all began.'

'Yes, Mr Latter?'

He rumpled his hair again, thrusting nervously at it as if it was something that he would like to brush away. He said,

'Something happened after that. It's not easy to tell you, but I've got to. The police know about it, because there was a girl who listened at the door—Joe Marsh's wife. She's no good, and I'm sorry for him. I don't know what Lois saw in her, but she would have her here. I never cottoned to her myself—and she listened at the door—'

'What door, Mr Latter?'

His eyes shifted. They looked past her.

'My cousin Antony's—the one who met you. He came down on business. I asked him to—made rather a point of it—so he was here. It was just after the quarrel. Lois was angry. She must have been very angry, or she wouldn't have done it. Antony says so, and I think he's right.'

Miss Silver coughed.

'What did she do?'

'I think she wanted to make me angry by flirting with him. He'd been in love with her, you know, but she refused him and she married me. I'm sure I don't know why—Antony's a much better chap. I don't want you to think any of it was his fault, because that wouldn't be fair. He asked her to marry him, and she said no, and that was the end of it as far as he was concerned. He went away and got over it, and—well, now he's engaged to someone else—to Julia—Julia Vane, you know.'

Miss Silver inclined her head.

'Pray continue.'

'So it wasn't his fault,' said Jimmy Latter in a dead voice. 'It was pretty late, but I hadn't gone to sleep. I was wondering whether I would go and see if Lois was awake too. I thought perhaps we might make it up. Her room is the other side of the landing. I was just going to open my door, when I heard hers open. When you've lived a long time in a house you know just where a sound comes from, and I've got very quick ears. I thought perhaps she was coming to me, but she wasn't. I came out of my room and saw the door of her big clothes-cupboard shutting on the far side of the landing. It's a room really. It used to be the dressing-room of the room Antony has, and there's a door through. I went after her. She didn't hear me, because by the time I got there she was in Antony's room talking to him.' The dead voice fell a tone. It had no expression except that it began to drag on the words. 'I heard her say, "It's two years since you kissed me. Don't you want to kiss me now?" ' His eyes came suddenly back to her with a look of defiant misery. 'The police have got it all written down. That girl was listening at the other door—she's got it all pat. It wasn't Antony's fault. He said she was my wife now, and he said he wasn't in love with her any more. She said he usedn't to be such an icicle, and she called him Joseph, laughing at him. That's when I went in. He was asking her if she liked the idea of being Potiphar's wife.

She was in her nightgown. I told her to go back to her room, and she went. That was the last thing I ever said to her.'

'When did this happen, Mr Latter?'

He put his head in his hands.

'It must have been Tuesday—yes, Tuesday night. Today is Friday, isn't it?'

She said, 'Yes, Friday.'

'Then it was Tuesday. Antony went away in the morning before anyone was up. I went out all day and most of the next. I didn't sleep—I couldn't seem to think—I didn't know what to do. Lois and I didn't speak. We met at dinner, but we didn't speak. I came into the drawing-room both evenings and took some of the coffee—because of what you said about her not taking anything that other people didn't have. They were sending in two cups of coffee, and I was having one of them.'

Miss Silver coughed.

'Were the cups poured out before they came in, Mr Latter?'

He nodded.

'I took one of them. That's what the police keep harping on—how could anyone know which one I was going to take? The police have got it all down—they'll tell you what happened. I went back to the study as soon as I'd drunk my coffee. Julia went for a walk. Ellie and Minnie went to bed. Lois stayed in the drawing-room. She was all alone. When Julia came in and found her it was too late. We got a doctor, but it was too late.' He lifted his head and stared at her. 'It was a dreadful thing to happen to a woman, my coming in like that and finding her with Antony. And I let two days go by—I didn't go near her, and I didn't speak. I left her alone—even that last evening I left her alone. If that's why she took the stuff, then I killed her, didn't I? I don't want you to tell me I didn't if I did. I only want you to find out the truth.'

Miss Silver returned his gaze with a very steady one. She said,

'I will do my best, Mr Latter.'

TWENTY-ONE

When Miss Silver came out of the schoolroom she stood for a moment, her hand fallen from the door which she had closed behind her. Under the surface her thoughts were grave and disturbed, but at the moment she was wondering what she had better do next. It was her custom when she came into a household professionally to make contact as soon as might be with every member of it. As the experienced cashier in a bank takes the feel of the coins which run through his fingers and knows the counterfeit by touch, so she had over and over again found her instinct serve her in these first contacts. Being temperate in all things, she did not give undue weight to her impressions, but held them in balance with observation and reason. She might have quoted from the Victorian poet whom she so much revered, in his summing up of different types of men: 'For good ye are and bad, and like to coins, some true, some light.'

Of the people in this house, she had met only the two men, Jimmy Latter and his cousin Antony. She glanced at her watch. Just on seven o'clock. She would doubtless meet the rest of the family at the evening meal. It was no part of her method to seek any set interview, but rather to observe the give and take of family life under conditions as nearly natural as could be. It would be pleasant to go up to her room, unpack her case, and adjust her toilet for the evening, but she had first to ascertain whether Chief Inspector Lamb and Sergeant Abbott were still upon the premises, and to break to them her presence in a tactful manner. She had not wished to see them until she had interviewed her client, but, having learned from him that he had in no way prepared them for her coming, she was now anxious that there should be no delay. They might, of course, have left the house, but this did not seem very likely.

Antony Latter had indicated the position of the study when he brought her in, mentioning that the police officers were using it. The room from which she had just emerged was the old schoolroom. He had mentioned that too—'My cousin has taken refuge in the old schoolroom.'

She began to walk down the hall in the direction of the study, and was almost level with it when the door opened and the massive figure of Chief Inspector Lamb emerged. Frank Abbott, following him, saw her face light up with a welcoming smile. Her hand came out to meet a somewhat reluctant clasp, whilst in tones warm with kindness she declared her pleasure at this encounter. The extraordinary thing was that the pleasure was so perfectly genuine. She really was delighted to meet an old and respected friend. Her enquiries after his family were sincere. She remembered that Mrs Lamb had been ill in the summer, and hoped so much that all was well with her again. She knew all about the three daughters and showed a deep interest in hearing the latest news of them. She remembered that it was Myrtle who had been in the W.A.A.F.S, Violet in the Wrens and Lily in the A.T.S. Lily was now married. Miss Silver knew all about that too. The young man had a nice position in a solicitor's office, and they were very happy.

Frank's smile, if sardonic, was admiring. The ice in which the Chief had encased himself was by this time completely melted, the barometer was at *Fair and warmer,* and he was informing Miss Silver that he hoped to be a grandfather in the spring.

With her congratulations these preliminaries came to an end. The compliments were over, but the atmosphere remained genial. Lamb's voice was friendly as he said,

'And what brings you here, if I may ask?'

Miss Silver looked about her. The hall appeared to be empty, but there was no harm in being careful. She passed into the study, and the two men followed her. When Frank had shut the door she said,

'Mr Latter is a client of mine. He came to see me last Saturday and told me that his wife thought someone was trying to poison her.'

Lamb stared.

'Oh, he did, did he?'

Miss Silver's manner became slightly more restrained.

'That is what I am telling you, Chief Inspector. If you can spare the time, I will acquaint you with what passed. But of course I do not wish to detain you.'

Lamb said, 'No, no—let's have it.'

Frank Abbott produced a chair. They all sat down.

Miss Silver coughed.

'Naturally, I recommended him to go to the police.'

Frank's eyebrows rose. He bit the corner of his lip. Lamb's 'Naturally!' tried his gravity a good deal. Sarcasm wasn't really in the Chief's line. One was reminded of an elephant doing tricks.

'His wife was not willing that he should do so.'

'That's what he said?'

'That is what he said. I will give you as accurate an account of our interview as I can.'

She did so, speaking in her clear, measured voice. From their knowledge of her, both men were aware that the account would be meticulously correct. She would waste no words, but she would omit no detail. The interview with Jimmy Latter took form in both their minds. She said in conclusion,

'I do not know what you will think, but I was very strongly of the opinion that Mrs Latter's attacks, which were obviously not of a serious nature, were the result of a spiteful trick. The symptoms were such as would be produced by a simple emetic like ipecacuanha, and except as indicating the presence of ill will towards Mrs Latter, I did not consider the attacks of any real importance. Mrs Latter was contemplating extensive changes in the household. I expect you are aware that Mrs Street and Miss Mercer were leaving, and that a regular staff was to be installed. Mr Latter was opposing this. Or perhaps that is too strong a word—he was not happy about it. It seemed to me that relations in the household were strained, and that the sooner the parties separated the better. I advised him not to prolong the situation. I also told him that it would be as well if Mrs Latter were protected against any further tampering with her food by confining herself to what other people were eating and drinking. He agreed, but said, "She *will* have her coffee". As you probably know, she took Turkish coffee, made specially for her as the rest of the family disliked it. Mr Latter tells me that from Saturday evening onwards two cupfuls were made and poured out, and that he always took one of them—this being the case yesterday evening when Mrs Latter succumbed.'

Lamb said, 'Yes, there's a young woman here who has made a statement about those attacks. She's a flighty piece of goods and not what I'd trust as a witness, only as it happens nobody denies what she says. What I was wondering was whether we'd have heard anything about Mrs Latter's attacks if it hadn't been for this Gladys Marsh—I was just saying so to Frank. But now it seems that Mr Latter came to you about them, and you thought someone was playing a trick.'

Miss Silver coughed.

'That was my opinion then. I may say that I have not yet seen occasion to alter it.'

Lamb gazed at her with a perfectly stolid face.

'You think the preliminary attacks were not connected with the one which caused her death?'

'I am not prepared to be definite on the subject, but that is what I am inclined to think. They seem too trifling in their nature and effects to constitute a serious attempt upon Mrs Latter's life.'

Still with that stolid expression, Lamb said,

'With every respect for your opinion, there's more than one way of looking at those attacks. You might have a bungler feeling his way—you might have a clever criminal drawing a red herring across the trail—you might have someone who hated Mrs Latter beginning with a trick and, finding out how easy it was to bring it off, going on to murder.'

Miss Silver inclined her head.

'I would agree with that as a general statement. I do not know enough about the evidence in this case to say how any of these theories would agree with it.'

Lamb cleared his throat, a sound which commanded attention.

'You say Mr Latter is your client. Are you here to prove that he didn't poison his wife?'

Miss Silver looked very much shocked. Her tone reproved him.

'I did not think it would be necessary to explain to you what I have put very clearly to Mr Latter. I am not here to prove anyone guilty or anyone innocent. It is my endeavour in every case I undertake to discover the truth, and to serve the ends of justice.'

Lamb's colour rose. He said, 'Yes, yes,' in an uneasy voice. And then, 'No offence meant. But you know, your position— well, I'm within my rights in asking to have it defined.'

'Perhaps you would care to define it, Chief Inspector.'

If the words were formal, the smile which accompanied them had a surprising charm. He felt himself consulted, deferred to. His prickles lay down, his colour came back to its normal crimson. He produced an answering smile.

'Well, if you were a friend of the family and Mr Latter had a great respect for you and would naturally turn to you for advice—and if you were willing to co-operate with the police—'

Miss Silver made a gracious inclination.

'I should find that perfectly satisfactory.'

Frank Abbott covered his mouth with his hand. The Chief walking on eggshells was a ponderous sight. It was accomplished, and without anything being broken, but the performance lacked grace. Maudie, of course, remained perfectly at her ease, dispensing frowns and smiles at the appropriate moment.

He got back to his Chief Inspector, who was speaking.

'Well now, bearing in mind what I said about a red herring, I'd like to ask you whether Mr Latter coming to see you last Saturday and telling you someone had been trying to poison his wife—whether that mightn't have been a put-up job. Suppose he'd made up his mind to get rid of her?'

'With what motive?'

'Jealousy—'

Miss Silver coughed.

'He had no cause for jealousy until Tuesday night, when he found her in his cousin's room.'

Lamb stared.

'Oh, you know about that?'

'Yes. He had no cause for jealousy until then.'

Lamb looked at her shrewdly.

'Well, that's all we know. There may be quite a lot we haven't heard about. Or it mayn't have been jealousy at all. Mrs Latter came in for a large fortune from her first husband. We don't know how it's been left—not yet. It may go back to his family, or it may not. Mr Latter says there was some dispute about the will, and a settlement was made out of court—Mrs Latter and the relations divided the money. Mr Latter thinks she got her share unconditionally, but he doesn't know for certain. He says he never talked to his wife about money, and didn't even know if she had made a will. Well, that sounded like poppycock to me. I got him to ring up her solicitor. There's a will all right, and they're posting a copy—it should be here in the morning. If Latter is down for anything considerable, there might be a motive in that. He might think it a pretty clever piece of work to come to you with a story of someone trying to poison his wife, and go away to play the devoted husband sharing his wife's coffee so that no one should tamper with it . . . Well, what do you think of that?'

Miss Silver looked at him very seriously.

'Do you know what is Mr Latter's chief concern?' she said.

He gave a short laugh.

'I can't say I do, but I suppose you are going to tell me.'

She said, 'Yes. All he wants is an assurance that she did not commit suicide.'

Lamb pushed his chair back a couple of inches.

'What's that?'

'He wants to be sure that his wife did not commit suicide. It is weighing on him very much that she may have done so. If she did, he thinks that he would be responsible for her death. After the scene in Mr Antony's room there was a complete breach between husband and wife. He let two days go by without speaking to her. He is afraid—I believe quite desperately afraid—that she took the morphia herself.'

Lamb thumped the table.

'He wants us to prove that someone murdered her?'

Miss Silver coughed.

'I do not think that he has got as far as that. His mind is fixed upon the dreadful thought that he may have driven her to suicide.'

Lamb leaned forward, a hand on either knee.

'I'd want more than his word before I'd believe that! I'm not saying he's guilty, but I'm not saying he's innocent. He'd the strongest motive of anyone, and the best opportunity of making sure that he didn't get the poisoned cup of coffee himself. Now what you say about his state of mind may be true, in which case he's an innocent man, and I'm sorry for him. Or he may be the clever criminal I said we might have to look out for, in which case all this about wanting to be sure it wasn't suicide—don't you see how it might be just a smokescreen?' He pushed his chair farther back and got up. 'Well, I shan't convert you, and you won't convert me—not tonight. We're at the Bull in the village, and if it's as bad as I think it's going to be, I shall be glad when the job's over. One comfort is, Frank's going to like it a lot less than I do!' He laughed heartily. 'If you like, he can step up after supper and let you look through the statements as far as we've got. Only mum's the word.'

Miss Silver beamed.

'That will indeed be kind.'

Lamb shook her warmly by the hand.

'Mind you, there's an advantage you've got over us that's as good as a running start. We come down, and we see people just about as much on their guard as they can be. In a murder case they've most of them got something to hide—if it isn't about themselves it's about somebody else. They're thinking about every word they say, and they don't say more than they've got to—unless they're like this Gladys Marsh that's so full of spite she can't unload it fast enough. But you come in as a friend. You see them when they don't think anyone's watching them. They talk natural to you, a thing they don't do to a police officer. There's no denying you've an advantage over us, and that's why I'm willing to strain a point and let you know where we stand—as far as we can be said to stand anywhere yet. Well, Frank'll be up after supper, and I'll see you in the morning. Good night.'

Miss Silver coughed.

'I very much appreciate your confidence.'

TWENTY TWO

Antony walked out of the house with the feeling that if he didn't get away from it for a bit he might not be able to resist the temptation to plead business and catch the first train back to town in the morning. He wasn't very proud of the feeling, but there it was. He considered himself entitled to take half an hour off. He wondered where Julia was. She had gone to help Ellie wash up when supper was over, and he hadn't seen her since. After a dreadful meal during which he and Miss Silver maintained the conversation, and poor old Jimmy sat staring at an untouched plate, they had all separated. By common consent, Minnie was urged to go to bed. Whether she had done so or not, he didn't know. She certainly didn't look fit to be about. Abbott, the police sergeant, had come up to see Miss Silver. They were closeted in the schoolroom, leaving the study to Jimmy, to whom all rooms, all places were the same, since wherever he was the same prison of misery closed him in. Presently Antony would go back to him. Not that there was anything that he could do except be there. A foul business.

He went down over the lawn and through the rose-garden. Beyond the hedge which screened it there was a seat. He came round the corner, saw that Julia was there, and stood still, watching her. It was still quite light, the sun going down into a haze. A wide prospect of meadowland spread out on a gentle slope which tilted to the banks of a stream. Mist lay on the fields, but overhead the sky was a clear pale blue. Julia sat with her hands open in her lap, her face lifted to the sky. But she was not looking at it or at anything else. Her eyes were shut. He thought how pale she was, and how withdrawn. But there was strength in her pose, not weakness—the strength of control. She was still because everything in her was bent upon some image in her mind.

He stood there watching her, with the silence between them. Time flowed past. At last he moved, going towards her over the grass, and almost at the same moment she turned her head and saw him come. At least he supposed she saw him. Her eyes were open, but they were curiously blank. Then warmth came to them. She put out a hand.

'Come and sit down. It's nice here.'

That seemed to be all she had to say. There was something restful about being there together, with no need to talk.

After a time he touched her hand lightly, looking down at it. She spoke then.

'I was thinking—'

'Yes?'

'About yesterday—before it happened. We should have said, pretty well all of us, that things were about as bad as they could be. Jimmy and Ellie and Minnie were all desperately unhappy. I don't know about Lois. It must have been pretty grim for her too. And yet if we could turn the clock back and be where we were then, it would seem like heaven.'

The touch on her hand became a clasp.

'What are you driving at?'

She gave him a look dark with trouble.

'We can't drive anywhere, we can only drift. That's what is so horrible. I can bear it when there are things to be done, but there isn't anything that we can do. It's like being in a boat without a rudder and hearing something like Niagara pounding down over a horrible drop ahead of you.'

He gripped her hand hard and said,

'Don't be melodramatic, darling.'

She pulled to free herself, but gave it up as soon as she found that he did not mean to let her go.

'All right—it was rather—I'm sorry.'

'What had you in mind as Niagara? Perhaps you would like to elucidate.'

She gave him another of those looks.

'What's the good? Perhaps it isn't Niagara—only an endless sticky swamp for us all to drown in.'

'It sounds revolting. Darling, don't you think you'd better get it off your chest? I don't feel I can cope with any more metaphors at the moment.'

She pulled her hand away and swung round, facing him.

'All right, let's have it out. Either Lois committed suicide, or someone murdered her. If it's suicide,

Jimmy's never going to get over it—I don't see how he can. He's always going to think he drove her to it. Of course it's irrational and insensate to the last degree, but people don't reason about these things, they feel them. We've both known Jimmy all our lives. You know, and I know, how he's going to feel this—how he is feeling it. That's one alternative. The other is murder. Well then, who did it? The way Jimmy is going on, any policeman in the world is going to pick on him. We know he didn't do it. But he could have done it—you know that too. He had the motive, and the opportunity and everything, and if it turns out she's left him a lot of money, they'll be quite sure he did it. That frightens me more than anything.'

Antony said in a hard, angry voice,

'Don't talk nonsense! It wasn't Jimmy!'

'Of course it wasn't. I'm talking about the police, not about us. Jimmy rang up Lois' solicitors this afternoon. Did you know that? The Chief Inspector asked him to. Jimmy spoke to them, and then *he* did. They're sending down a copy of Lois' will—Jimmy told me. I'm horribly frightened.'

Antony said, 'Don't be a fool! It's ten to one the money goes back to her first husband's relations. Doesn't Jimmy know?'

'No, he doesn't. He didn't like her having so much money, you know. It upset him a good deal when he found out how much it was. The case wasn't settled when they were married—not till about six months afterwards. He didn't like it at all, and he didn't want to know anything about what she did with it. Ridiculous of course, but—well, that's Jimmy. Only of course the police don't know what he's like, so they'll think—'

'Rather jumping at conclusions, aren't you?'

'Yes—I'm an idiot. It all keeps going round and round in my head. It looks as if the best thing that could happen now is for the police to believe that it's suicide—and then what happens to Jimmy? Because if it's murder—it's one of us.'

Antony said quietly,

'You know, Julia, you can't hold your tongue about Manny. You'll have to tell the police. She did what she did, and she'll have to take the consequences. If she did anything more she'll have to take the consequences of that too. I'm not going to see Jimmy accused of murdering his wife just to save Manny, and that's flat. If she poisoned that coffee she'll have to go through with it. I don't believe that Lois committed suicide, and I never shall. Nothing would convince me that she did. Why should she? Since we are talking about it, let us be perfectly plain. She hadn't any motive for suicide. She didn't care a snap of her fingers for Jimmy. He provided her with a good social position and an attractive house in which to entertain her friends. At the time she married him there was a disputed will between her and her first husband's money. If it had come into court, she wasn't at all sure of the result, and she was on the rocks financially. That's why she married Jimmy. She as good as told me so. Do you suppose she'd have killed herself because he found her out? Not she! And as to any other motive, she cared no more for me than she did for Jimmy.'

'I wonder—'

'You needn't. She was bored, she was angry with Jimmy, she was annoyed because I had no intention of being whistled to heel, and she didn't take kindly to being crossed—you may have noticed that. But as for her having any real feeling for me, the idea is fantastic. Lois was very much too fond of Lois to do her an injury for any man alive.'

She did not speak, but she did not need to. What she might have said was there between them. He felt her holding to it obstinately. When the silence had lasted long enough he said in the voice that meant he had made up his mind,

'It wasn't suicide. Someone poisoned her. If it wasn't Manny, who was it? You? Jimmy? Ellie? Minnie? That's the field. Which are you going to put your money on? We know who the police are backing. As things stand, they can't do anything else. It's gone quite far enough. If you don't see Manny and tell her so, I will. The best thing would be for her to go and tell the police herself, but—they've got to be told.'

The sense of resistance ceased between them. One minute it was there, as hard and solid as a wall, with Julia on one side of it and he on the other. And then all at once it yielded and was gone. She looked at him and said in a soft, breathless voice,

'Tomorrow—Antony, please—I can't do it tonight—'

She had the most extraordinary power to move him. That look in her eyes, that tone in her voice, and he was ready to commit almost any folly, go down on his knees, take her in his arms, tell her—What could he tell here—and now? He was astonished at himself and at her—astonished at how hard it was to hold back all those things which clamoured in him.

What a moment to speak of love! A harsh determination sounded in his voice. He said,

'Tomorrow will do.'

He saw her eyes mist over, and turned his own away. All at once she leaned towards him, pressing her face against the stuff of his sleeve. After a moment he put his arm round her and held her like that. They sat there for a long time without speaking.

TWENTY-THREE

Julia woke up suddenly, and wondered what had waked her. She thought it must have been Ellie crying out in her sleep as she sometimes did, not loudly but with a catch of the breath like a sob. She spoke her name gently,

'Ellie—'

There was no answer. She listened, and could hear from her soft, regular breathing that Ellie was asleep. She might have cried out and yet have been asleep. She thought, 'It's so strange—we don't know where anyone is when they're asleep. I don't even know about Ellie. I don't always know where I've been myself.' She had the feeling of having come up out of a dream once she leaned towards him, pressing her face against the stuff which had left her only at the moment of waking. All that remained of it was a longing to go back again, to escape from the things which waited for them all in the day to come.

She wondered what time it was. She thought between two and three in the morning. The room was dark, but the two windows hung on the darkness like pictures on a black wall. The pictures showed an even tinge of gloom, like very old paintings in which all detail is lost and only the main mass of light and shade remains. But here there was nothing which could be called light. There were gradations in the shadow, that was all. Because she had slept in this room for as long as she could remember, she knew that in the blackest part of the shadow there were the shapes of trees, and that it became less dense as the branches thinned away towards the sky. It must be very dark outside, because she could not see any line where foliage ended and cloud began.

She had risen on her elbow, the bed-clothes pushed down to her waist, her hair pushed back. Now she lay down again, smoothing the sheet, pulling the pillow round a little. It was all right, Ellie was asleep. If anything had waked her, it must have been one of those night sounds which are common enough in the country—the cry of a bird, the bark of a fox, a badger calling. She had heard them all, lying here in this bed, on many nights running back through many years.

She put her head on the pillow, and the sound which had waked her came again. It wasn't badger, bird, or fox. It was the sound of a hand brushing over the outer panel of the door. She sat up, listening, and heard it still. It isn't a sound like anything else, it isn't a sound that you can mistake. A hand was groping at the door—sliding over it, softly, whisperingly.

Julia pushed the clothes right back and got out of bed. Her bare feet took her to the door. She stood, holding her breath to listen. But there wasn't anything to hear. The sound had stopped. All at once it came to her that it might be a trick. Someone had played a trick upon Lois, and Lois had died . . . But that was Manny. Manny wouldn't come here in the middle of the night to play a trick on Julia.

With a sudden movement she turned the handle and opened the door, stepping back as she pulled it towards her. The landing outside was light—a low-powered bulb burned there all night. Coming from sleep and from the darkness of her room, it dazzled her. There was a white figure standing about a yard from the threshold, staring. The impression came and went before she could take her breath, and she saw that it wasn't *someone,* but Minnie—Minnie Mercer in her nightgown, with her hair hanging down over it as far as her waist and her eyes fixed in sleep. She wasn't staring at Julia, because she wasn't seeing her. She wasn't seeing anything in Julia's waking world. What she saw and what she looked for was known only to the dream sense which had brought her here.

It went through Julia's mind that it was dangerous to wake people who were walking in their sleep. You had to try and get them back to bed—one of these things that are nice and easy to say and abominably difficult to do. Of course she would have to try. You couldn't have Minnie wandering all over the house, scaring people to death and perhaps starting that awful Gladys' tongue on a new scandal. Anyhow she wasn't going to have Ellie waked up. She came out of the room and shut the door behind her.

As if it had been a signal, Minnie turned and went towards the stairs, moving so fast that by the time Julia came up with her she had already taken the first step down and having taken it, continued to descend without pause or stay. If she didn't see where she was going, how was it she could move with so much certainty? She went down into the darkness of the lower hall, and Julia with her. It was like going down into dark water. When they were quite swallowed up in it Julia said in a low, insistent voice,

'Minnie—come back to bed.'

Something must have got through into her dream, for she stopped, there, at the foot of the stairs. Julia said it again.

'Come back to bed, Minnie.'

There was no response. She just stood there, barefoot in her nightgown, with her hair hanging loose. Julia came up close and put an arm round her.

'Min—do come back to bed.'

Whether it was the urgency in Julia's voice that reached her or whether it was that the impulse which had brought her so far was fading out, she turned and set a hesitating foot upon the bottom step. With Julia's arm about her, she drew the other foot up and waited there as if she didn't know what to do next. The arm urged her gently. She took another step, and so on step by step to the top of the stair. Sometimes there was a long pause when she stood so still she hardly seemed to breathe and Julia was afraid of using any force. Sometimes she mounted steadily.

When they were about half-way up she began to talk in a rapid whispered monotone. There were words, but they had no form. It was like listening to someone talking in another room. She wondered where Minnie was in her dream, and what she was saying.

At the top of the stair there was one of those long pauses. The murmuring voice sank into inaudibility and ceased. Julia said 'Min—*darling*—' and to her relief Minnie walked suddenly across the landing and in through the open doorway of her room. It was dark after the light outside, but she went straight up to the bed and sat down on the edge of it. Julia stood back to see what she would do.

All at once Minnie said in a lamentable voice, 'What have I done?'

Julia felt as if everything inside her had turned over. It wasn't only the words. They were bad enough, but they seemed to come on the very breath of despair. She said them again, her tone failing under them as if they were too heavy to be borne. Then as she drew two or three long sobbing breaths and groped for her pillow and lay down, Julia pulled the clothes over her with shaking hands. Her knees shook too. She stood there listening, and heard the sobbing breaths grow still. In less than a minute she could tell that Minnie was asleep. Whatever her dream had been, she had passed out of it into ordinary, everyday sleep.

In so far as Julia was capable of feeling relief it came to her. She turned from the bed and went towards the door. It was wide to the lighted landing. There was someone standing just outside. Julia came out into the light and saw that it was Miss Silver, in a dressing-gown of crimson wool, trimmed round the neck and sleeves with handmade crochet. There were black felt slippers on her feet, her hair was arranged very neatly under a net. She looked dreadfully intelligent and alert. Julia had never felt so near the end of her courage. She did not know that her own wide, dark gaze stirred all the kindness of a benevolent heart. She did somehow receive some assurance from Miss Silver's voice and manner as she said,

'If she is asleep now, I think it will be safe to leave her. I have never known of a case where a somnambulist has left his bed a second time. A trying experience for you, I am afraid, but there is no cause for alarm. Has she been accustomed to walk in her sleep?'

Julia put a hand against the jamb of the door. They both spoke very low. She said,

'I don't think so—not since I can remember. I think she did a long time ago, when she was a girl. It has all been a great strain.'

Miss Silver coughed.

'Quite so. And now, my dear, I think you should go back to bed. You are so very thinly clad, and the nights are cold. I do not think you need be afraid that Miss Mercer will disturb us again.'

Julia went into her room and shut the door. It seemed a long time since she had left it. As she lay down and pulled the bedclothes over her she found that she was shivering from head to foot. She was cold, but it was not only the cold that made her shake. She was very much afraid.

TWENTY-FOUR

Life would be much easier if it could be arranged as in a play or a novel, where the curtain may be rung down or a chapter closed, and the action or the narrative resumed after a lapse of days, weeks, or even years. In real life there are, however, no such intervals. Whatever happened yesterday, you have to rise and dress, endure a family meal, and face whatever the hours provide. If Julia could have rung down a curtain before her interview with Mrs Maniple, and rung it up again afterwards with what had been said between them relegated to the past, she would have confronted the daylight with a better heart. If it had to be done, she would do it. And if she had to do it, the sooner she got it over the better.

Nobody was disposed to linger over breakfast. The general gloom was definitely deepened by the arrival of the post. Jimmy looked down the table after opening the long envelope which bore his name and said in a dazed voice, 'She has left me all that damned money.' After which he sat there staring at nothing, until quite suddenly he pushed back his chair and went out of the room.

The Chief Inspector and Sergeant Abbott arriving, first interviewed him in the study, where the party was joined by Miss Silver, and then, after he had gone unhappily away, remained there with her.

Julia cleared and washed up the breakfast things, sent Antony off to walk Jimmy round the garden, and then went through to the kitchen feeling rather as if she was going to attend an execution.

She found Mrs Maniple weighing out the ingredients for a pudding, with Polly in attendance. It must be a special one, because Manny didn't weigh things as a rule, she just threw in butter, and flour, and milk, and eggs, and what not in a splendidly inattentive manner, and the result was a dream.

'Yes, Mrs Maniple,' said Polly, and fetched the lemon essence.

Julia came into the room with a dragging heart.

'Manny—could Polly go and give a hand upstairs? Miss Minnie had a bad night, I'm afraid—'

'Looks fit to drop,' said Mrs Maniple. 'Polly, you take and go along and see what you can do. There's nothing here I can't manage. No call for you to come back before eleven, so you get right on with the bedroom floors, and Miss Ellie can do the dusting.'

The table faced the long window looking into a stone-paved court with a very old chestnut tree growing in the middle of it. Julia stood and looked out at the tree. There was a story about it. A Cavalier Latter had hidden in the branches whilst the Roundheads ransacked the house for him.

Everyone in the village knew that he had come home wounded, but no one gave him away. It was an old story—

She turned round from the window, to see Mrs Maniple looking at her shrewdly.

'Well, Miss Julia, what is it? You may as well come out with it soon as late. It wasn't Polly you came after—was it?'

'No, Manny.'

'And no call to look as if we was at our own funeral neither. There's some that can be spared, and I'm not saying nothing about them, but no reason why you and me should cry our eyes out neither.'

'Manny—don't!'

Mrs Maniple had her hands in the pudding-bowl. There was a dusting of flour on her strong arms. The sleeves of her lilac print dress were rolled above the elbows. She wore it high to the neck with a little turndown collar of the stuff, and it fastened with hooks and eyes all down the front like dresses used to when she first went into service. An out-sized apron with strings to it was tied in a bow at the back of what had once been a waist. Her hair was still very thick. It stood up strongly from her forehead and was coiled into a large knot behind. It was iron-grey in colour, and if she had allowed it to curl it would have curled. Under it black eyebrows gave a very decided look to eyes which were as nearly black as eyes can be. She turned them defiantly on Julia.

'Now, Miss Julia, what's the good of saying that? I don't hold with speaking ill of the dead no more than you do, not without there's a reason for it, but I don't hold with pretending neither, nor yet with crocodile's tears which isn't my way, as well you know. And no good your coming here and saying, "Don't, Manny!" '

Julia took hold of herself. It wasn't any good thinking of all the times she had watched Manny breaking eggs, and stoning raisins, and buttering tins as she was doing now, to the accompaniment of the village news and all the stories of everything that had ever happened to everyone in it. It wasn't any good. She found she was saying the words out loud.

'It isn't any good, Manny.'

Mrs Maniple tossed her head.

'Nor never will be if you go looking at it the way you're looking at me! I always did say you'd the heartrenderingest way of looking I ever did see, right from a child in arms. And I'll thank you not to, Miss Julia, for there's quite enough to do in the house without your turning the milk and making my pudding go sad.'

She was scooping it into the buttered tin as she spoke. When she had finished she went over and put it in the oven. Then she went through to the scullery, ran the cold tap over her hands and arms, and dried them on the roller towel behind the door.

Julia stood where she was and waited till she came back.

'It isn't any good, Manny, I've come to talk to you.'

Mrs Maniple's round apple-red cheeks took on a deeper shade.

'And what was it you was going to say, Miss Julia?'

'I think you know.'

'And what I think is you'd better say it straight out and be done with it. If there's a thing I can't abide, it's hinting, which wasn't never my way nor it usen't to be yours. So if you've anything to say, you come out with it and let's have done!'

Julia said, 'Very well then, I will. The police have got to be told about those sick attacks that Lois had. They've got to be told you gave her ipecacuanha.'

Mrs Maniple's colour had deepened to plum. Her bright black eyes looked steadily at Julia.

'And who's going to tell them?'

Julia wouldn't look away. She didn't know how white she was. She wouldn't look away. She said,

'They've got to know.'

Mrs Maniple came up to the table and put the lid on the flour-bin with a steady hand.

'Then you can tell them—if you don't think there's trouble enough in the house already. What I give her didn't have no more to do with what she died of than the turkey we had for Christmas, and well you know it—a drop of ipecac that wouldn't have harmed a child—and the last she had going on for a week before she died! Go and tell them my dear—the sooner the better! I'm not asking you not to.'

Julia said in a different voice,

'They think Jimmy did it—'

Mrs Maniple dropped a spoon. It fell clattering into the mixing-bowl, but she took no notice.

'They darsn't!'

'They think it was Jimmy. You know they had quarrelled.'

'No chance of anyone not knowing that with Gladys Marsh

in the house—telling everyone what I wouldn't repeat, though you know it as well as what I do! Like mistress like maid, and not as much shame between them as would lie on a three-penny bit!'

Julia said steadily, 'They know about what happened the night Antony was here. They think it gave Jimmy what they call a motive. They'll think he had another motive too. He got a copy of Lois' will from her lawyer this morning. She has left him a lot of money. He didn't know anything about it, but they won't believe that. Manny, it's very, very dangerous—they really may believe he did it.'

Mrs Maniple said, 'More fools they!' in a loud, brisk voice. Then she began to roll down her sleeves and fasten the hooks and eyes at the wrists. 'And if I'm took, you'll have to see to the lunch. There's the cold meat can go into a stew, and Polly can do the vegetables. That's a slow oven I've put the pudding in and you don't want to touch it. And when the baker comes, tell Polly to take two fresh and one stale.'

'Manny—'

'What's wrong now? I'm doing what you wanted, aren't I? Seems to me about time someone up and told those policemen not to make more fools of themselves than they can help. Mr Jimmy indeed! Why, he'd have laid down on red-hot coals and let her walk over him if she'd wanted to, more's the pity!' She put a firm hand on Julia's shoulder. 'Don't you take on, my dear, for I'll never believe Mr Jimmy'll be let come to harm for what wasn't much better than a common bad woman with no more heart in her than what you'd find in a rotten nut. You make yourself a nice cup of tea and don't take on. And don't let that Gladys Marsh into my larder. As likely as not she'll try it on so soon as my back's turned—and I won't have it, and that's flat!'

TWENTY-FIVE

In the study Chief Inspector Lamb sat in Jimmy Latter's writing-chair with a hand on either knee, looking sometimes across the table at Frank Abbott, and sometimes to his right where Miss Silver, a little detached from the proceedings, was knitting. She was half-way through one of the useful grey stockings destined for her niece Ethel's second boy, Derek. The needles clicked busily. A portrait in oils of the late Mr Francis Latter looked down from over the mantelpiece and gloomed upon the scene. Considered by all who knew him to be a depressingly accurate likeness, it raised the question as to how near relations could have so little in common. No one could have supposed him to be Jimmy Latter's father. Francis Latter stood there, tall, dark, and haggard. There was a hint of his nephew Antony, but Antony had not the tragic look which was, however, very appropriate to the present occasion.

Lamb was speaking.

'It looks pretty black for him—you'll admit that?'

Miss Silver coughed.

'I am not prepared to contradict you, but I would ask you to bear in mind some of Lord Tennyson's wisest words. He observes that—

'any man that walks the mead,
In bud, or blade, or bloom, may find,
According as his humours lead,
A meaning suited to his mind.'

Lamb's eyes bulged visibly.

'Well, I don't know about meads and buds and blooms, but when I see a man that's got every reason to think his wife isn't any better than she ought to be, and when that man has to admit she'd made a will leaving him a fortune, I don't have to ask Lord Tennyson's leave to suspect Mr Jimmy Latter of having two very good motives for poisoning Mrs Latter.'

Miss Silver's needles clicked.

'Two motives may be one too many, Chief Inspector.'

Frank Abbott's look sharpened to interest.

'Meaning that if he was knocked off his balance by jealousy he wouldn't be thinking about the money, and if he was all out for the money he wouldn't have been knocked endways by that scene in Antony Latter's room.'

Lamb thumped his knee.

'That's just where you're wrong then! That's where you young chaps can make a big mistake. People aren't all that simple—they're all mixed up. You'd be surprised if you knew how many different things a man can have in his mind at the same time, first one thing coming up on top and then another. Say a man's jealous about his wife, but not jealous enough to kill her—he has a quarrel with her about something else. He begins to see that she means to take her way about everything and leave him to take his. He remembers that she holds the purse-strings, and that gets his goat. There are sharper and sharper differences about family affairs—he wants to keep the family together, and she wants to split them up. He's pretty hard up—it's doubtful if he can run the place without her money—it's an old place that's been in the family a long time. That pulls at him. The way she's carrying on pulls at him—she wants to break up the family, and she's setting her cap at his cousin. They're heading for a breach, and if there's a breach, perhaps he won't be able to carry on. Then overnight the breach becomes inevitable—he finds her in his cousin's room. Don't you see how it all works in together? If it weren't for the money, he could let her go. If she hadn't gone too far for him to overlook it, the money by itself mightn't have got him to the point of murdering her. I say there are two motives here, both of them strong in themselves, and the way they come to bear on this case each of them strengthens the other.'

Miss Silver gave her slight cough.

'You illustrate my quotation perfectly, Chief Inspector. You have found a meaning suited to your mind.'

His florid colour deepened.

'I use my mind to get a meaning—is that what you're after? And if there's any other way of getting a meaning, I'd like to know about it. To my mind that will of Mrs Latter's is very damaging—you can't get away from it. And on the top of that comes this report from Smerdon. Miss Mercer's medicine-chest has been examined by the police surgeon. Besides the ordinary household remedies which you'd expect, there's a quarter-full glass bottle of morphia tablets. He says they're of German manufacture and much stronger than what you could get in this country. Now all the things in the medicine-cupboard have got Miss Mercer's fingerprints on them—some old, some fresh, which is just what you'd expect. This bottle of tablets has a very good set of her prints. But it's got Mr Jimmy Latter's prints on it too. They're a bit smudged, as if she'd taken hold of it after he had, but they're his all right. He'd been to that chest, picking things over. There's a very clear set of his prints on another very similar bottle with quinine pills in it. I'd say he was looking for the morphia and picked the other one up by mistake. There's a bottle of ipecac there too, but no fingerprints on it. If you're right, Miss Silver, about those preliminary attacks—well, I'd say he was being careful to start with. Wiped the bottle, or wore gloves—something like that. I don't know why he should have risked the attacks at all, but I daresay we shall find out before we're through. Well, I didn't put any of this to Mr Latter when we had him in here just now, because I thought I'd like to see what Miss Mercer had to say about it first. She handled that morphia bottle after he did, and I want to see what she's got to say about it. She may have moved it to get at something else, in which case I'd like to know if it was out of its place. Or—' he looked hard at Miss Silver—'it may be that she was in on the job. She may have been—there's no saying.'

There was a knock upon the door. Lamb said, 'Come in!' and there entered Mrs Maniple, very majestic in the almost visible panoply of more than fifty years service, her head high, her colour steady, her manner dignified and purposeful. She came round to the far end of the writing-table and stood there, the Chief Inspector on her right, Sergeant Abbott on her left, and Miss Silver in her direct line of sight. There was something about her entry which proclaimed an occasion of the first magnitude. No one spoke until she did. She put her hands down flat on the table edge and said,

'There's something I've got to say.'

Lamb swung round to face her, moving his whole big body. He said,

'You're the cook, aren't you—Mrs Maniple?'

She said, 'Yes.'

Frank Abbott got up and brought her a chair.

'Won't you sit down?'

She looked at him, sizing him up, and said,

'No, thank you, sir.'

For once in his life Sergeant Abbott was abashed. He went back to his seat with some colour in his face and busied himself with writing-pad and pencil.

The Chief Inspector looked grimly at the old woman who had kept her 'sir' for his subordinate. He knew what it meant quite as well as she did. Something in him respected her. Something else made a mental note that Master Frank mustn't be allowed to get wind in his head. He said,

'I see you have something to say, Mrs Maniple. Will you tell me what it is?'

She stood there very upright.

'That's what I've come for. Before Mrs Latter died she was taken sick two or three times. I've come to tell you—those turns she had, they were along of what I put in her coffee.'

There was a short electric silence. Miss Silver stopped knitting for a moment and gave her a long, steady look.

Lamb said, 'If this is a confession, it is my duty to warn you that anything you say may be taken down and used in evidence.'

There was no change in Mrs Maniple's expression, nor in her voice when she spoke.

'I've no objection to anything being taken down—I wouldn't be here if I had. And I'm not confessing nothing about what Mrs Latter died of, only about those sick turns she had, which was along of ipecac—in her coffee mostly, but there was once I put it in the fruit salad.'

Lamb leaned back in his chair, his face as expressionless as her own.

'What made you do a thing like that?'

The answer came grim and short.

'To punish her.'

'Why did you want to punish her?'

'For what she was doing to everyone she come in contact with.'

'As what?'

'It 'ud take a long time to tell the half of it.'

'Never mind about that. You tell us why you thought she ought to be punished.'

She drew her black brows together briefly.

'Very well, then. I'll put it as short as I can. There was what she did to Mrs Marsh.'

'Do you mean the young woman, Gladys Marsh, who was acting as Mrs Latter's maid?'

'No I don't. I mean her husband's mother, Lizzie Marsh, that's a cousin of my own and as that there Gladys got sent away to the workhouse. Institute they may call it now, but workhouse is what it is. And Mrs Latter backed her up. She wouldn't have darsn't do it, nor Joe Marsh wouldn't have let her, if it hadn't been for Mrs Latter backing her up and telling Mr Jimmy all manner of lies.'

'And you put ipecacuanha in her coffee because of that.'

'Not for that by itself. It was for that and other things. There was Miss Ellie—Mrs Street—that she worked to death like I wouldn't have stood for any housemaid being worked, and when she'd taken all the strength out of her she was turning her out—wouldn't let her have her husband Mr Ronnie here to look after. And the same with Miss Minnie that's been here ever since the old doctor died. Worked her pretty well to death, and then out she could go, and it wasn't Mrs Latter that 'ud care whether she lived or died. And more lies to Mr Jimmy, making him think Miss Minnie wanted to go. That's why I done it. Maybe I didn't ought to, but that's why I done it. And it wasn't done for no more than to punish her—drop of ipecac like you'd give a child that had swallowed something. And no harm done. That's what I come to say.' She took her hands off the table and turned to go.

Lamb stopped her.

'We can't leave it quite like that, you know. I think you'd better sit down.'

She came back to her former position.

'I can stand well enough.'

'Well, that's just as you like. I want to ask you some questions. You needn't answer if you don't want to.'

'I'll tell you when I hear them.'

'Well, we'll start with an easy one. How long have you been here?'

There was pride in her voice as she said,

'It'll be fifty-three years at Christmas.'

'You didn't leave to be married?'

She stood up very straight.

'I'm single. The Mrs is what is only right and proper when you've turned fifty in a position like what mine is.'

'I see. Very fond of the family, aren't you?'

'Wouldn't anyone be after fifty years?'

'Very fond of Mr Jimmy, as you call him?'

She said, 'I saw him christened.' And then, 'Anyone 'ud be fond of Mr Jimmy—he's one that's got kindness for all. There isn't anyone for miles round that don't love Mr Jimmy.'

Lamb shifted his position, leaning forward with an arm along the table.

'Well now, suppose you tell us about the times you put this ipecac into Mrs Latter's coffee. When did you start?'

He noticed that she did not have to stop and think. Her answer came pat.

'It was the evening Miss Julia come down, and Mr Antony. They hadn't neither of them been here for two years, and I thought, "Well, they shall have their evening the same as it was before Mrs Latter come". She'd been up to her tricks with

Miss Ellie that evening, wanting her to do the flowers all over again when anyone could see she was ready to drop—and she'd done them lovely. And I thought to myself, "No you don't, my lady!" for I knew how it 'ud be, Miss Ellie and Miss Julia, they wouldn't get a moment's peace, neither with Mr Jimmy nor Mr Antony. I tell you she couldn't abear to see anyone noticed if it wasn't herself, so I took and put some ipecac in her coffee, she being the only one that took that nasty Turkish stuff, and it made her sick and kept her quiet like I thought it would.'

Frank Abbott turned a page and went on writing. Lamb said,

'Well, that was the first time. When did you do it again?'

'Next day at lunch. There was fruit salad in separate glasses, with cream on the top. Mrs Latter never took cream, so there was one glass without. I put the ipecac in that.'

'And after that?'

'There was once when Mr Jimmy was away seeing after Miss Eliza Raven's affairs down in Devonshire, and there was once more after he come back—I think it was Tuesday last week. And then on the Saturday Mr Jimmy come down from London, and he says to send in two cups of Turkish coffee because every time Mrs Latter has it he's going to have it too. So then I stopped.'

'You didn't put any more ipecac into the coffee?'

Her eyes met his.

'Do you think I'd have risked making Mr Jimmy sick?'

'Well, I don't suppose you would. So you didn't use any more ipecac. How did you get hold of the morphia?'

Her gaze never wavered. It was perfectly steady and perfectly blank.

'I don't know what you mean.'

'The stuff that was in Mrs Latter's coffee on Wednesday night—the stuff that killed her—it was morphia. How did you get hold of that?'

'I don't know nothing about it.'

'Mrs Maniple—did you put anything into the coffee on Wednesday night? You needn't answer if you don't want to.'

There was a touch of scorn as she said,

'Why shouldn't I want to? I didn't put nothing in, and Miss Julia can tell you so. She stood there watching me all the time—she can say what I did. And if I'd wanted to murder Mrs Latter a hundred times over, do you think I'd have put poison in one of those cups and let Miss Julia go through with the tray and put it down for them to help themselves—Mrs Latter, and Mr Jimmy that I couldn't love more if he was my own child—and not know which of them 'ud take the poison? Do you think I'd have done that? If I'd got the length of making up my mind to poison her, do you think I'd have risked Mr Jimmy's life, with no saying who would take which cup? It's not sense, and you know it!'

He said, 'Maybe.' And then, 'I'd like to take you through Wednesday, Mrs Maniple. Mrs Latter kept her room in the morning, didn't she? That means her breakfast went up to her. Who took it up, and what did she have?'

Mrs Maniple leaned a little forward on her hands.

'Gladys Marsh come down for the tray and took it up. She had toast, and fruit—it was an apple on Wednesday.'

'Not much of a breakfast. Well then, what happened after that? Did she come down for lunch?'

'Yes, she come down. I didn't know what she was going to do, so I sent Polly up to ask, and she said Mrs Latter would come down.'

'So she had the same for lunch that everyone else did. What did they have?'

'Mince and two vegetables, with a trifle to follow.'

'What about tea?'

'Mrs Latter took her car out after lunch. She didn't come in till getting on for seven o'clock—she wasn't here for tea.'

'And dinner—what did you give them for dinner?'

'There was fish—baked haddock—and a sweet omelette. And hardly a bit of anything ate.'

'They were all too much upset?'

'Seems like it.'

'And then you made the coffee and Miss Vane took it in?'

'Miss Julia watched me make it.'

'Well now—one thing more. Where did you get the ipecac you put in Mrs Latter's coffee? Did you get it out of the medicine cupboard in Miss Mercer's room?'

'Not then, I didn't.'

'What do you mean by that?'

'It was a bottle she give me when I had a cough in the spring. I'd put a drop or two with some honey and vinegar and sup it. And she said to keep the bottle—it wasn't above half full.'

'You knew she had a medicine cupboard in her room?'

'Everyone in the house knows that.'

'It wasn't kept locked, was it? Anyone could help themselves?'

Mrs Maniple drew herself up.

'There wasn't no one in the house wouldn't do that—without it was Gladys Marsh. There's never been no need to lock things up in this house, thank God! But it's proper a medicine cupboard should be locked.'

'You didn't take anything out of that medicine cupboard yourself?'

'I'd no call to, nor wouldn't if I had. If I'd wanted anything I'd have asked Miss Minnie.'

'Did you ask her for anything from that cupboard?'

'No, I didn't.'

Lamb pushed back his chair.

'All right, Mrs Maniple. Now Sergeant Abbott will run those notes of his off on the typewriter and read them over to you, and you can sign them.'

TWENTY-SIX

Miss Silver gathered up her knitting and left them to it, but almost at once the Chief Inspector followed her out of the room. When she glanced round and saw him he made what she described to herself as a grimace, walked on as far as the drawing-room door, which he opened, and beckoned her in. When he had shut it again he said confidentially,

'Well, what did you make of that?'

Miss Silver stood, her hands clasped on the new knitting-bag which her niece Ethel had sent her for her birthday in July—a capacious affair in a chintz with a pattern of honey-suckle and humming-birds. It had been much admired not only by its recipient but by several of her oldest friends. A primrose lining showed here and there where the frill at the top fell over. She took a moment before she said,

'I thought Mrs Maniple was speaking the truth.'

Lamb nodded.

'Well, so did I. I don't see why she needed to say anything at all if she wasn't going to tell the truth. A silly trick to get up to, and one we could run her in for. I'd do it like a shot too if I thought there was any chance she poisoned Mrs Latter. The trouble is, I'm pretty well sure she didn't.'

'I agree.'

'For one thing, she'd never have admitted the ipecac if she'd gone on to the morphia—not without she was going to confess the whole thing. That's my first reason for thinking she didn't do it. The second one's stronger. She hit the nail right on the head when she said she'd never have risked Mr Latter's taking the poisoned cup. As the evidence stands, neither she who made the coffee nor Miss Julia Vane who took it in had any control over who took which cup. They weren't either of them in the room when the coffee was shared out. So the murderer was either someone who didn't care whether it was Mr or Mrs Latter who was poisoned, which makes nonsense, or else it was someone who was right here in this room and was able to see that there were no mistakes, and that the cup with the morphia in it got to the person it was meant for. And that means just one of three people—Mrs Street, Miss Mercer—and Mr Jimmy Latter.'

Miss Silver inclined her head.

'I agree with you as to the facts.'

He laughed in a good-humoured way.

'Well, isn't that nice! I don't know when you agreed with me last over a case. Live and learn, as we used to say.'

Miss Silver's manner became a trifle remote. She coughed.

'I may agree with your facts without accepting the conclusions you draw from them.'

He laughed again.

'Oh, yes—Mr Latter is your client, isn't he? You won't admit he did it. That leaves Mrs Street and Miss Mercer. Which of them do you fancy? They were both being turned out of what had been their home for twenty-five years—if Mrs Street is as old as that. And she's got a husband she'd like to have here, only Mrs Latter wouldn't have it. Well, that's some sort of a motive for each of them, but I don't think it would cut much ice with a jury. No, I'm afraid things look very bad for your client. Come now—what do you think yourself? You may as well own up.'

Miss Silver looked at him without any expression at all.

'At the moment I have no opinion to offer.'

She left him smiling to himself and passed into the hall. It was in her mind that she would like to talk to Julia Vane, but she decided that that could wait. There seemed to be an excellent opportunity of a conversation with the kitchenmaid, Polly Pell—rather a shy girl, and so constantly at Mrs Maniple's beck and call as to make it very difficult to get hold of her.

She made her way into the pantry, and at once became aware that she would not find Polly alone. The door through into the kitchen was ajar, and the high-pitched voice of Gladys Marsh was plainly audible.

'I'll get my picture in the papers—you see if I don't.'

As a gentlewoman, Miss Silver deplored a professional necessity. Gentlewomen do not eavesdrop, but it is sometimes very useful to be able to do so. In her professional character she did not hesitate to avail herself of opportunity when it came her way. She provided herself with a tumbler and stood with her hand on the drinking-water tap. What she heard she found very interesting—very interesting indeed.

A cautious glance round the edge of the door showed her Gladys Marsh sitting across the corner of the kitchen table swinging her legs. She had a cup of tea in her hand. Polly was not in sight. Her voice came hesitating, not much above a whisper.

'I don't know that I'd care about that.'

Gladys took a noisy gulp of tea.

'Well, I would. You just watch me and you'll see. There's a couple of reporters been at me already, but I'm not making myself cheap. I told them so. I've said what I know to Chief Inspector Lamb from Scotland Yard—that's what I told them. And he says I'll be called at the inquest, and not to say nothing to nobody, so I'm not. "Come to think of it," I said, "why should you boys get the money for my story? I can write it myself, can't I?" And the cheeky one with red hair—they're all cheeky, but he's the worst—he said, "You don't mean to say they taught you to write?" and I said, "Yes, Impudence—and a lot more besides." And he said, "You bet!" and he took two photographs. But I didn't tell him nothing, only a lot of stuff about the house and the family, and about Mrs Latter being such a lot admired, and all that. If they want anything more they can pay for it—and if they won't there's plenty that will.'

There was a murmuring sound from Polly. Gladys drained her cup and reached for the teapot.

'Oh, come off it!' she said. 'What's the good of being alive if you don't have a good time when you're young? You start thinking if there isn't something you can tell the police and get called at the inquest! That'll be only a village affair, but when it comes to the trial—'

Polly's voice came in with a frightened sound.

'Who will they try?'

'Dunno. But I can guess. Can't you?'

'What do you mean?'

Gladys laughed and swung her legs.

'Who spied on her and caught her in Mr Antony's room? Who comes into a lot of money now she's gone? She told me that herself no longer ago than the Wednesday morning—said she wasn't going to stay here the way things were going, and the first thing she was going to do when she got up to town was to alter her will. She'd have taken me with her too. Gosh—what a chance!'

'I don't know that I should care about London.'

Gladys said contemptuously,

'More fool you! You don't know what's good for you. I didn't when I married Joe Marsh and tied myself up to live in a hole like this.'

'Weren't you—weren't you fond of him?'

Gladys laughed. Really, Miss Silver thought, a most unpleasant sound.

'Fond of him! I'd been ill and I was out of a job, and he was getting good money. I was a damned fool. If I'm one of the chief witnesses in a big murder trial, why I'll get dozens of offers—girls do. I'd be able to pick and choose, and marry where there's some money going and a chance of a good time if I hadn't tied myself up to Joe. However, 'tisn't for always nowadays—that's one comfort. I'll do better than Joe with this trial to boost me.'

'You didn't ought to talk like that.'

Gladys laughed again. The sound really quite got on Miss Silver's nerves.

'Oh, I didn't, didn't I? Well, you wait and see, Polly Pell! There's more than that I can say if I choose, but I'm not saying it yet. I'm keeping it back to make a splash with—see?'

'What do you mean?'

'I mean I can put the rope round somebody's neck if I choose, and I'm going to choose all right. There's someone in this house that's going to swing for what they done, and it's me that's going to put the rope round their neck. And get my photo in all the papers, and everyone talking about me! I'll say this for those reporter chaps, they give you a good write-up. "Golden-haired, blue-eyed Gladys Marsh"—that'll be me, when I'm not a "beautiful blonde". You see, I'll be right in the news, and if I can't make something out of it, my name's not Gladys Marsh. And won't you wish you was me!'

Polly achieved emphasis.

'No, that I don't!' she said.

TWENTY-SEVEN

At the sound of footsteps coming from the direction of the hall Miss Silver set down the tumbler she was holding and walked briskly to meet them. It was Julia Vane whom she encountered. It did not escape her that, in addition to being unusually pale, Julia had a look of endurance which had not been there when they met at breakfast. Whatever may have been her errand, Miss Silver forestalled it.

'I should appreciate a short conversation with you, Miss Vane, if you can spare the time.'

She had shut the door behind her. Julia looked past her in that direction.

'I was going to see Mrs Maniple. Is she in the kitchen?'

Miss Silver shook her head.

'Oh, no—she is still in the study with Sergeant Abbott. I will not detain you for long. Perhaps the drawing-room would be suitable.'

Julia preceded her there in dumb rebellion. The house was no longer their own—it certainly wasn't Jimmy's. Their lives, their actions, their time, the words they spoke, the words they dared not speak, were all conditioned by this timeless nightmare in which they lived and moved. She turned, to see Miss Silver looking at her kindly. Her voice too was kind as she said,

'Truth is always best, Miss Julia.'

The bitterness she felt for Manny, for Jimmy, for all of them, came out in her voice as she answered,

'Is it?'

Miss Silver said, 'I think so. It is not always easy to see it at the time. That is one of the things which makes the conduct of a murder case so difficult. People with something to conceal persist in trying to conceal it. It may be a serious matter, or it may be quite trifling, but the result is the same—the issues are obscured. People who are habitually truthful are tempted to depart from the truth. They are not usually very successful. It requires a good deal of practice to deceive an experienced police officer. It is much easier, as well as much safer, to tell the truth.'

The words which formed themselves in Julia's mind dissolved as she looked at Miss Silver. They were what anyone might suppose. 'Do you think I'm telling lies? Why should I? I haven't got anything to hide.' They were in her mind, but they never reached her lips. She looked at Miss Silver, and lost sight of her primness and her dowdy clothes. She didn't see them any more. She was aware of intelligence and strength. She was intelligent enough herself to recognise these qualities, and strong enough to value them. She said in a quiet, humble voice,

'I'm not hiding anything—really.'

Miss Silver's smile came out.

'Thank you, my dear. I shall be very glad if you will trust me. Concealments are of no real benefit. The innocent cannot gain by them, nor can the guilty. There is no worse punishment than a seeming impunity in crime. That is why I said that truth is best. If you are wondering why I wished to speak to you, it is about Miss Mercer.' She saw all the muscles of Julia's face go taut, and added, 'You see, I heard what she said.'

Julia's lips were stiff. She had to force them to move. She said,

'What did you hear?'

'I heard her say, "What have I done—what have I done?"'

'She was asleep—she was dreaming—she was talking in her sleep.'

Miss Silver made a slight inclination of the head.

'Is she in the habit of walking in her sleep?'

'I think she used to—after her father died.'

'Was his death a sudden one?'

Julia nodded.

'Yes—a car accident—at night. It was a great shock.'

'And under similar conditions of grief and shock the sleepwalking has returned. But perhaps I should not have mentioned grief. Perhaps there is no personal grief on Mrs Latter's account. You can inform me as to that, can you not? Or, shall I say, you can confirm my impression that Miss Mercer felt no affection for Mrs Latter?'

Julia's wide, sad gaze did not falter. She said,

'No. None of us did.'

Miss Silver coughed.

'Then it was shock that brought about a recurrence of the sleep-walking. When I first came out of my room you were following her down the stairs. When you caught her up and stopped her she had her face turned in the direction of this room. It would have been interesting to see what she would have done if she had entered it. As it was, your touch broke the thread of her thought. I withdrew into my room and watched you both come back and enter hers. I reached the door in time to hear her say, "What have I done?"'

After her last words Julia had turned away. There was a ruined vase of roses on the mantelpiece. The room had not been done since Wednesday, nor the flowers changed. There was a scatter of crimson petals on the shelf. Julia swept them together, and as she did so remembered how she had seen Minnie stand just here where she was standing when she looked into the room on Wednesday night. In her mind she could see her as plainly as if it was all happening again—Minnie half turned from the room, bending a little as if she were too tired to stand upright, picking up the fallen petals one at a time in a small trembling hand—With an abrupt movement Julia broke the picture. The rose leaves fell to the hearth in a crimson pool as she swung round crying,

'She didn't do it!'

Miss Silver had been watching her closely.

'If you were quite sure about that, there would be no need for you to feel so much concern.'

Julia drew a stormy breath.

'I *am* sure! Anyone who knew her would be sure!' She checked herself and went on in a different tone. 'Miss Silver, there are things people can do, and things they can't. When you know someone, you know what it would be possible for them to do. It wouldn't be possible for Minnie to kill anyone. You can't kill unless there's something that lets you. People either have that something, or they haven't. Anyone with a hot temper could kill, I suppose, if the provocation was enough to break through a normal self-control. I've got a temper myself. As a rule I've got hold of it—I've always known I mustn't let go. I suppose if I did, I might—kill. But Minnie hasn't got a temper. I've known her all my life, and I've never seen her angry. There's no wild beast in her to get loose like there is in me. Then the other sort of killing, the slow, cold-blooded sort—she couldn't do that any more than I could. None of us could. You see, you don't know her. She's one of the people who is born unselfish—she just doesn't think about herself at all. She's always been the same ever since I can remember. She's kind, and patient, and gentle, and really, truly good. She never had a hard word even for Lois. She'd have been fond of her if it had been humanly possible, because it's her nature to be fond of people. You see, she's *good.* She could no more poison anyone than she could suddenly turn into a hyena. It's just one of those things that are right off the map.'

Miss Silver smiled disarmingly.

'She has a very good friend, my dear,' she said.

TWENTY-EIGHT

Julia went out of the room and up the stairs again. She had just reached the landing, when the door of Lois' bedroom opened and Ellie came running out. Julia gazed at her in amazement. There was a pink flush in her cheeks and her eyes were blue and shining. It was quite obvious that she was running because she couldn't wait to walk. She ran right up to Julia and caught at her with both hands.

'Oh, Julia—isn't it marvellous! Jimmy says I can have Ronnie here as soon as all this is over! Isn't he an angel! I hugged him—I feel as if I could hug everyone I meet! I've just been through to Matron on Lois' extension. Those policemen never give one a chance of getting near the telephone in the study, and I felt I couldn't possibly wait, so I rang up and told her, and she said it wouldn't be worth sending Ronnie down to Brighton unless he was going to stay there. She sounded grim and said it was putting out all the arrangements—and I suppose I let her see just how much I cared about that, because she got a lot grimmer and began to talk exactly as if I was a V.A.D. again. I very nearly said to her, "Well, you know I'm not, and I hope I'm never going to be any more", only I thought it wouldn't exactly oil the wheels, so I didn't. I just said things like "Oh", and "No", and "That's very kind of you, Matron", until she simmered down and said oh, well, she supposed they would have to manage.'

She let go and threw her arms round Julia's neck.

'Darling, isn't it marvellous!'

Time had swung back. This was the old Ellie with the quick blood in her cheeks, light in her eyes, every bit of her quivering with life. Julia had a moment of giddiness. You can swing too fast and too far to keep your balance. Ellie must have lost hers. She stepped back and said in a ringing voice,

'It's an ill wind that blows nobody any good, isn't it?'

Someone was coming up the stairs behind Julia. She could just hear the sound of quiet footsteps. She said '*Ellie*—' in a warning voice, but it wasn't any good. Ellie stamped her foot and cried,

'I don't care! Lois wouldn't have had him here—*ever*!'

Then she saw Miss Silver coming up behind Julia. She stood for a moment, her colour bright, her eyes wide, but before Miss Silver reached the landing she turned, ran into the room she shared with Julia, and shut the door.

Miss Silver coughed reprovingly.

'That was not very wise.'

Julia said, 'No.' And then, 'She wasn't thinking about being wise, you know. She was just being natural. She hasn't got anything to hide. She has been very unhappy about him. It just hasn't occurred to her that she mustn't let anyone see that she is happy because he can come here now.'

Miss Silver said thoughtfully,

'Wisdom is to be commended as well as harmlessness. There is Scriptural warrant for that, you know, Miss Julia.' She crossed the landing to her own room and entered it.

Julia followed Ellie. She found her rubbing cream into her face. Ellie began to talk at once.

'I'll go over and see him this afternoon. I'm trying the cream Minnie makes. If my colour would only keep like it is now, I wouldn't need to put any on, but the bother is I can't trust it. I'd better be on the safe side, don't you think?'

Julia went and stood by the near window. Looking out she said,

'I expect so.' And then, quickly, 'Ellie, what possessed you to say that about Lois? Miss Silver heard you.'

'I don't care if she did. It's true.'

Julia's dark brows had met. She said,

'Ellie, you've got to be careful—we all have. Those police-men don't think Lois committed suicide—they think she was murdered.'

'Don't!'

'I must. We've got to be careful of everything we say or do. What you said just now could very easily be twisted.'

Ellie's colour had gone out like a candle in the wind.

'You mean they could think I did it?'

Julia turned round. She had no colour to lose.

'I mean you've got to be careful not to give them anything to think about. If you put it into their heads that Lois was in your way, and that you're glad she isn't there any longer—well, it isn't going to be so good, is it?'

Ellie went on rubbing cream into her face mechanically. She said,

'That's nonsense.' Her shoulder jerked.

Julia walked over to her, and took her by the arm.'

'Use your head, Ellie! Think! You and Minnie and Jimmy were in the drawing-room when she took that coffee. You can't afford to start the police thinking about you.'

Ellie pulled away.

'It wasn't the police—it was Miss Silver.'

'It's all the same thing.' Julia's voice had a discouraged sound. Now she had made Ellie think her unkind. She didn't want to frighten her, she only wanted her to be careful. It was like having to pick your way among eggshells. She wondered if she had said enough. She didn't see her way to saying any more. She thought she had better go downstairs again and see whether the police had finished with Manny.

Ellie was wiping the cream off her face. She didn't turn round or look up.

Julia went out of the room with the feeling that she might just as well have held her tongue.

TWENTY-NINE

Miss Silver, having fetched a fresh ball of grey wool from her bedroom, proceeded downstairs with it. She had left her knitting-bag on a table in the hall, and it was while she was slipping the wool into it and hanging the bag on her arm that the door of the study opened and Mrs Maniple came out. The dignity of her bearing was unimpaired. She crossed the hall and made her way down the long passage which led off it to the kitchen wing.

As soon as she was out of sight Miss Silver entered the study. The Chief Inspector, who was on his feet, was saying, 'Well, you'd better go and get her, and Miss Silver too. I don't want—' He broke off at the sound of the closing door. 'Well, there!' he said, 'How did you know you were wanted? I was just sending Frank for you.'

Miss Silver smiled agreeably.

'For me—and also, I think, for someone else. May I enquire who else was to be summoned?'

He said briefly, 'Miss Mercer. I was going to ask her about those fingerprints, and as she looks as if it wouldn't be any trouble to her to faint, I thought I'd have you handy.'

A shade of distance tinged Miss Silver's manner. She did not regard herself as something to be kept handy, nor did she expect to be so regarded. Frank Abbott, gathering up his papers, suppressed a smile.

Miss Maud Silver reached the chair which she had occupied before, altered its angle slightly, and sat down. As she disposed the knitting-bag on her lap and drew out Derek's half-finished stocking, she observed,

'I am always pleased to do anything I can to assist you, Chief Inspector.' She made a light but impressive pause and continued. 'I would, however, ask you to defer Miss Mercer for the moment. I have just overheard a conversation between Gladys Marsh and the young girl Polly Pell. When I have repeated it to you, you will, I think, agree that it would be as well to question Gladys without delay.'

Lamb gave a snort of disapproval.

'What's she been saying?'

'I will tell you. I was in the pantry, with the door ajar into the kitchen. I heard Gladys boasting that she was going to be a witness, and that if it came to a trial she would have her photograph in all the papers. She regretted that as she was already married she would not be able to avail herself of the many offers of marriage which she anticipated. She had, however, the effrontery to indicate that the difficulty might be surmounted.'

Frank Abbott looked over his shoulder to say,

'We shall certainly want you here as a chaperon if we're going to interview Gladys—shan't we, Chief?'

There was an impudent gleam in his eye which drew a frown from his superior officer. Lamb said gloomily,

'I suppose that wasn't all, or you wouldn't be wanting us to see her.'

Miss Silver was knitting with great rapidity.

'It was by no means all,' she said. 'After boasting that she would be one of the chief witnesses in a big murder trial, she went on to use these words, "There's more than that I could say if I choose, but I'm not saying it yet—I'm keeping it back to make a splash with." Polly asked her what she meant. In reply Gladys said that she could put the rope round somebody's neck if she chose, and she was going to choose all right. She added, "There's someone in this house that's going to swing for what they done, and it's me that's going to put the rope round their neck, and get my photo in all the papers and have everyone talking about me."'

The Chief Inspector pursed up his lips as if he were about to whistle.

'She said that?'

'Word for word.'

'Then we'll have her in and find out what she meant by it. It mightn't be very much, you know, if she was boasting like you say. No, there mightn't be very much to it, but we'll have her in. Where did you say she was—in the kitchen?'

Miss Silver coughed.

'She was there. But Mrs Maniple having returned, I think it probable that Gladys will now be somewhere else.'

Wherever she was, it did not take Frank Abbott long to locate her. She could be heard giggling before he opened the door and ushered her into the room, where she looked impudently at Miss Silver, rolled her eyes at the Chief Inspector, and tripped round the table to sink gracefully upon the chair which had been placed for her. Seated, she crossed her legs, bringing a brief skirt several inches above the knee. The blue eyes rolled in Frank's direction, glanced coyly down at the expanse of silk stocking, and then swam back to his extremely unresponsive profile.

Lamb, reflecting that someone had missed the chance of spanking her when young, thumped the table with a formidable hand, and rapped out,

'Please pay attention, Mrs Marsh! Sergeant Abbott isn't here to look at you—he's here to take down what you say, so be obliged if you'll give your mind to it.'

He received a languishing gaze and a giggle.

'You haven't asked me anything yet—have you?'

'You needn't trouble about that—I'm going to. Now, Mrs Marsh, you'll be so kind as to give me your whole attention. About a quarter of an hour or twenty minutes ago you were in the kitchen talking to Polly Pell—'

Gladys pouted her scarlet lips.

'That's right—we were having an elevens. Anything wrong about it?'

She didn't get any answer to that. Lamb looked at her as stolidly as if she had been a rag doll. He said,

'Your conversation was overheard.'

Gladys raised her plucked eyebrows and said in a genteel voice,

'Reelly? I don't know how people can lower themselves to listen at doors—do you? It isn't what I'd call naice myself.'

This was too much for Lamb. His eyes bolted perceptibly, and his voice rasped as he said,

'That's quite enough of that! You were heard to say that you knew more about Mrs Latter's death than you had disclosed to the police. You said you could put a rope round the neck of someone in this house and you were going to do it, but you were holding back what you knew because you wanted to make a splash.'

The blue eyes ceased to languish. They showed a calculating gleam.

'You don't say!'

'Will you explain what you meant?'

'Well—I dunno—'

'I think you'd better. Ever heard of an accessory in a murder case? It means someone who knows something about the murder, either before or afterwards—a person who participates by advice, command, or concealment.' He repeated the last two words in a slow, weighty tone—'Or concealment, Mrs Marsh. And an accessory can be put in the dock and tried with the principal.' His manner changed suddenly. 'But there—I expect you were just doing a bit of boasting, trying to impress that girl Polly. If you really knew anything, a smart girl like you wouldn't be getting herself into trouble keeping it back. You'd look a lot better in the witness-box than you would in the dock—but I needn't tell you that. Come now, out with it! You were just boasting, weren't you?'

She tossed her head.

'It's a free country, isn't it? I can say what I like!'

He kept his easy manner.

'You said you could put a rope round somebody's neck. You can't say that sort of thing in the middle of a murder case and not be asked what you mean by it. Now—did you mean anything, or didn't you? If you did, you can only tell it once, you know. No good saving it up to make a splash like you said and finding you've landed yourself up to your neck in trouble.' He let her have a moment, and then came back at her with a point-blank, 'Have you got anything, or haven't you?'

She gave him a bright, bold stare.

'Well then, I have.'

'All right, let's have it.'

Frank Abbott pulled a block towards him and took up his pencil. Gladys watched him out of the corners of her eyes. He was going to take down what she said in shorthand. Then he would type it out, and they would ask her to sign it like they did before. She didn't care—she might as well tell it now as later. She didn't want to get into trouble with the police—they could make it ever so nasty for you if you got on the wrong side of them. Good-looking chap that Sergeant Abbott—looked cold enough to freeze you, but you couldn't always tell by looks—she wouldn't mind having a date with him. He must be bored stiff at the Bull. . . She re-crossed her legs, hitching her skirt a little higher. A good thing she'd got those new long stockings. Mrs Latter hadn't liked the colour and she'd passed them on. Funny to think of her being gone and the stockings still here. A feeling of sincere regret that the source of so many favours should have been removed gave impetus to her decision. She tossed back her mane of hair and said,

'I dunno who heard me talking to Polly, but I don't need to take any of it back. I know what I heard and I know what I saw, and I know what I think about it. But I didn't know at the time, so there's nothing for me to get into trouble about.'

The Chief Inspector was bluff.

'You won't get into trouble if you haven't done anything wrong.'

'*Me!*' She swept her lashes up, and down again—an accomplishment very carefully practised before her looking-glass. 'I'm a good girl, I am—anyone'll tell you that.'

Lamb controlled himself with difficulty.

'Well now, suppose you tell us what you heard and saw.'

'I'm going to. It was on the Tuesday evening—'

'You mean Tuesday this week?'

'Yes, last Tuesday—the day after there was that turn-up in Mr Antony's room, and the day before Mrs Latter was poisoned.'

'All right, go on.'

'Mrs Latter stayed in her room most of the day. Mr Latter was out pretty nearly all day. I didn't know he was in until I come out of Mrs Latter's room about seven o'clock and I heard him in Miss Mercer's bedroom—'

'What's that?'

Gladys looked through her lashes.

'He was in Miss Mercer's bedroom on the other side of the landing. The door wasn't fastened.'

'You listened?'

She tossed her head.

'Seemed funny to me. I thought Mrs Latter might like to know. Seemed he'd made a lot of fuss about her being in Mr Antony's room, and here he was, in with Miss Mercer. Seemed funny to me.'

Lamb stared at her.

'There's quite a difference between twelve o'clock at night and seven o'clock in the evening, isn't there? Well, you listened—'

'I thought Mrs Latter would like to know what they were saying. Ooh—I did get a start!'

'Why?'

'Mr Latter was crying—he was reelly—down on his knees with his head in Miss Mercer's lap.'

'How do you know?'

'Because I looked round the door. They was a great deal too taken up with themselves to notice if I'd come right into the room, but I just took a look and back again, and there was Miss Mercer in the little low easy chair, and Mr Latter down on his knees with his head in her lap, and her stroking his hair and saying, "My poor Jimmy!"' Gladys sniffed virtuously. 'And I thought to myself, "How's that for goings on!"'

Miss Silver looked across her clicking needles and said in a repressive voice,

'You are doubtless aware, Chief Inspector, that Mr Latter and Miss Mercer were brought up together like brother and sister.'

He said, 'Yes, yes,' and put up a hand for silence. 'Go on, Mrs Marsh.'

'He went on crying for a bit, just like a big baby. And then he said all of a sudden, "I've got to sleep. I'll go mad if I don't—or I'll do something I'll be sorry for. You've got to give me something to make me sleep. What have you got?" I took another look round the door, and he'd gone over to the medicine cupboard she had in her room—the police took it away, but it used to hang right over the middle of the book-case. He'd got the door open, and I saw him take a bottle out and look at it.'

'What kind of a bottle?'

'One of those flat ones with a screw top. He said, "This'll make me sleep", and Miss Mercer come up to him and took it away. She said, "Oh, no—that's morphia. You mustn't have that—it's dangerous." And he said, "As long as I sleep, I don't care if I never wake up again."'

'Sure he said that?'

She nodded.

'Of course I'm sure! I heard it, didn't I?'

'Go on.'

'Miss Mercer put the bottle back. She said something about it oughtn't to be where it was. Seemed she thought she'd put it away out of sight. She took out another bottle and tipped something out into her hand. She gave it to Mr Latter and said, "Take these when you go to bed. They won't do you any harm." And he said, "All the harm's done, Min." And I come away, because it looked like he was getting ready to go.'

Miss Silver gave a short dry cough. She addressed Gladys Marsh.

'Mrs Latter came down to the evening meal, I believe.'

Without troubling to look at her Gladys said,

'Yes, she did.'

'Did you go back into her room to help her dress?'

'What if I did?'

'Nothing at all, Mrs Marsh—I should merely like to know.'

Gladys was inspecting a row of scarlet fingernails. With scant attention and no attempt at politeness, she said languidly,

'Well then, I did.'

'And did you acquaint her with what you had overheard?'

Gladys threw up her head with a jerk and enquired of the Chief Inspector,

'Look here—who's she anyway? I don't have to answer her, do I?'

His voice was grim as he told her,

'You don't have to answer anyone—not till you come before the Coroner. But if you haven't done anything wrong, what's your objection? It's a simple question enough. Perhaps you'll answer me if I put it to you. Did you tell Mrs Latter what you had overheard?'

She rolled her eyes at him.

'What do you think?'

'I think you did.'

'Clever—aren't you!'

He went on as if she had not spoken.

'But I'd like to hear whether you did or not. Come along—out with it!'

Her hair had fallen forward again. She tossed it back.

'Well, of course I did! That's what I listened for, wasn't it?'

Lamb said,

'That's what you said. So you told Mrs Latter there was a bottle of morphia tablets in Miss Mercer's room—you did mention that?'

Gladys looked sulky.

'I told her what I heard and saw, same as I told you.'

'You mentioned the morphia?'

'I don't know what you're getting at. Of course I did!'

Lamb was silent for a moment. Then he said,

'Sure you've told us all you heard and saw?'

'Isn't it enough for you?'

'I'm asking you whether you've told us all you heard and saw.'

'I saw Mr Latter with the morphia bottle in his hand, and I heard Miss Mercer tell him the stuff was dangerous. That's something, isn't it?'

He said, 'Yes—that's something.'

THIRTY

All right' said Lamb, 'you can go. Sergeant Abbott will type out your statement and you can sign it presently. It may be important, or it may not—it depends on what other people have to say. You've done right in making it, but I'm warning you to keep your mouth shut, or you may find you're in trouble. You mustn't go about saying you can put ropes round people's necks, you know.'

Gladys tipped her chair back and got up. As she passed Frank Abbott she contrived to brush against him. She seemed to stumble. Her hand caught at his shoulder, and a long flop of yellow hair fell down and tickled his cheek. He became disgustedly aware that it wanted washing. Something in his expression, something in the way he handed her off, brought the blood to her cheeks. She gave him a stabbing look and rounded on Lamb.

'I'm to hold my tongue, am I? So you can hush it up, I wouldn't wonder! If it had been me, there wouldn't have been any hushing up! But because it's Mr Latter of Latter End nobody's to let on he poisoned his wife! And I'll tell you all something—Mrs Latter was a very good friend to me, and you can't shut my mouth! I've got my rights like other people!' She reached the door, jerked it open, and turned on the threshold to deliver a final volley. 'My tongue's my own and I'll say what I like with it—so there!'

The door banged. The Chief Inspector pursed his lips in a soundless whistle. Frank Abbott took out an immaculate handkerchief and wiped his cheek. Miss Silver continued to knit.

Lamb spoke first. He said,

'There's times when it cramps you, being a police officer—there's no doubt about that.'

Frank crumpled the handkerchief and put it back in his pocket.

'A few branding-irons and things, Chief? You know, somehow I don't feel you'd really be at home in a torture chamber.'

Lamb fixed him with an awful eye, and then relaxed.

'What she wants is a good smacking,' he said. 'Pity somebody didn't do it for her when she was a kid.'

Miss Silver coughed.

'An exceedingly badly brought up young woman. As Lord Tennyson so truly says, "The tongue is a fire". But she will make a good witness, Chief Inspector.'

He slewed round in his chair.

'In what way?'

Derek's sock revolved briskly.

'She is intelligent and, I think, accurate. Perhaps sharp would be a better word than intelligent. When you very kindly afforded me the opportunity of reading the statements which have been made, I was a good deal struck by her account of the scene in Mr Antony Latter's room on the Monday night. It was clear, vivid, and so accurate that neither Mr Antony nor Mr Jimmy Latter have challenged it in any respect. This argues a gift of aural memory which is not very common. In listening to her just now, I was confirmed in my opinion. Her evidence was, of course, tinged with spite, but it was presented very clearly, and the essential points were stressed. I should be very much surprised if her account of what took place in Miss Mercer's room is not perfectly correct.'

Frank Abbott was looking at her with a good deal of attention. The Chief Inspector let his hand fall heavily upon his knee.

'Looks bad for your client, Miss Silver. She'll go into the box and swear he knew where he could lay his hands on a dangerous dose of morphia. I agree she'll make a good show there—always provided there aren't too many women on the jury—the way she rolls her eyes won't do her any good with them. No—it doesn't look too good for Mr Jimmy Latter.'

Miss Silver coughed.

'You are not, I suppose, overlooking the fact that Gladys Marsh will also have to swear that Mrs Latter knew where she could lay her hands upon that morphia?'

Lamb frowned. He drew his fingers up into a bunch, and then suddenly spread them out again as if he were letting something go. He said in a bluff voice,

'One for you, and one for me—is that it?'

Miss Silver's needles clicked. She said primly,

'The implication that we are taking sides is not one which I can accept, either for myself or for you, Chief Inspector.'

He said. 'Well, well—' and turned to Frank Abbott. 'We'd better be getting a move on. Tell Miss Mercer I want to ask her a few questions.'

Whilst they were waiting he picked up a stick of sealing-wax and began to fidget with it. When presently it snapped in his hand he turned to Miss Silver with an abrupt movement and said,

'You're a very obstinate woman, you know.'

She allowed her eyes to meet his with a faint smile in them.

'I hope not.'

'No good hoping.'

'Obstinacy is an impediment to the free exercise of thought. It paralyses the intelligence. Conclusions based upon preconceived ideas are valueless. It is only the open mind that really thinks. I endeavour to keep my mind open.'

He turned back to the sealing-wax, picked up the two bits, frowned at his own attempt to make the broken ends fit, glanced suddenly over his shoulder, and said,

'Look here, have you got anything up your sleeve ?'

'Nothing whatever, I assure you.'

'You haven't got the murderer there by any chance?'

'No, indeed.'

He threw down the sealing-wax and turned to face her.

'If it comes to a trial, the defence will be suicide. The way things are shaping, it lies between the husband and wife. They both knew about the morphia. Either he gave it to her, or she took it herself. You've read all the statements, and you've been mixing with the family in a way the police don't get a chance of doing. You've talked with them, I don't doubt, and you've formed an opinion of Mrs Latter from what they've said. I don't suppose it's very different from the opinion I've formed myself. Without any beating about the bush—are you going to tell me you think it's at all likely that she committed suicide?'

'Likely? No. But unlikely things do happen, Chief Inspector.'

'Are you going to tell me that in your opinion she did commit suicide?'

She said, 'No—' in a very thoughtful tone. And then, 'Pray do not misunderstand me. I have at this time no opinion to offer—I have an open mind. I agree with you that Mrs Latter does not sound at all the sort of person who would be likely to commit suicide, and I agree that if she had been going to do so she would have been much more likely to take the morphia after she had gone to bed. But, as I said, unlikely things do happen, especially when people have suffered a shock or some violent mental disturbance. We really do not know much about Mrs Latter's state of mind. Externally she was a hard, spoiled woman with a habit of getting her own way, but we do not know what was going on underneath. It has been rather stressed that her feeling for Mr Antony was of a wilful and casual nature, and that in her pursuit of him she was actuated by anger against her husband and a desire to punish him. Mr Antony specially stressed this point of view. It is, of course, quite natural that he should do so. He is very much attached to his cousin, and he desires to minimise the importance of what took place on Monday night by representing it as a sudden

LATTER END   241

angry whim. But it is quite possible that Mrs Latter's feeling for him may have been of a much more serious character.
She was a woman who was not accustomed to being crossed.
Suppose her to have been actuated by one of those dangerous passions which so often precipitate a tragedy—suppose
her to have become aware that she has a rival in Miss Vane.
This would be a very formidable combination. What happens?
She is not only refused, but the refusal occurs in her husband's
presence, and in circumstances calculated to give a very violent
shock to her self-respect. I remember many years ago being
very much impressed by the statement that crimes of violence
by women are apt to follow directly upon some sudden lower-
ing of their self-respect.'

Lamb said, 'That's right enough. Well, you say you haven't
got an opinion, but it seems to me you've been giving me one.'

She made a slight negative gesture.

'It is merely a theory, Chief Inspector. It is not an opinion.'

THIRTY-ONE

As Minnie Mercer seated herself in the chair recently occupied by Gladys Marsh it is probable that each of the other three people present was visited by a sense of contrast. Miss Mercer not only looked ill and strained, but she had an appearance of fragility which rather alarmed the Chief Inspector. Her eyes had a haunting look of distress. She folded her hands in her lap and leaned against the high back of the chair.

Lamb was leaning back too, his pose easy, his manner quiet. He had obviously no desire to alarm Miss Mercer. 'Just a few questions', was what he had said as she came into the room. He waited now until she was settled, and then said,

'You've been a long time at Latter End?'

There was an almost inaudible 'Yes'.

'Twenty-five years?'

'Yes.'

'Never thought of leaving?'

A still more inaudible 'No'.

'But you are leaving now—or shall we say you were leaving at the time of Mrs Latter's death?'

'Yes.'

'Why?'

Her hands took hold of one another.

'Mrs Latter was making other arrangements.'

'She gave you notice.'

There may have been a purpose behind the bluntness of his speech. It brought a faint colour to her cheeks. There was a gentle dignity in her manner as she answered him.

'It was not quite like that. Mrs Street and I had been doing the housework between us, owing to the difficulty of getting any staff. It was a temporary arrangement. Mrs Latter—' her voice caught on the name—'Mrs Latter had succeeded in finding a butler and two maids.'

He looked at her shrewdly.

'You haven't answered my question, have you? Let me put it another way. Did Mrs Latter ask you to leave, or did the suggestion come from you?'

The faint flush was gone. It is always rather horrifying to see a fair skin quite drained of colour. She opened her lips to speak, and shut them again.

'Well, Miss Mercer?'

Her lips parted. This time she had found words.

'My work here was over.'

Lamb said, 'Yes—I suppose so. Now, to go back a little— what was your position here before Mr Latter's marriage?'

'It is rather difficult to say. I looked after the house. I—until Mrs Street married and Miss Vane went away to do war work—I—there were two young girls in the house—they needed someone after their mother died—'

'You took Mrs Vane's place?'

She said, with warmth in her voice for the first time,

'No one could do that. I did what I could.'

'Would you say that you were on the same footing as a relation would have been, running the house, looking after the two girls?'

'Yes, I think so.'

'But you received a salary.'

Colour in her face again, quickly come, and very quickly gone.

'Yes.'

'Have you any private means?'

'No.'

'Have you another post in view?'

She shook her head.

'What salary did you receive?'

'Sixty pounds—since Mrs Vane's death.'

A brief glance from Frank Abbott met his Chiefs. Sixty pounds a year—to cover those wartime years when wages and salaries had soared!

Lamb said bluntly,

'That's very low. You didn't think of asking for a rise?'

'Oh, no!'

If anyone had had the leisure to look in Miss Silver's direction, it would have been observed that she was frowning, and that her lips were pressed together in a manner which suggested distaste. She was, in fact, exercising a considerable degree of restraint upon herself. She had a good deal of respect for the Chief Inspector, but sometimes he lacked the finer shades. Miss Mercer was a gentlewoman. This was no way to speak to a gentlewoman. Like David in the Psalms, she held her tongue, but it was pain and grief to her.

Lamb, unconscious, pursued his enquiry.

'Then I take it you haven't saved very much?'

'No.'

'You didn't expect to have to make a change?'

She said in a gentle, tired voice,

'One doesn't expect changes—but they come.'

Lamb nodded.

'And that brings us back to where we started. I want to know who suggested this particular change. Was it Mrs Latter, or was it you?'

'It was Mrs Latter. I was expecting it.'

'I see. But Mr Latter was under the impression that it was you who wished to make a change. Who told him that? Was it Mrs Latter?'

'Yes.'

'You didn't undeceive him?'

She shook her head.

'He was distressed at your going—he asked you to stay? You let him think you wanted to go? Why?'

She said very gently,

'It was the best way. I couldn't stay if she wanted me to go. I didn't want there to be any trouble over me.'

'I see—you didn't want to be the cause of a quarrel. Is that it. Did they often quarrel?'

'Oh, no.'

'But you thought they might quarrel about this?'

'I didn't want to make any trouble.'

He leaned forward.

'Miss Mercer, you know what happened on Monday night—with that girl Gladys Marsh in the house, there's no one who doesn't. You know Mrs Latter went into Mr Antony Latter's room, and her husband found her there. I'd like to know when you heard about that, and who told you.'

The knuckles stood out bone-white on her clasped hands. She leaned forward too.

'Mr Latter told me. I heard people moving about, and I looked out of my room. I saw him come back. I thought something had happened. He turned, and saw me looking out. He told me what had happened.'

'How did he seem?'

She said, 'Dazed—' Her voice ceased. After a moment she went on again. 'I got him to go into his room, and I went down and made him some tea. I took it in to him and got him to take it.' She looked at him with an earnest, direct gaze. 'He wasn't angry—he was just—heart-broken.'

'How long did you stay?'

'Not very long. I hoped he would go to sleep.'

'Well now, that brings us to Tuesday. Did you have any more conversation with him on the Tuesday?'

'He was out nearly all day.'

'But he came home in the evening. Did you have any talk with him then—at about seven o'clock in the evening, when he came to your room and asked you to give him something to make him sleep?'

Her eyes widened. After a moment she said,

'I gave him some aspirin—two tablets. He hadn't slept.'

'Yes we know about that. He came to your room about seven, didn't he? Will you tell us just what passed between you?'

Into those wide eyes there came a look of remembered pain. She had to force her voice. Even then it made very little sound.

'He came in—he had been out all day. He was a good deal—distressed. He wanted something to make him sleep.'

'Yes?'

'I have—that is, I had—a small medicine cupboard in my room—the Inspector took it away—'

'Yes, that's all right.'

'Everyone comes to me if they want anything. That's why Mr Latter came. I gave him two aspirins.'

Lamb said,

'That wasn't quite all that happened, was it?' He looked round at Frank Abbott. 'Could you run through Mrs Marsh's evidence from your shorthand notes?'

'Yes, sir.'

Minnie Mercer took a faint gasping breath.

Frank Abbott began to read in an agreeable expressionless voice. She listened because she had to listen. There was no way of stopping her ears. She had to know that what she and Jimmy had said had been overheard, and by Gladys Marsh.

There was no way in which she could close her mind or shelter Jimmy. It was like being stripped naked. The room filled with a light wavering mist. Sergeant Abbott's voice seemed to come from a long way off. Then it stopped.

The Chief Inspector said, 'Is that a correct account of what took place between you and Mr Latter?'

'I think so—'

Until she heard the words she wasn't sure that she had spoken.

'It is substantially correct? He went to the cupboard and took out a bottle of morphia tablets, and you said, "Oh, no—that's morphia! You mustn't have that—it's dangerous"? '

'Yes.'

'And he said, "As long as I sleep, I don't care if I never wake up again"?'

'Yes.'

'Now, Miss Mercer—what did you do with that bottle?'

'I put it back in the cupboard.'

'Was it in its right place when Mr Latter took it out?'

'He turned round from the cupboard with the bottle in his hand.'

'Mrs Marsh says you said something about the bottle not being in its right place.'

She looked blankly at him for a moment. Then,

'I don't remember what I said. I must have thought he had taken it from the front of the shelf. It oughtn't to have been there.'

'How did you come by it?'

'My father had it—he was a doctor. When I came here I brought the medicine cupboard with me. The bottle of morphia tablets was in it.'

'You knew that they were strong enough to be dangerous?'

'Yes.'

'Yet you kept them in an unlocked cupboard where anyone could lay hands on them?'

She said, 'No. I kept it locked.'

'It wasn't locked when Mr Latter went to it?'

'No. I'd been getting some cold cream out for Mrs Street.'

'But as a rule you kept that cupboard locked?'

'Oh, yes.'

'Where did you keep the key?'

'It was on my bunch.'

'And where did you keep your bunch?'

'Inside my handkerchief-case, in the dressing-table drawer.'

Lamb grunted.

'And I suppose everyone in the house knew where you kept it.'

She said in quite a firm voice,

'There is no one in the house who would go to my drawer and take my keys.'

'Well, we don't know about that. And you don't know where the morphia bottle was when Mr Latter found it. But I suppose you know where it ought to have been.'

'Yes. There's a cardboard box at the back of the shelf. It should have been inside the box.'

'Sure about that?'

'Oh, yes, quite sure.'

'Is that where you put it when you returned it to the cupboard?'

'No—not then.'

'Will you explain that?'

She hesitated, but not painfully. It was more as if she was uncertain.

'I think—I wanted to give Mr Latter—something quickly. I thought I would look at the bottle afterwards when he was gone. I left it on the front of the shelf.'

'Why did you want to look at it?'

'I thought—I had an idea—' She stopped.

'Go on.'

She gave him a wide, piteous look.

'I can't be sure about it.'

'You mean you had an impression, but you were not sure that it was correct. Is that it?'

She relaxed and said, 'Yes.'

'Well, suppose you tell us about this impression. What was it?'

'I thought the bottle wasn't full enough.'

Lamb pursed up his lips as if he were going to whistle.

'Thought it wasn't full enough? How could you tell?'

She said, 'I did look afterwards—and I can't be sure. I've never used any of those tablets since my father died. With anything like that—anything that was dangerous—he wrote the number of tablets in the bottle on a strip of paper pasted down the back. Every time he took a tablet out he crossed the old number out and wrote a new one, so he always knew just how many tablets there were left in the bottle. I was going to count the tablets and see whether they were right, but when I came to look for the number on the strip of paper it was too smudged to read.'

'What did you do with the bottle after that?'

'I put it back in the cardboard box.'

'Did you lock the cupboard and put away your keys?'

'Yes, I did.'

He leaned forward.

'Miss Mercer—could Mr Latter have removed any of those tablets without your seeing him?'

She was as startled as if he had struck her. It wasn't only her voice that said 'No!', it was her whole body.

'No—no! Oh, no!' And then, 'There wasn't time. He went to the cupboard and I followed him. I saw his hand come back from the shelf with the bottle in it. Oh, no—there wasn't any time at all!'

He let her go.

When the door had shut behind her he said,

'I wonder whether she thought that up for herself, or whether Mr Jimmy Latter put it into her head.'

Miss Silver coughed.

'You refer, I suppose, to Miss Mercer's implication that some of the tablets might already have been removed when she and Mr Latter handled the bottle on Tuesday evening.'

Lamb gave a short laugh.

'You might call it an implication, and I might call it a try-on. I don't know that I do, but I might. Whichever way you look at it, it's clever. What I'd like to know is, who is being clever? You wouldn't think to look at them that either Mr Latter or Miss Mercer were what you'd call sharp enough to cut themselves or anyone else. Of course it's easy to see she'd do anything she could to get him off—that's as plain as a pikestaff. I only wish a few other things were half so plain. But unless she's a lot deeper than she looks she wouldn't have thought up that line about some of those tablets being missing. It's clever, and she put it over cleverly too—didn't overdo it. You know, I've had an idea all along that there was a clever brain behind all this. If Miss Mercer didn't think that up for herself, I'd like to know who did.'

Miss Silver coughed in a deprecating manner.

'You would not be inclined to consider the possibility that she may have been telling the truth, Chief Inspector?'

THIRTY-TWO

Julia had a brief, exasperating interview with Mrs Maniple.
If she expected to find her at all cast down she was mistaken.
Coming back to her own domain to find 'that Gladys Marsh'
sitting on her kitchen table, Mrs Maniple had, to use her
own expression, 'set her to rights'. For all her impudence,
Gladys met her match. She retired with impertinence upon
her tongue, it is true, but quite in a hurry. Polly, silent and
quaking, was set to scrub vegetables in the scullery, the door
into the kitchen being then shut so firmly as to suggest a
bang.

Julia was received in an extremely lofty manner which put
her back again to somewhere about five years old.

'Manny, what's happened?'

'I'm making a cake, Miss Julia.'

'Manny! I mean in the study. Please tell me.'

Mrs Maniple looked over the top of her head.

'There's nothing to tell that I know about. I went in, and I come out. I told them that you made such a point of their being told, and what good it's going to do them or anyone else, I don't know. But there it is—you can't say I've kept anything back. And the stout policeman, he said to stay on the premises in case I was wanted. I could have told him it wasn't any hardship to me, seeing I'm on them all the time, and have been for more than fifty years if it wasn't for church of a Sunday, and down into the village, and once in a way into Crampton, but I wouldn't demean myself. I come out, and if the lunch is spoilt it won't be my fault. And I'll thank you to let me have my kitchen to myself, Miss Julia.'

It was some time later that she met Jimmy Latter coming in from the garden.

'They want to see me again,' he said.

'The police?'

He nodded.

A sharp fear pricked Julia. They couldn't be going to arrest him—or could they? In this nightmare world there were no landmarks. It stretched all round them with no way of escape. Any path might dissolve beneath your foot, any bridge might crumble, any word or any action might precipitate disaster. And all the while they were being watched.

Jimmy was saying in a grey, hopeless tone, 'I don't know what they want me for—they've asked me everything already.' He went past her with a dragging step.

It was perhaps because Manny had pushed back the years that Julia found herself running out of the house. If they were going to arrest Jimmy, she couldn't be there, she couldn't see it. She had to find Antony. It was all quite unreasoning and instinctive.

When the impulse failed she was horribly ashamed of it. It had taken her almost as far as the rose-garden. She stood still and looked around her. It was a lovely morning, the early mist all gone, the air fresh and delicate with the scent of flowers, and a promise of warmth to come. There was not a cloud in the sky. She saw Antony coming towards her and waited for him. Even in the middle of a nightmare Antony was real.

He came up to her, slipped a hand inside her arm, and said, 'What's the matter?'

'I don't know—I'm frightened. They've sent for Jimmy again. I thought—' Her voice died away. She caught his hand in a convulsive clasp. 'Do you think—they're going—to arrest him?'

He said quite coolly, 'I shouldn't think so—not at present. But it isn't the end of all things if they do. Don't look like that. I expect they only want to ask him some more questions. There's that damned will—'

'They had him in there for ages about that as soon as they came this morning.'

He began to walk her up and down. There were big bushes of musk rose on either side of the path, full of their early autumn bloom—pink buds and creamy flowers, and a heavenly smell. It didn't seem real. But Antony was real.

They walked up and down and talked. She told him about Manny, and he said,

'I wonder if it will make any difference.'

That frightened her, because she had been building on it, and because she and Antony had made Manny do it. They had made Manny go and accuse herself, and if it wasn't going to be any good, then why had they done it? Everything inside her mind seemed to slip. It gave her a dreadful feeling of giddiness. Words went past her without meaning anything.

When she got hold of herself again Antony was saying in a voice with an edge to it,

'He's got to rouse up. This will has just about put the lid on everything. When he comes out I'm going to tackle him. You'd better stay and lend a hand. Up to now it's all been "poor old Jimmy", and the family hushing themselves up and walking round him like a lot of cats on hot bricks. It's got to stop. Jimmy's in a damned dangerous position. The sooner he realises it and begins to put up a bit of a fight, the better.'

'What can he do?'

'He can stop saying Lois didn't commit suicide every time he opens his mouth.'

Julia turned to look up at him.

'Does it matter what he says?'

'Of course it does! We've all been fools. We ought to have backed up the suicide idea for all we were worth. If they've let Manny go, it means they're not taking her confession very seriously. And why? It seems to me there are two reasons. The first is that she hadn't any possible opportunity of making sure that Lois got the poisoned cup, and she would never have chanced Jimmy getting it. The second is they think Jimmy did it. He's got to be made to realise where he stands. He's got to rouse up and come out of all this self-accusation about Lois' death. At the moment he's giving such an extraordinarily good imitation of guilt and remorse that if it was anyone but Jimmy, I might be carried away by it myself. Look here, Julia, is it possible that the stuff wasn't in the coffee? Did Lois have anything at dinner—anything at all—that the rest of you didn't have?'

She shook her head.

'The police have been over every mouthful we ate or drank. The coffee was the only chance—the only thing she had that the rest of us didn't have too. There's no way out there.'

They had reached the corner of the walk where it came out upon the lawn. Jimmy Latter was coming towards them over the grass. He looked ill and desperately forlorn. When he came up to them he said in a halting voice,

'I don't know why they wanted to see me. It all goes for nothing.'

Antony had dropped Julia's arm. Standing back, he seemed to loom up over her and Jimmy, very tall and bleak, brows drawn together in a frown. He said sharply,

'What did they ask you?'

'Something about Min giving me some aspirins.'

'When was that?'

'On Tuesday evening. I hadn't slept—I felt as if I should go mad if I didn't sleep. But she wouldn't give me the morphia—she said it was dangerous. I didn't care whether it was or not—I only wanted to sleep. But she took it away and gave me the aspirins instead. They didn't make me sleep.'

Julia felt as if she was standing in ice-cold water. Antony said in a new, cutting voice,

'Minnie had morphia in her cupboard? You talked of it, handled it? Both of you? Do the police know this?'

Jimmy lifted vague, unhappy eyes.

'That girl Gladys Marsh was listening at the door. She told them.'

Antony's hand came down hard on his shoulder.

'Then you'll have to rouse up and fight—if you don't want to hang.'

The cold came up as high as Julia's heart. She saw Jimmy's face twitch. A deep flush came up in it, more distressing than the pallor had been. He said something inarticulate.

Antony went on harshly.

'Good God, Jimmy—can't you see how you stand? It's one thing after another. You have a serious breach with your wife, and within forty-eight hours she dies of morphia poisoning. Either she committed suicide, or one of three people poisoned her— Ellie—Minnie—you. No one else could have done it without running the risk of your getting the stuff instead. You keep on saying it can't be suicide and wanting us to say so too. You come in for a lot of money under Lois' will. And now you tell me the police have got a witness to the fact that you and Minnie were handling a bottle of morphia on Tuesday night. Wake up, man!'

Jimmy Latter seemed to steady himself. He said quite quietly,

'What can I do?'

Antony took his hand away.

'That's better! Keep it up! You can stop being so sure it wasn't suicide, to start with.'

'You said it wasn't yourself—you said she wouldn't. I'd give my right hand to be sure about that.'

Antony said, 'I've been a fool—we all have. We'd better stop, especially you. The other thing you can do is to think—really think—about who shared out that coffee on Wednesday night. Julia took in the tray with two cups on it and put it down on the table. Minnie says they were still there when she came through. She says Lois was putting the sugar in. They both went out on to the terrace. Ellie came in next. She says she didn't notice the cups. You came in and found her there. Then she went out to call Lois and Minnie. Now, Jimmy, think—think hard! Were those two cups still on the tray?'

Jimmy put up a finger and rubbed his nose.

'I don't know—I don't remember. I don't believe I noticed them—I wasn't thinking of things like coffee-cups.'

'Well, there must have been a time when you began to think about them—at least about your own, because you picked it up and drank the coffee. You did, didn't you?'

'Yes, I drank it. The cup was on the table by my chair.'

'You remember that. Well, how did it get there? And when did it get there?'

Jimmy shook his head.

'I don't know. It was there and I drank it.'

'Was it there before the others came in from the terrace?'

'I don't know. I didn't go and sit down in my chair till after they all came in.'

'What were you doing?'

'I was over by the paper-table turning over the papers.'

'With your back to the room?'

'Yes—I suppose so.'

Antony said in an exasperated voice,

'Don't you remember anything?'

'I remember that the coffee was on the table by my chair, and that I drank it. I don't remember anything else.'

'You mean it was there when you eventually went to your chair and sat down?'

'I suppose it was.'

Antony controlled himself.

'You don't remember?'

'I don't remember anything, except that I drank the coffee. It's no good badgering me. I wasn't thinking about what was going on—I wasn't noticing. I was trying to think what I was going to do—'

'*Do?*'

Jimmy nodded.

'About Lois. We couldn't go on. I had to think—to make up my mind—'

Antony caught him by the arm.

'For God's sake don't say that sort of thing to the police!'

'Well, you asked me. That's what I was thinking about. I didn't notice anything until I picked up the cup, so it's no use worrying me about how it got there.' He paused, ran a hand through his hair, and said with a kind of absent-minded irrelevance, 'They're having the inquest tomorrow afternoon—at the Bull.'

THIRTY-THREE

Some time in the afternoon Miss Silver again requested a few words with Julia Vane. She had, as a matter of fact, contrived to have a few words with several other members of the family either before or after lunch. She found Julia in the old school-room alone. Coming in with her knitting-bag on her arm, she closed the door and remarked brightly upon the pleasant view from the windows and the number of familiar books upon the shelves.

'Charlotte Yonge—how perfectly she recreates the mid-Victorian period. Lifelike in the extreme. No one has ever pre-sented with such fidelity those large families which are now, alas, a thing of the past. Really most vivid. *The Heir of Redelyffe* is rather too sad, but the many tears which were shed for that poor young man are certainly a tribute to her art. I must own to a preference for a happy ending, but one cannot cavil when so much faith and courage are inculcated. One day I believe that Miss Yonge will be admitted as the equal of Trollope, if not his superior. Will you not sit down, Miss Vane?'

Julia did so. Since the day had to be got through some-how, it didn't seem to matter very much whether she gazed idly from a window or discussed Victorian novelists with Miss Silver. Antony had taken Jimmy for a tramp. Ellie had gone over to see Ronnie Street. Minnie, she hoped, was lying down. She took the nearest chair and raised tragic eyes.

The preference which she had just expressed for happy end-ings induced Miss Silver to return the look with a very kind one.

'All this is very trying,' she said. 'Pray do not think me unsympathetic if I ask you once more to tax your memory for some details about Wednesday evening.'

'I don't think there is anything more to tell you.'

Miss Silver coughed.

'Perhaps not. In the course of my professional experience I have found that those nearest to a tragedy do almost invariably know more than they have told. Sometimes what they do not tell is held back of design because they are afraid that if it is told it will injure someone whom they love. Sometimes they do not realise that they have anything to tell. In the present case it is certain that some knowledge is being withheld. I do not say why it is being withheld, or who is withholding it. I do not know. But I am quite sure that here in this house, there are, let us say, scraps and fragments of knowledge which, brought together, would provide a solution of this tragic problem. I am going to ask you to let me have any such fragments as you may possess. Pray do not withhold anything because you are afraid. Fear is not a satisfactory motive.'

Julia's eyes had remained fixed upon her. She said,

'I don't think I am keeping anything back."

Miss Silver had begun to knit.

'We will see. I am anxious to have as much information as possible about the state of Mrs Latter's mind on Wednesday evening.'

'I didn't see her between lunch and supper.'

'Did she come straight down into the dining-room?'

'Yes. Ellie rang the bell and I came out of my room. Lois caught me up on the stairs and we went down together.'

'How did she seem? Depressed—nervous?'

'Not in the least. She seemed just as usual.'

'You must remember that I had not the pleasure of her acquaintance. Will you do your best to give me an idea of her usual manner?'

Julia frowned.

'I didn't like her,' she said bluntly—'I expect you know that. You've seen her photographs. She was very good looking. Everything about her was very finished—her hair, her skin, her nails—her manner. Everything in perfect control. If I'm cross or rude, it's because I'm tired, or I'm unhappy, or I'm angry. If I quarrel with anyone, it just happens. Lois wasn't like that. If she was rude, it was because she meant to be rude. Things didn't just happen with her—she made them happen. I daresay I'm not being fair to her—you can't really be fair when you dislike anyone. I looked at her through my dislike. I'm telling you how I saw her.'

Miss Silver gazed thoughtfully in her direction.

'Control?'

Julia nodded.

'Yes—all the time. I don't think she ever let up.'

Miss Silver coughed.

'She caught you up on the stairs. Had you any conversation with her?'

'She talked about Jimmy.'

'Will you tell me exactly what she said—word for word if you can?'

Julia pushed back her hair. The scene rose in her mind, a picture on a lighted screen. Lois catching her up. Lois talking about Jimmy. The words spoke themselves again. She repeated them.

'She said, "Another lively meal! You'll have to help us through. You know, I'm really worried about Jimmy. We've had a row. Everybody in the house must know that by now, the way he's advertising it." I said something—I don't know what it was. And she said, "He looks awful. I've never seen him like this before—have you?" I said, "Not quite so bad", and she said, "Well, I wish he'd come off it. It's giving me the creeps"—' She stopped.

Miss Silver said, 'Was that all?'

'Yes.'

'At the time were you aware of the reason for the quarrel between them? Did you know of the scene in Mr Antony Latter's room on Monday night?'

'No.'

'You thought it was an ordinary quarrel?'

'I thought it was about old Hodson's cottage. Lois had been telling a lot of lies to get him out of it, and Jimmy had found her out. Hodson stopped him in the road and told him. I was there.'

'You thought that was enough to account for the breach between them?'

'I thought it was enough to account for a pretty bad quarrel. Jimmy hates lies. And he worshipped Lois—he thought she was an angel. It was a pretty bad shock.'

Miss Silver said, 'I see—' She knitted for a while in silence, and then said suddenly and directly, 'Miss Vane, you are very intelligent. You were in contact with these people immediately before the poisoning took place. You say Mrs Latter was as usual. Did that continue throughout the meal?'

'Yes. She talked—chiefly to me, sometimes to Ellie.'

'What did she talk about?'

'A play I had seen. She asked me if it was good. I made the subject last as long as possible. She told a story about some friends of hers taking a house and not being able to get the previous tenants out. It was just talk, you know.'

'And Mr Latter?'

'He sat there. He didn't talk, and he didn't eat.'

'Mrs Latter did both?'

'Oh, yes.'

With every word the weight on Julia's heart grew heavier. She had held nothing back. And what did it go to prove? Could she herself believe that Lois meant to take her own life—that as she talked, as she ate and drank, she knew that she had only an hour or two to live? It wasn't possible.

Jimmy's image rose—his pallid face, his reddened eyes, the hand which shook as he tilted the whisky decanter. The worst fear she had known came in like a flood.

Miss Silver said quickly, 'Are you all right?'

Julia said, 'Yes. But that's all. I don't know any more.'

She got up and went out of the room.

One of her short sentences remained, to burn like a small, clear light in Miss Silver's mind.

THIRTY-FOUR

Miss Silver waited until the house was quiet that night. Then she got out of bed and set the door ajar. If there was to be any more sleep-walking, she wished to make sure of being an interested spectator. If she had come out of her room a little sooner the night before she would certainly not have permitted Miss Vane to intervene. Miss Mercer had had some purpose in her mind. It would have been interesting to discover what that purpose was. It had roused her from her bed, and had taken her to the foot of the stairs. If Miss Vane had not checked her there, it might have taken her a good deal farther. Perhaps as far as the drawing-room. She was certainly facing in that direction.

Miss Silver looked at her watch by the light of the bedside lamp. It was half past eleven. She was in her dressing-gown, her hair neatly coiled under a rather stronger net than the one she wore by day. She had had the dressing-gown since before the war, a circumstance upon which she congratulated herself. It would be some time before materials returned to that standard. To the pre-war price, she feared, they would never return. This crimson wool, so light, so warm, so durable, would however last for quite a number of years, and the hand-made crochet with which it was trimmed, and which was now in its second tour of service, would still be available for further use. Crochet really did wear remarkably well. It would certainly trim another dressing-gown. Perhaps next time she would choose a nice deep blue. She put her slippers handy and got into bed, arranging the pillows so that she could sit up comfortably, and reflected with gratitude that her excellent hearing would immediately inform her if any of the other bedroom doors were to open.

Prepared at all points, she now allowed herself to review the progress of events. They were not satisfactory. They were not progressing in a manner at all favourable to her client. The Chief Inspector had, indeed, been in two minds as to making an immediate arrest. Whilst deprecating this course, she could not deny that the circumstantial evidence against Mr Latter had accumulated in a very formidable manner. She could not really have blamed the Chief Inspector if he had decided to make the arrest. Yet in the end he had made up his mind to await the result of the inquest. A relief. But the time was short, very short indeed. It would have been so very much pleasanter if the arrest could have been avoided. The publicity would be so very painful for Mr Latter. There was just the chance that to-night's vigil might bring something to light. That there were hidden thoughts and motives, actions still screened from view, she was assured. How far they reached, what part they had played or still might play, she did not know, but the feeling of secrecy was there.

As she sat in the half darkened room with the house so still about her, she turned her thoughts first to one and then to another of the people sheltered there. Some would be sleeping. Did the sleeping thought give up its secrets? Some would be awake—in fear, in grief, in torment. She thought of them one by one—Jimmy Latter—his cousin Antony—Julia Vane—Ellie Street—Minnie Mercer—Gladys Marsh—Mrs Maniple—the little pale kitchenmaid Polly Pell—

The clock in the hall downstairs struck twelve—first four strokes to mark the hour, and then after a pause twelve more, the strokes solemnly spaced, not noisy or ringing but with a quiet, deep tone which enriched the silence of the house without jarring it. If anyone slept, it would not waken him. If anyone waked, it would be a friendly, companionable sound.

Of the nine people at Latter End only Miss Silver counted the twelve strokes on this particular night. Jimmy Latter would say in the morning that he had not slept. There is a borderland state in which, whilst consciousness remains, control is lost. The mind drifts without aim or rest. In a shifting world between waking and sleeping his thoughts had slipped the leash and went questing after shadows, themselves too shadowy to know what they followed or why they followed it. Only always there was the sense of strain, of effort, of something lost beyond recall, of fevered striving to bring back what was gone. Shadow-play on the broken surface of consciousness—broken shadows passing, dissolving, coming again—nothing stable—nothing clearly seen—just shadows—

Ellie Street was dreaming, her body relaxed, her left hand under her cheek, as she had slept ever since she was a child. Her dream-self walked in a garden. She didn't know the place, it was quite strange to her. At first it was sunny and pleasant, but after a little she came to a high thorn hedge, and she knew that she couldn't get out. The hedge was twenty feet high, and she couldn't get out. Ronnie was on the other side, and she couldn't get to him. She began to break the thorns with her hands. The twigs snapped like sticks on a frosty day. They tore her hands and the blood ran down, and all at once they were not thorns any more, but icicles—the whole hedge was made of ice. She stood in snow up to her knees, and the blood ran down upon the snow and froze, so that some of the icicles were white and some were red. She couldn't get to Ronnie.

In the bed beside her Julia was dreaming too. She had on a white dress and a long white veil. She was being married to Antony. An unbearable joy filled her. He lifted her veil and bent to kiss her lips, and a great roaring wind came and carried her away into a dark place where she was quite alone.

On the other side of the swing-door Gladys Marsh was asleep, with her face well creamed and her hair in curlers. She had taken the cream out of Mrs Latter's bathroom together with a good many other oddments. If questions were asked— why, Mrs Latter had given them to her, and no one could prove she hadn't. She was having a really vivid and exciting dream in which she was wearing a diamond necklace with ever such big stones and standing up in a high thing like a pulpit to give her evidence. There was a judge in scarlet with a great grey wig, just like she'd seen him when they had the assizes at Crampton. He looked at her over his glasses, the way any man looks at a pretty girl, no matter whether he's a judge or a juryman. The jury were on the other side. They looked at her too. Everybody looked at her . . .

Mrs Maniple was also sleeping. She wore a voluminous calico nightgown which was five yards round the hem and fearful to behold with gussets and stitchery. In her young days a nightgown was an Undertaking. She still undertook her own, which she made on her grandmother's pattern. From the same source she had accepted the conviction that an open window after nightfall induced an early death. Night air wasn't wholesome, and you shut it out except perhaps in what she called the 'heighth' of summer. This being the autumnal season, her window was hermetically sealed. The room smelled strongly of camphor, furniture polish, and lavender.

In Mrs Maniple' dream the smell was transmuted into a mingled scent of bergamot and rosemary, of which she held a tight bunch in a small, plump hand. The hand belonged to little Lizzie Maniple who was six years old. It was hot as well as plump, and the herbs smelled lovely. Most of the children brought bunches to Sunday school and gave them to the teacher, who was old Miss Addison. She lived in a small square house on the Crampton Road, and she was young Dr Addison's aunt and very much respected. She was teaching the children their catechism, and they were doing the long, difficult answer to the question, '*What is my duty to my neighbour?*' Echoes floated through Mrs Maniple's mind. '*Learn and labour truly to get my own living—*' Melia Parsons was getting that bit. '*Do my duty in that state of life—*I've always done that. I don't care what anyone says, I've always done that.' In the dream Miss Addison was looking at her with those very bright blue eyes. She said, 'Now, Lizzie—' and little Lizzie Maniple piped up—'*To hurt nobody by word or deed, to bear no malice or hatred in my heart.*'

In the room next door Polly Pell lay flat on her back. Her thin childish body hardly raised the bedclothes. Her window stood wide to the night. A light breeze rustled the leaves of the tree outside. The sound passed into Polly's dream and became the rustling of hundreds of newspapers. She tried to run away from them, because they all had her picture right up on the front page for everyone to see. Everyone looking at her, everyone staring. She couldn't bear it—she really couldn't. She tried to run away, but her feet wouldn't carry her. They had grown into the ground. When she looked down she couldn't see them any more, and she couldn't move. The rustling papers came nearer, and nearer, and nearer. She gasped, and woke to hear the wind moving the leaves of the chestnut tree. The summer had dried and ripened them. They rustled in the wind with a papery sound. Her forehead and her hands were wet.

Antony did not dream at all. He lay in a profound sleep which blotted out yesterday and veiled tomorrow. Perhaps there is something in us which does not sleep—some spark of consciousness burning on amid the surrounding dark, unknown even to ourselves. If we could see, by its light we should know the innermost thought and intent of the heart. Sometimes without sight this knowledge comes to us in sleep.

Minnie Mercer was dreaming—

At the first sound from the room next to hers Miss Silver threw back the bedclothes and stepped down on to the floor, sliding each foot expertly into a waiting slipper. She left the bed-side lamp burning, and reached the door, which she had set ajar, as the clock in the hall struck the quarter after midnight. For a moment its vibrations drowned everything else. Then, as the air settled back into quiet, the same sound that had brought her out of her bed was heard again—the sound of bare feet on a polished floor, the sound of a hand sliding over a polished surface.

Miss Silver stood on the threshold of her room and heard Minnie Mercer's hand go groping in the dark. It must be very dark in her dream. Her hand went feeling in this darkness for the handle of her door. Miss Silver saw it turn, slowly, slowly. Then the door opened. Miss Mercer came out, barefoot in a white nightgown, her fair hair hanging over it. Her eyes were open and set. They were so widely open that they caught the light. It made them look very blue. Now the door was out of her way, her hands hung down. She walked slowly across the landing, stood for a moment at the top of the stairs, and then began to descend them, taking one step at a time with the right foot and bringing the left down after it like a child who is afraid that it may fall. She did not touch the balustrade, but kept the middle of the stair, and so went slowly down.

Miss Silver followed her, but not too closely. She was, of all things in the world, most anxious not to encroach upon this dream or break it. At the foot of the stairs Miss Mercer stood quite still. Perhaps she would turn, as she had yesterday, and come back.

It was while she was waiting in some anxiety that Miss Silver heard a door open on the landing above. She turned with her finger on her lips and saw Julia Vane looking over the head of the stair. Julia nodded and began to come down. She was barefoot and made no noise. Before she could reach them, Minnie Mercer moved, walking slowly across the hall in the direction of the drawing-room. It was all dark down here, with the light from the upstair landing dwindling and dying as they moved away from it.

Miss Silver made a swift decision. To the sleepwalker, hall and drawing-room would be light or dark according to the colour of her dream, but if she herself and Julia Vane were to see what happened they must have light to see it by. It was not difficult to out-distance those hesitating feet. She reached the drawing-room door and went in, leaving it open behind her. The first switch she tried gave too bright a light, full in the face of anyone coming into the room. The next set two pairs of shaded candles glowing, one on either side of the mirror above the mantelpiece. The light was reflected in the glass. It showed the whole room in a kind of golden twilight.

Minnie Mercer came as far as the open door and stood there. She looked into the room, her hands caught together, the fingers twisting. All at once she said in a low, distressed voice, 'No, no—he doesn't like it.' Then she lifted her head and stared at the curtained windows. In her dream there were no curtains there. It was a fine sunny evening and the glass door to the terrace stood wide. Someone was moving towards that open door. She watched the moving figure pass out on to the terrace, pass out of sight. Then she herself began to move. Past the table where Julia had set down the coffee-tray. Standing beside it for a moment and then going on. Turning a little to the right and standing by Jimmy Latter's chair. The small table beside it was the one upon which someone had placed his cup of coffee on Wednesday night. Minnie's hand went out to it now with a groping movement. She might have been putting down a cup. She might have been taking one up. She lifted her hand, turned back, paused for a moment by the table where the tray had stood, and again put out her hand. When she had drawn it back she took a sighing breath that was almost a groan and said in a shuddering voice, 'What have I done! Oh, God—what have I done!'

Miss Silver stood before the hearth. She could see the open doorway, and Julia Vane with one hand touching the jamb. They could both see Minnie Mercer, and they had both heard what she said. Julia had a stunned look. As Minnie left the table and came towards her, she drew back into the dark hall. Minnie went past with a sighing breath and an indistinguishable murmur of sound. In her dream she was grieving, grieving—She crossed the hall and went up into the light of the landing, and so to her own room.

Miss Silver came out of the drawing-room, switching off the light and shutting the door. She touched Julia's arm and found it cold.

'Go back to bed, my dear.'

She felt rather than saw the intensity of Julia's gaze.

'Miss Silver, she *couldn't*!'

'Go back to bed, my dear.'

'It isn't true!'

Miss Silver said very kindly,

'What is not true will not harm her or anyone else. We want the truth for everyone's sake. What has happened tonight has, I believe, brought us nearer to it. Will you trust me when I tell you not to be so much afraid of it? The truth sometimes inflicts a shock, but no one is really benefited by a state of deception. Believe me, it is better to see clearly, even if what we see is—somewhat unexpected. Go back to bed. And pray do not be afraid. Miss Mercer will sleep now, and you should do the same.'

Julia opened her lips to speak, and closed them again. What was there to say? Better say nothing at all. Better go back to bed and wait for the morning. The morning—and Jimmy's arrest? A long, slow shudder went over her. She turned away, went up the stairs, and into the room where Ellie lay asleep.

Miss Silver followed. When she was in her own room she took off the red woollen dressing-gown and laid it neatly across the chair upon which her clothes were folded. Then she dropped her slippers side by side and got into bed, all very deliberately and rather as if her thoughts were somewhere else. Before she put out the light she took up the shabby black Bible in which it was her custom to read, and turned to the thirty-seventh psalm. She perused it with gravity, giving particular attention to the seventh and fifteenth verses:

Fret not thyself because of him who prospereth in his way, because of the man who bringeth wicked devices to pass.

Their sword shall enter into their own heart, and their bows shall be broken.

THIRTY-FIVE

It was half past seven next morning when Polly Pell knocked lightly and came in to draw the curtains and set down an early morning tea-tray. The room had two windows, but only the nearer one had been screened. As Polly turned round from it, there was plenty of light to show how pale she was, with no colour anywhere except in the reddened lids.

Miss Silver turned her thoughts away from the consideration of early morning tea as an indulgence—but such a very pleasant one—and focused them upon Polly Pell. She had already wished her good-morning and received a shy response. She now said,

'Please come here for a minute.'

Polly wanted to run out of the room, but she had not had two years training under Mrs Maniple for nothing. She blinked at the light, wished it a good deal less bright, and came to stand by the bed and pleat her apron.

'You've been crying, Polly. What is the matter?'

Polly blinked again, but a tear got past her lashes and began to trickle very slowly towards her chin.

'It's all so dreadful, miss!'

Miss Silver looked at her kindly and searchingly.

'Yes—murder is dreadful. But it lays a duty upon us all. If everyone does his duty and tells all he knows, the truth will come to light. If anyone does not do his duty, an innocent person may suffer.'

She had spoken in general terms, but now the expression in Polly's eyes arrested her very particular attention. She had seen fear too often to mistake it. The child was sick with terror. No girl looks like that unless she has something to hide. If there was one thing overwhelmingly obvious besides the fear, it was Polly's anguished desire to get out of the room. She said in a small, breathless voice, 'If you'll excuse me, miss,' and then stopped short with a quiver, because Miss Silver had taken her by the hand.

'Sit down, Polly—I want to talk to you. Yes, here on the edge of the bed. I shall only keep you a very short time. And pray do not be frightened. If you have done nothing wrong you have nothing to be afraid of. You know that.'

The original tear was now quite drowned by those which followed it. In a choking whisper Polly was heard to say,

'It's not true they're going to arrest Mr Latter? They couldn't do a thing like that, could they—not to Mr Latter!'

Miss Silver coughed.

'I cannot tell you that. Why are you so frightened, my dear? Is it because you know something and have been keeping it back? If you are doing that, it is very wrong of you, and I do not wonder that you are unhappy. What will you feel like if Mr Latter is arrested?'

Polly choked back her tears, sniffed desperately, and whispered,

'They'd put my picture in the papers—'

'What did you say, my dear?'

The sobs broke out again.

'Gladys—said—they—would—Gladys Marsh. She wants—to have—her photo took and put in the papers. But I never. I feel as if I'd die—having everyone look at me—and having to stand up and swear. Oh, miss, I couldn't! Oh, miss, don't make me!'

Miss Silver patted the hand she was holding. Then she took her own away, produced a clean folded handkerchief from under her pillow, and gave it to Polly.

'Blow your nose, my child, and wipe your eyes. And stop thinking about yourself. We have to think of Mr Latter, who is in a very dangerous position, and we have to find out whether you know anything which will make his position less dangerous.'

Polly blew, dabbed, sniffed, and dabbed again.

'Oh, miss!'

'That's a good girl. Now listen to me. What would you feel like if Mr Latter should be arrested?'

'Oh, miss!'

'And because you were only thinking about yourself you let him go to prison?'

Polly was past words. She could only gulp.

'Are you going to let him be hanged?'

The gulp turned to an anguished sob.

'Oh, no! Oh, miss!'

Miss Silver let her cry until she thought she had cried enough. Then she said very briskly indeed,

'Now, my dear, that is quite sufficient. Crying will not help you. If you know anything that might prevent his arrest, do you not think it would be more sensible to tell me what it is?'

Polly scrubbed at her reddened eyes and nose. The handkerchief was quite wet through.

'I dunno if it would stop them taking him to prison. Gladys, she says she wants to have her photo in the papers, but—Oh, miss!'

Miss Silver said in a kind, firm voice,

'You have not to worry about that. You have to think about Mr Latter, and to tell me what you know, then you will have done what is right, and you will feel a great deal happier.'

Polly gave a last sob and said,

'It wasn't none of my doing. Mrs Maniple sent me up.'

Miss Silver's mind worked quickly at all times. It worked very quickly indeed now. Without any appreciable pause, she had gone back to the Chief Inspector's interview with Mrs Maniple, detached one piece of evidence, assimilated it, and was saying,

'Mrs Maniple sent you upstairs on Wednesday morning just before lunch to ask Mrs Latter whether she was coming down.'

It was no bow drawn at a venture. It was the result of rapid, accurate deduction. At that moment and no other would Polly have been brought into contact with Lois Latter. At that time, and at no other time, would she have had the opportunity of seeing or hearing something which might throw a light upon the impending tragedy.

Polly stared at her and said,

'Oh, yes, she did.'

Miss Silver coughed.

'Then you had better tell me just what happened. No, you are not going to cry any more—you are going to be a sensible girl. Just tell me exactly what you did.'

Polly managed to stop everything except the sniff.

'Mrs Maniple, she told me to go up and find out whether Mrs Latter would be wanting a tray took up, so I come upstairs and I knocked on the door. I knocked twice and there wasn't any answer. There was a kind of a hammering sound going on like as if it was in the bathroom. There's a door through from Mrs Latter's bedroom, you know. It's her own bathroom and nobody else doesn't use it. Well, I thought, "She's in the bathroom hammering something, and she won't hear me knock." '

'What kind of a hammering sound was it, Polly? Was it loud?'

'Oh, no, miss—only just so as I could hear it. But she would be close up to it, and I don't knock very loud.'

Miss Silver smiled.

'No—I have noticed that.'

Polly sniffed.

'I don't seem as if I can—it seems so kind of rude.'

Miss Silver nodded.

'Go on, my dear, you are doing very nicely. You heard the

knocking, and you thought Mrs Latter might be in the bathroom. What did you do then?'

'I opened the door a little and looked in. Mrs Latter wasn't there. The door to the bathroom was a bit open, and the hammering came from there. I went across the room to knock on the bathroom door.'

'Go on, Polly.'

Polly looked at her round-eyed.

'I don't know if you've been in Mrs Latter's room, miss. The gentlemen from the police locked it up, but it was open again yesterday. Mrs Huggins is going to turn it out today.'

'Yes, I have been into it.'

'Then you know, miss, one side of the room's all looking-glass, and the bathroom too. Mrs Latter had it done as soon as the war was over. If the bathroom door's a certain way open, you can see the bath in the looking-glass that's in the bedroom. I hadn't gone no more than a few steps, when I could see the bath and I could see Mrs Latter.'

'You mean you could see her reflection?'

'Yes, miss.'

'What was she doing?'

'She was stooping over the bath. There's a ledge runs all round it. She'd got a piece of white paper on the ledge, folded over, and she'd got her shoe off, hammering the paper with the heel. That was the knocking I'd heard.'

'Yes, Polly?'

'I didn't know what to do. I thought I'd wait. She stopped hammering and opened the paper. There was a lot of white powder in it, and one or two bits that wasn't quite powder yet.

There was a box on the ledge. It's a little box Mrs Latter has on her dressing-table. It used to be a snuffbox. She took it up and opened it. I could see right inside. There were some white tablets. She took them out and put them down on the white powder, and folded the paper over and hammered them with the heel of her shoe. I didn't ought to have stood there and watched her, miss—I dunno what come over me to do it—I was kind of frightened.' She caught her breath and twisted the corner of her apron with thin, nervous fingers. 'I dunno what come over me—indeed I don't. It didn't seem as if I could move, not anyways.'

Miss Silver gave a gentle cough.

'How much of Mrs Latter could you see, Polly? Could you see her face?'

Polly looked at her with frightened eyes. All the colour seemed to have been cried out of them and out of her face. Only the tip of her little thin nose was red. Her voice jerked and the words stumbled.

'Not at first I couldn't, not when she was bending over and hammering on the ledge, but when she'd finished and she was putting the powder into the box, I saw her then.'

'How did she look?'

Polly twisted the corner of her apron and shook.

Miss Silver laid a hand on her knee.

'Come, my dear, if you saw her face you can tell me how she looked—grave—sad—unhappy?'

Polly went on shaking.

'Oh, no, miss, she didn't.'

'Then how did she look?'

Breaking, stumbling, catching on the words, the small scared voice said,

'Oh, miss—she looked—ever so pleased.'

'Are you quite sure about that?'

'Oh, yes, miss. It frightened me ever so—I dunno why.'

'There is no need to be frightened. Did Mrs Latter see you?'

'Oh, no, miss. When she finished putting the powder in the box I run out on the landing again and shut the door, and I knocked on it real hard and loud. And Mrs Latter, she come and asked me what I wanted, and I said Mrs Maniple wanted to know was she coming down to lunch, and she said she was, and I come away. Please, may I go, miss?'

Miss Silver looked at her encouragingly.

'Not just for a minute, Polly. You say Mrs Latter put the powder into the little box. Had she taken all the tablets out of it? Was the box empty?'

'Yes, miss.'

'Have you seen this box since Wednesday?'

'No, miss.'

'Will you describe it to me?'

'It isn't very big, but it's ever so pretty—about two inches long, and all gold round the sides and underneath, with a painted picture on the top—a lady with nothing on but a sash, and a little boy with wings and a bow and arrow. It's ever so pretty.'

'Just one more question, Polly.' Miss Silver's voice was so equable that no one could have guessed how anxiously she awaited the answer to this question. 'Just one more, and you shall go. Did Mrs Latter take a bath when she dressed for dinner on Wednesday evening?'

'Oh, no, miss—she wouldn't do that. Mrs Latter, she always had her bath when she went to bed at night. The water had to be kept hot for her to have it then.'

Miss Silver said, 'Thank you, Polly.' A sober gratitude filled her.

THIRTY-SIX

As soon as Polly had hurried away Miss Silver put on her dressing-gown, went downstairs to the study, and called up the Bull. When Frank Abbott came on the line, it was to tell her that the Chief was breakfasting with a view to an early start for Crampton, where he was meeting the Chief Constable and Inspector Smerdon.

Miss Silver coughed in a manner which informed him that she had not come to the telephone to listen. In grammatically correct but unmistakably home-made French she informed him that he should lose no time in repairing to Latter End.

Frank whistled.

'It's really important?'

Miss Silver coughed.

'It clears my client,' she said, and replaced the receiver.

Sergeant Abbott reported to his Chief Inspector, who was putting away bacon and eggs and looking forward to toast and marmalade. The beds at the Bull had exceeded Frank's worst fears—lumpy flock mattresses, short sheets, and narrow blankets. The bacon was underdone, but the eggs, being local produce, were fresh. Lamb was not so fastidious as his Sergeant. When he went to bed he slept, and when he sat down to a meal he ate with good appetite. He looked up now as Frank took the chair beside him, observed his expression, and said,

'Well, what is it?'

Sergeant Abbott lifted an eyebrow and said, 'Maudie!', adding after an explosive pause—'in French! All very hush-hush.'

Lamb's shining morning face had become decidedly over-cast.

'What's she want?'

Frank was smiling.

'You, sir—or, shall I say, us. I told her you were meeting the Chief Constable. She says evidence has turned up which will put Latter in the clear.'

Lamb's voice said in its deepest growl,

'Tell you what it was?'

'No, sir.'

'Mare's nest,' grunted Lamb. He added gloomily—'as like as not.'

'It sounded a good deal more like the ace of trumps.'

Lamb banged the table.

'Go on—back her up! That's what you're here for, isn't it? Who do you take your orders from?'

'You, sir.' Voice and manner were deferential in the extreme.

His Chief Inspector looked at him sharply and said,

'Just keep on bearing that in mind, will you!' Then, after a pause, 'Well, you'd better go along and see what she's got. I can be back by half past ten. If there's anything urgent, you can give me a ring—Crampton 121.'

Sergeant Abbott had his breakfast, eschewing the bacon and playing for safety by ordering two boiled eggs. He then betook himself to Latter End, and after a short interval rang up the Chief Inspector, who was not best pleased.

'Well, what is it? I'm talking to the Chief Constable.'

'Well, sir, you told me to ring you up if the new evidence was important—and it is. I think you'd better come out here as soon as you can. Meanwhile I've got specimens of a white powder taken from the lady's bathroom which ought to be analysed without delay. I've sealed them up, and the local constable is bringing them out on his bike. We ought to have a report before the inquest opens.'

'Probably toothpowder!'

'I don't think so, sir.'

The Chief Inspector said, 'Tchah!'

THIRTY-SEVEN

Polly had told her story for the third time. Every time she told it she minded less. Probably no one but Miss Silver, with her peculiar mixture of unwavering kindness and unwavering authority, would have made the original breach in a crust of secrecy which was her protective armour. But having spoken once, it was easier to speak again. She told her story to Frank Abbott, and repeated it in front of the Chief Inspector with hardly an alteration in the order of the words. Those who have a small vocabulary are often extremely accurate. Children will repeat a story word for word, partly because there is for them no choice of words. One is reminded of ballads from the childhood of the race, in which gold is always red, and ladies fair. In a village this simplicity of thought persists.

Polly told her story in the only words she knew. By the time she told it to the Chief Inspector she didn't even want to cry, though she still pleated her apron. When she had finished, and

Lamb had asked her as many questions as he wanted to, he let her out of the room and turned to Miss Silver.

'Well, that's just about upset the apple-cart! I suppose I've got to be grateful you dug it out of her before we started on the inquest.'

Miss Silver coughed. She opined that it might be considered as providential.

Lamb was looking at her with a curious mixture of irritation and respect. He gave a short laugh and repeated her last word.

'Providential? Well, I don't know about that—unless you mean that heaven helps those who help themselves. You're first-class at doing that, I should say. But what I want to know is, what made you think the girl had anything to tell? She wasn't near the drawing-room, and in the ordinary way she hadn't anything to do with Mrs Latter. What made you think she knew something?'

Miss Silver's hands were busy with her knitting. Derek's stocking, now of a substantial length, revolved.

'She was afraid.'

Lamb nodded.

'That's where you've got an advantage. When we come into a house after a murder, everyone's afraid of us, everyone's watching his step, nobody's normal—to look for a frightened person is like looking for a pin in a packet of pins. Now you mix with the family. They're not afraid of you because they don't know what you're up to. You sit there with your knitting, and they think that's all you've got on your mind. They don't bother about you. It gives you a pull, you know.'

She inclined her head.

'I have no doubt, Chief Inspector, that if Polly had been bringing your early tea instead of mine, you would have discerned, as I did, that she had something to conceal.'

Lamb glowered.

'I don't take the stuff! But there you are, it's just what I said—you've got a pull. Frank, ring up Crampton 121 and ask whether they've identified that powder yet. If it's morphia it shouldn't take long.'

He sat back in his chair while Frank got the number—listened to his question; listened, frowning, to the vague buzz of the reply; heard Frank say, 'Quite so,' and then, 'All right, I'll tell him.'

He hung up.

'It's morphia all right.'

Miss Silver's needles clicked. Lamb lifted his hand and let it fall again upon his knee.

'Then she committed suicide. Well, I'm blessed! If that doesn't beat the band!'

Miss Silver gave her slight arresting cough.

'I think it would be as well if you were to see Miss Mercer.'

Lamb turned to face her.

'Miss Mercer? What's it got to do with Miss Mercer?'

Miss Silver knitted equably.

'I should like to put some questions to her in your presence if you have no objection.'

Frank Abbott was looking at her too. There was a faint sarcastic sparkle in his eye. He murmured,

'You can't go on pulling aces out of your sleeve, you know.'

Miss Silver smiled above the clicking needles.

Lamb said roughly, 'A little less of your lip, my lad! Better go and get her.'

When the door had closed he turned his reproof upon Miss Silver.

'When I let you in on this case I thought you undertook not to conceal evidence from the police.'

She met his frown serenely.

'But I have concealed nothing, Chief Inspector. Polly's evidence only came to me this morning. I went straight from her to the telephone. The incident about which I should like to question Miss Mercer occurred in the middle of the night. I have purposely refrained from asking her about it until I could do so in your presence.'

He opened his mouth to speak, and shut it again with an exasperated 'Tchah!' After which he drummed on his knee, and Miss Silver continued to knit until the door opened and Minnie Mercer came in with Frank Abbott behind her. She looked perceptibly more worn than she had done yesterday. There was, if possible, less colour in the tired gentle eyes and in the blanched fair skin. The smudges under the eyes were deeper and more like bruises. She sat down on the far side of the table, folded her hands in her lap, and looked at the Chief Inspector. He shook his head.

'It's Miss Silver who has something she wants to ask you about.'

Minnie Mercer moved, slipping round in the chair until she was leaning against the arm instead of the back. It seemed as if she needed something to lean against. Frank Abbott had the impression that without it she might just have slipped down on to the floor. She turned the same dumb, acquiescent look upon Miss Silver as she had done upon the Chief Inspector.

Miss Silver did not keep her waiting. She said very kindly and gently,

'Miss Mercer, do you know that you sometimes walk in your sleep?'

She was certainly startled. A faint tremor went over her. She said with a catch in her voice,

'I did when I was a girl—after an illness I had. I didn't know that I ever did it now.'

Miss Silver went on knitting.

'You have done it twice in the last few days—on the night before last, and last night.'

She said, 'I didn't know—' The words were so faint that they could only just be heard.

'On the first occasion Miss Vane followed you down into the hall. She put her arm round you and brought you back to your room. I was watching from the landing. She was very kind and careful, and you did not wake, but just as you got into bed you said in a very distressed voice, "What have I done!"'

Lamb was sitting so that he could see both women. He was still frowning, but the character of the frown had changed. It indicated concentration now instead of anger. He saw that faint tremor pass over Minnie Mercer again. She did not speak.

Miss Silver continued.

'Last night you walked in your sleep again. I was prepared, and I followed you. You went down into the hall, and just as you reached it Miss Vane came out of her room. By the time she had joined us you were crossing the hall in the direction of the drawing-room. When I saw where you were going I passed you and put on a light. You did not need it, but it was necessary that Miss Vane and I should be able to watch what you did. You were dreaming. Miss Mercer, do you remember your dream?'

'I don't—know—'

'I will tell you what you did. You stood and looked into the room. You seemed distressed, and you said, 'No, no—he doesn't like it!' Then you went to the small table near the middle of the room. That is the table upon which Miss Vane placed the coffee-tray on Wednesday night.'

Minnie Mercer said, 'Yes—' The sound just carried and no more.

'You put out your hand towards the table. You stood there for a moment. Then you turned a little to the right and went over to Mr Latter's chair. The table beside it is the one upon which his coffee-cup was placed on Wednesday night. You put out your hand again. You put out your hand as if you were holding something—you put it out as if you were setting something down. Miss Mercer—on Wednesday night did you take a cup of coffee from the tray and carry it over to the table beside Mr Latter's chair?'

Minnie looked at her with dilated eyes. She made the sound that she had made before. They thought the sound was 'Yes—'

'When you took that cup from the tray, were there two cups there, or only one?'

Minnie said, 'One—'

'When you went over to the table by Mr Latter's chair, was there a cup there already?'

'Yes—'

'What did you do?'

'I changed the cups.'

'You put down the one you had brought from the tray and took up the other?'

'Yes—I changed the cups—'

'Will you tell us why you did this?'

A long sigh lifted her breast.

'Yes—I'll tell you. Oh, I didn't want Jimmy to know—but it can't be helped—'

Lamb said, 'Miss Mercer, it is my duty to warn you that what you say will be taken down and may be used in evidence.'

She gave him a fleeting glance and shook her head.

'It's not like that. I'll tell you how it was.'

Frank Abbott took up his pad and began to write.

She spoke quite calmly, almost with an air of relief, her voice exhausted but quite audible now.

'When I made my statement I didn't say anything that wasn't true. I didn't say everything, because I didn't want Jimmy to know. When I came to the door on Wednesday night Mrs Latter was standing by the tray just as I said in my statement. I thought she was putting sugar into one of the cups—I really did think so. She was tipping it in out of a little ornamental snuffbox she has. I never thought about its not being sugar, or glucose—one of those things. I just thought it was some new kind of fancy sweetening stuff. She was like that, you know—always trying new things. And sometimes she would go in for slimming—I thought perhaps it was something to do with that. She put all the stuff into the cup and stirred it up. Then she put two lumps of sugar in and stirred them up too. And she took up the little bottle of cognac and put in quite a lot. I thought it was her own cup, but she took it over and put it down by Jimmy's chair. I thought how he would hate it.' She paused, closed her eyes for a moment, and then went on again. 'He doesn't like things very sweet—he doesn't take more than one lump in tea or coffee. I thought Mrs Latter ought to have known that—I thought she *must* have known it. Everyone knew how much he disliked her Turkish coffee, and that he only drank it because she said she thought someone was trying to poison her. Everybody knew that. I am afraid I thought that she was putting all that sugar in out of spite—to make it as nasty as possible for him. I couldn't bear it, and I changed the cups.'

Lamb said in his solid voice,

'Did you see her put anything into the second cup?'

'No.'

He leaned forward, a hand on either knee.

'You say she tipped this powder into the cup from a little ornamental snuffbox. Can you describe it?'

'Oh, yes. It was French—eighteenth century I believe—about two inches long and not quite so wide—silver-gilt, with a picture of Venus and Cupid on the lid, painted on porcelain.'

He said, 'Hm! What did she do with it?'

'With the box?'

'Yes. Did you see what she did with it?'

There was a feeling of expectancy. Frank Abbott held his pencil poised. Miss Silver ceased to knit. Minnie Mercer said,

'Yes, I saw where she put it. She had the coffee-cup in her right hand and the box in her left. When she had put the cup down she took up some of the dried rose-leaves from the bowl on the table and filled the box. Then she opened the table drawer and slipped the box inside.'

'What did you think of her doing that?'

She said without hesitation, 'I didn't think about it at all—not at the time. Of course afterwards—'

He said, 'I'm coming to that. Miss Mercer—just when did you realise what you had done?'

'As soon as I knew that Mrs Latter was dead.'

'Not before that?'

'Oh, no—how could I?'

'You might have noticed that she was ill—drowsy—sleepy.'

She shook her head.

'No—there was no opportunity. I was—very tired. As soon as they had finished their coffee I took out the tray and washed the cups. I didn't go back to the drawing-room again. I went up to bed.'

'Yes, of course—it was you who washed the cups. Nothing strike you when you were doing it—sediment at the bottom of a cup?'

She said, 'No. You see, it was Turkish coffee—there are always the grounds—you wouldn't see any sediment.'

'You didn't notice anything unusual?'

'No.'

'And you went up to bed. Did you go to sleep?'

'Yes—I was very tired.'

'What waked you?'

'The disturbance in the house after Julia had come in and found Mrs Latter.'

'You were downstairs when the doctor came?'

'Yes.'

'And later on when Inspector Smerdon arrived?'

'Yes.'

'And by this time you had realised that Mrs Latter had drunk the coffee which she intended for her husband?'

She looked for a moment as if she were going to faint. Then she said in an extinguished voice,

'I was—beginning—to realise it—'

He fixed a reproving look upon her.

'Then why didn't you speak up and say what you had done? You say your statement wasn't an untruthful one, but when you suppress a lot of critical evidence, it comes as near being untruthful as makes no difference. Why didn't you speak up and save us all a lot of trouble?'

A wavering colour came into Minnie Mercer's face. She sat up straight.

'You can't take things back when you've said them. I had to think—but the more I thought, the less I knew what I ought to do. I had to think what was going to be the best thing for Jimmy.'

Miss Silver coughed.

'The truth is always best. Falsehood really helps no one.'

Minnie took no notice.

'I had to think about Jimmy. I thought it would kill him if he knew that his wife had tried to poison him—I was afraid of what he might do. And then I was afraid of what he might do if he thought she had committed suicide—he would have believed that it was his fault. And then I began to be afraid that you were suspecting him. There didn't seem to be any way out, and I didn't know what to do.'

Frank Abbott wrote that down. Lamb turned round to him.

'Get along to the drawing-room and see if that box is where she says it ought to be!'

THIRTY-EIGHT

Jimmy Latter took it hard. But in the very completeness of the destruction which it brought to all that he had ever believed or thought about Lois there was some hope for the future. No man can cling sentimentally to the memory of a woman who has tried to poison him. The shock of learning what she had done was tremendous. It smashed his married life and its memories so entirely that there was nothing left. Presently, when the dust and fragments had been cleared away, there would be a space on which to build again. Even now, in these first hours, there was an undercurrent of relief. With so much else the fear that had ridden him was gone. It wasn't he who had driven Lois to her death.

The inquest opened at four o'clock in the afternoon. The Coroner, old Dr Summers, handled it very firmly. He had had a session with Chief Inspector Lamb, with whom he had found himself very much in accord. The evidence would be limited to what was strictly necessary, and sensational elements would not be encouraged. A sober jury sat with him—mostly local farmers, with the landlord of the Bull, a middle-aged spinster who bred dogs, and one or two tradesmen thrown in. The village hall was packed—reporters squeezed into a solid mass by sheer pressure of village interest; both moral and physical temperatures high and rising; the latter strongly tinged with varnish and the smell of hot humanity.

Police and medical evidence first. No doubt about the cause of death—morphia. The number of grains stated.

Then Dr Summers called Jimmy Latter.

'You had been married two years?'

'Yes.'

'You were on good terms with your wife?'

From the other side of the gulf which had opened in his life, Jimmy Latter said,

'Yes.'

'But this week there had been a serious breach?' Dr Summers settled his pince-nez and said firmly, 'I do not propose to enquire any further into this breach, but I feel obliged to ask you whether it was indeed a very serious one.'

Since the whole village already knew from Gladys Marsh that Mrs Latter had been found by her husband in Mr Antony's room in the middle of the night, with Mr Antony saying no—such a nice gentleman and engaged to Miss Julia—it had quite enough inside knowledge very heartily to endorse Jimmy Latter's 'Yes'. There was a murmur of whispered talk. Dr Summers quelled it.

'Would you say that the breach was of such a serious nature that it might have led to a separation?'

Jimmy Latter said 'Yes'. After which he was taken briefly through the events of Wednesday evening and dismissed.

Julia was called, to describe how she had found Lois Latter in a collapsed condition.

Then Polly Pell.

On this fourth time of telling her story the words came almost of themselves. She described the scene in the bathroom, her voice a child's voice, low and shy, but quite audible. Perhaps she remembered that on this very platform she had tripped as a fairy in selected scenes from *A Midsummer Night's Dream,* or stood on guard over a manger in a long white nightgown and a pair of wings. She had a pretty singing voice, and one year she had sung the Page to the sexton's Good King Wenceslas. This didn't frighten her too much, because in private life the sexton was Uncle Fred and she had known everyone in the hall since she was a baby. These memories may have had a supporting influence.

The Coroner told her she was giving her evidence very nicely. She was shown the snuffbox after she had described it, and said at once, 'Yes, that's the one.' At the end he asked her the same question as Miss Silver had done—had she seen Mrs Latter's face, had she noticed her expression? She gave the same answer.

'Oh, yes, sir. She looked ever so pleased.'

The close air in the hall seemed to stir. Everyone there except the gentlemen of the Press had known Lois Latter, by sight at least. Most of them had spoken to her one way or another. They all knew about the looking-glass walls in her bathroom and bedroom at Latter End, the general verdict being that it wasn't quite nice. They could all make a picture of her like the picture which Polly had seen reflected from the bathroom wall—the beautiful Mrs Latter hammering upon a folded paper with the heel of her shoe, and looking 'ever so pleased'. To the more imaginative the picture conveyed a rather sinister thrill. There was that stir in the air.

Polly went back to her seat.

The Coroner called Minnie Mercer.

She had no black to wear for Lois Latter, but she had put on the darkest dress she had, the navy cotton which she had been wearing all the summer whenever it was hot enough, and the dark blue straw hat in which the village had seen her in church on every fine Sunday since April. Between hat and dress her face showed so thin and bloodless that the Coroner looked at her with concern. He had been her father's friend, and there had been a time, some forty years buried in the past, when she used to sit on his knee and feel in his waistcoat pocket for peppermints.

He took her through her story very kindly. The history of the morphia first.

'It was part of your father Dr Mercer's stock of drugs?'

'Yes.'

'Where did you keep it?'

'In the medicine cupboard in my room.'

'Did you keep the cupboard locked?'

'Yes.'

'And where did you keep the key?'

'In my dressing-table drawer.'

Her voice was like her face, quite drained of life and expression, but it was audible.

The Coroner went on.

'Did you notice that the bottle containing the morphia tablets had been moved?'

'Mr Latter came to ask me for something to help him sleep. The cupboard was open because I had been getting some facecream out of it. He took up the morphia bottle, and I took it away from him at once and said it was dangerous. I think it was in front of the shelf when he picked it up, instead of at the back inside a box.'

'You saw Mr Latter pick it up?'

'Yes.'

'He didn't take anything out of it?'

'Oh, no—he just picked it up. I took it away at once.'

'Did you notice this bottle was out of its place when you were getting out the face-cream?'

'No. It was on a different shelf, amongst several other small bottles of the same kind. I didn't notice it till Mr Latter picked it up.'

'Did you notice anything about the bottle after you had taken it from Mr Latter?'

'I thought it wasn't as full as it ought to have been. I couldn't be sure, because it was a long time since I had looked at it, but I thought it was emptier than it had been.'

'What did you give Mr Latter to help him to sleep?'

'Two aspirins.'

'You locked the cupboard again after that?'

'Yes.'

'And put the key in the usual place?'

'Yes.'

'Did he see you put it away?'

'Oh, no.'

'When did all this take place?'

'On Tuesday evening.'

'That would be rather more than twenty-four hours before Mrs Latter's death?'

'Yes.'

Dr Summers settled his pince-nez.

'We will now come to the events of Wednesday evening. Will you tell us just what you saw and what you did when you came into the drawing-room after supper?'

In the same dead voice she repeated the story which she had told to Lamb that morning. The jury could make their picture of her standing there in the drawing-room doorway to watch Lois Latter tip a white powder from an old French snuffbox into one of the coffee-cups upon the tray. They could see the coffee stirred, lump sugar and cognac added, the cup carried over to the table by Jimmy Latter's chair. They could see the box packed with rose-leaves and slipped into the table drawer.'

The hall was dead still. Each of the low words fell into the stillness like a stone falling into water. In the middle of that hot, breathless afternoon more than one person shivered or felt a cold drop run trickling down the spine. They all knew Mr Jimmy. The older ones had known him for as far away back as he or they could remember. And it was Mr Jimmy's wife who had tipped that white powder into the cup and set it down where it would be handy for him to pick it up and drink it.

In the same strange hush they heard Minnie Mercer tell the Coroner, the jury, and all of them there in the hall how she had changed the cups. They all knew Miss Minnie. She had taught their children in Sunday school, she had gone in and out of their houses as a friend ever since she was a child herself. Behind her story there was the life which she had lived before them for eight-and-forty years. The light that beats upon a throne is nothing to the light that beats upon a village. It never entered the head of any of those village people that Miss Minnie's story was anything but the simple truth. It did not enter the Coroner's mind either, but he put a few questions just to make things quite clear to the gentlemen of the Press.

'It didn't occur to you that the powder which Mrs Latter was putting into the cup could be anything but sugar?'

'I thought it was sugar, or some sweetening compound—something like saccharin. She went in for slimming treatment sometimes. I thought she was sweetening her own cup—she liked her coffee very sweet.'

'And when she took it over and set it down by—Mr Latter's chair—what did you think then?'

Her voice faltered for the first time.

'I thought—she was angry with him. I thought she had—done it on purpose. He doesn't like his coffee with more than one lump in it. That is why I changed the cups.'

'That was your only reason?'

'Yes.'

She was asked to identify the snuffbox.

'It is the one from which you saw the powder tipped into the coffee, and which Mrs Latter afterwards filled with rose leaves?'

It lay on the table between them, bright with its silver-gilt and its painted lid—a coquettish French Venus with a blue riband floating and roses in her hair—a laughing Cupid taking aim with a toy bow and arrow. Such a pretty trifle to carry poison.

Minnie looked at it and said, 'Yes.'

The police analyst, recalled, deposed to having examined the box, and to having discovered particles of a white powder adhering to the sides and bottom under the dried rose-leaves. Traces of morphia had been found. The powder was identical with specimens from Mrs Latter's bathroom.

There were no more witnesses.

The Coroner summed up briskly. The jury retired. The hall broke into sound.

The party from Latter End sat silent whilst the village hummed. They did not even speak to one another. Julia looked once at Minnie, and hoped with all her heart that she wasn't going to faint. Jimmy Latter looked at no one. He sat on the end seat of the front row with the wall on his left, pitch-pine and sticky with varnish, and his cousin Antony on his right. All that anyone else could see of him was the back of his head, and perhaps a glimpse of ear and cheek. He sat there and looked down at the boarded floor. The boards had sprung a little and there was dust in the cracks. A very small spider came up out of the dust and ran along one of the boards. It ran a few inches and then stopped, crouched down and shamming dead. Jimmy watched it with a strained attention. Would it go on, or would it stay where it was? What made it come out of the crack, and why did it stop and pretend to be dead? What made people do any of the things they did do? What made Lois try to poison him?

The spider moved, ran another inch or two, and went dead again. He went on watching it.

The jury were only out for a quarter of an hour. Their foreman, a big hearty-looking farmer, said his say in a very slow, weighty, and deliberate manner. He had a paper in his hand, and he read from it.

'We find that the deceased lady died of morphia poisoning—that the morphia was in the coffee which she prepared for her husband and placed beside his chair—that Miss Mercer exchanged the cups without knowing that there was poison in one of them, and that she is in no way to blame for what happened. And we would like to say that we are quite satisfied that she took all proper precautions about keeping the morphia locked up, and that she is in no way to blame.'

There was a murmur of applause, immediately checked by the Coroner.

'That is a verdict of Accidental Death.'

'Yes, sir. But we want it put on record that there was no one else to blame. And we'd like, if it's proper, to express our sympathy with Mr Latter.' Jimmy Latter got up and went out by the side door. Antony went with him. A moment later the rest of the party followed them. The village of Rayne was left to the discussion of the biggest sensation it had had since Cromwell's troopers stabled their horses in the church.

THIRTY-NINE

Antony came out of the study. He met Minnie and Julia, and was in two minds about delivering his message. She looked as if she had come to the end of her strength, almost to the end of everything. Julia said, 'What is it?' and it was to her he spoke.

'He wants to see Minnie—but she doesn't look fit.'

Minnie Mercer straightened herself. When we think we have come to the end, there is always something left. She couldn't have found it for herself, but she found it for Jimmy.

She went into the study and shut the door. He was standing by the window with his back to her. He didn't turn round. When she had come up to him he moved to make room for her. They sat down side by side upon the window-seat. It was some time before he spoke. Whilst that time went by, her fear was passing too. It had tormented her day and night since Lois died—the fear that Jimmy would hate her for what she had done. She had done it innocently, but perhaps he would never be able to forget that she had done it. If he had had the thought, she would have known it, sitting there beside him with the silence round them. She had known him so long and so well, and had loved him so deeply, that he could not have hidden the thought. It came to her with a clear certainty that there was nothing to hide. He was desperately hurt, desperately unhappy. He needed comfort, her poor Jimmy. And he needed her.

He said at last, 'It's a bad business, Min.'

'Yes, my dear.'

After another pause he put out a hand and touched hers.

'You saved my life.'

She couldn't speak. The touch had been withdrawn at once. After a moment he said,

'I don't seem to take it in yet. I've been a great trouble to everyone. They've all been so good to me. Will you tell them, and say I'm going to do my best? Everybody's been so good.'

'Yes, I'll tell them.'

He leaned back against the window jamb. She felt that he was relieved—that he had said something that was difficult to say and it had relieved him. She knew as well as if he had put it into words that what he had really said was, 'You saved my life. I won't throw it away.' The most terrible weight of all was lifted from her.

After a little he began to talk about Ronnie Street.

'I've told Ellie she can bring him here any time after the funeral. It won't be too much for you, will it, if Mrs Huggins comes in every day?'

'No, it won't be too much. She's been coming the last few days.'

He rubbed his nose with the old familiar gesture.

'If you want more help, will you arrange about it? You and Ellie mustn't do too much. Julia said you were doing too much. I want you to arrange about everything just as you used to . . . You won't go away, Min?'

'Not if you want me.'

'I've always wanted you. I want you to take everything over. I don't want those people who were coming, the butler and the two maids. Will you see about that—pay them something and say we're making other arrangements? We don't want strangers here just now. Only you and Ellie mustn't do too much—I can't have that.'

'I'll see about everything, Jimmy. Connie Traill would come in for an hour or two in the morning if we wanted her. It might be a good thing—until Ronnie is on his feet again. It would give Ellie a rest.'

They slipped into a discussion which was so like old times that both of them were taken back to the days before Lois came.

FORTY

Miss Silver never returned from a case without experiencing a very deep and heartfelt gratitude. For many years of her life she had lived permanently in other people's houses. For many years of her life she had seen no prospect before her of doing anything else until, too elderly for her services as governess to be any longer in request, she retired to exist on the few shillings a week which her savings might bring in. You cannot save very much from the salary which governesses at that time received. To think of this, and then to see the front door of her little flat thrown wide with her faithful Emma waiting to welcome her, to come into her sitting-room and to behold its modest comfort—the pictures on its walls, the rows of photographs framed in plush, in beaten metal, in silver filigree, all speaking of valued friendships—never failed to evoke feelings of thankfulness.

If it made her happy to have these things for herself, it made her still happier to be able to share them with others—to pour

tea from a Victorian silver teapot, and to dispense the sandwiches
and little cakes in the making of which Emma Meadows excelled.

On the day after her return from Latter End, Sergeant
Abbott dropped in to tea. For him Emma provided three separate kinds of sandwich, as well as drop scones which melted in
the mouth, and a honeycomb which she would not ordinarily
have produced for a visitor.

Frank gazed at the loaded cake-stand and groaned.

'If I came here as often as I'd like to I should be getting a
Chief Inspector's figure, and then as likely as not they'd never
make me one.'

Miss Silver beamed upon him.

'My dear Frank, you are if anything too thin. Pray make a
good tea.'

He proceeded to do so.

It was at about the third cup of tea and perhaps the tenth
sandwich that he broke into Miss Silver's best tea-table talk.
He had been abstracted from what she was saying, but to the
best of his subsequent recollection it was a computation of the
variations in temperature between the September weather of
this and several preceding years. He stretched out his hand for
another sandwich and said,

'When did you first begin to suspect Mrs Latter?'

Miss Silver set down her cup and reached for her knitting.
She had begun a new grey stocking, the first of Derek's second
pair. Three inches of ribbing showed upon the needles. She
began to knit, her expression thoughtful.

'That is a very difficult question to answer. The conflict
between what I may call the material and the immaterial facts

appeared to be complete. I do not recall any case where this has been so marked. If Mrs Latter's death was to be considered as suicide, there was the evidence of everyone who knew her that she was the last person in the world to throw away a life which she thoroughly enjoyed. If, on the other hand, she was murdered, there were only three people who could have made certain that it was she and not Mr Latter who drank from the cup which had been poisoned. They were Mr Latter himself, Mrs Street, and Miss Mercer. The more I thought about these alternatives, the less could I persuade myself to accept either of them. I talked about the dead woman to each member of the family. Innumerable small touches made up the picture of a hard, determined woman who would stick at nothing to get her own way—a persevering woman. There were many small instances of this. A cool and calculating woman. Not at all the type to be abashed before her husband, or to commit suicide because she had been rebuffed by Mr Antony, whom she might have married two years ago if she had chosen. She had independent means, she had magnificent health and self-confidence. She had as little sentiment and affection in her composition as anyone can have. She was handsome, and attractive to men. I could not bring myself to believe that she had committed suicide.'

Frank took another sandwich.

'Two minds with but a single thought—you and the Chief! Two hearts that beat as one!'

Miss Silver had a weakness for impudent young men. She coughed indulgently.

'When I considered the other alternative I was equally at a loss. If it was murder, was it Mr Latter, or Mrs Street, or Miss

Mercer who had murdered her? Here again the physical and the psychological evidence were in contradiction. According to the former any one of the three might have done it. According to the latter not one of them. I will begin with Mrs Street. When I realised how unhappy she was making herself over the separation from her husband, and how intensely she had desired that he should be received at Latter End, I gave some thought to the possibility that, regarding Mrs Latter as an obstacle, she might have removed her. I discerned that she was terribly afraid that she might be losing her husband's affection. She was overworked and overwrought. In fact she was in just the kind of nervous state in which some loss of mental balance might have occurred. If you add to this that Miss Mercer when interrogated about the medicine cupboard stated that it was open on that Tuesday evening because she had been getting out some face-cream for Mrs Street, you will see that I really did have food for thought. You will remember it was shortly afterwards that Miss Mercer noticed that the morphia bottle had been moved. I had to consider whether it was Mrs Street who had moved it.'

'Well?'

Miss Silver regarded him intelligently.

'I became convinced that it was not in Mrs Street's character to commit a cold-blooded, premeditated murder. She is a gentle, not very efficient girl, and she is generally lacking in resource and initiative. She has, I imagine, been accustomed all her life to rely for these things upon her sister Julia, a very intelligent and forceful young woman. If Julia Vane had turned her attention to crime she would, I am convinced, have been most efficient. Fortunately for herself and for others, she has good principles and a warm and generous nature. Mrs Street is of the type which drifts and suffers. I could not believe her capable of definite and ruthless action. I was really unable to believe in her as a poisoner.'

Frank Abbott nodded.

Miss Silver continued to knit.

'Mr Latter, of course, had a very serious motive. It was quite natural that the Chief Inspector should have suspected him. He had indeed great provocation—just such provocation as has brought about so many crimes of violence. In the presence of strong conjugal jealousy few would look past the injured husband for a suspect. I myself was fully aware of my client's dangerous position, but after he had talked to me I was able to reject the idea that he had poisoned his wife. He was in great agony of mind, and full of self-reproach because he was afraid that she had committed suicide. The one hope he clung to was that I might be able to prove that she had been murdered. I found him as open and as simple as a child, and of a kindly and forgiving nature. Whatever the evidence might be, I considered him incapable of murder.' She paused, coughed, and said, 'Miss Mercer also had a very strong motive.'

Frank's eyebrows rose.

'Would you call her motive so strong?'

She inclined her head.

'Yes, Frank—the strongest which a woman of her type could have. She loved Mr Latter devotedly. It was impossible not to be aware of it. Unfortunately, I suppose it had never occurred to him. He had lived too close to her and become too much accustomed to her presence and to her affection to notice it until it was about to be withdrawn, when he became, according to all accounts, extremely unhappy. They are exactly suited to one another, and if they had married twenty years ago, it would have been an admirable thing for them both. Bearing all this in mind, you will see how strong Miss Mercer's motive might have been. She saw Mr Latter being made exceedingly unhappy, she saw Mrs Latter determined to come between Mr Antony and Miss Julia, she saw her set upon a course which threatened to disrupt the family. Yes, the motive might have been very strong. There was also the undoubted fact that she was in a state of mental distress even beyond what the situation warranted. I was convinced that she was concealing something, and that whatever it was, it was causing her great agony of mind.'

'Did you never think she had done it?'

Miss Silver met his look.

'I could not do so. Real goodness is a thing quite impossible to mistake. In Miss Mercer's case it was present as the motive power of all her thoughts and actions. It was the atmosphere in which she lived. She was suffering very deeply, but it was the suffering of innocence in the presence of evil. This was my constant impression. I was therefore brought to the point at which I could not accept Mrs Latter's death either as the result of suicide or of murder.'

'In the absence of the Chief, we may perhaps call it an *impasse*. He won't let me use French words, you know. He considers them uppish.'

'I have a great respect for Chief Inspector Lamb,' said Miss Silver reprovingly. 'A man of real integrity.'

Sergeant Abbott blew her a kiss.

'It's nothing to the respect I have for you. Continue, revered preceptress.'

Miss Silver gave a very slight cough.

'Really, my dear Frank, you sometimes talk great nonsense. When, as you say, I had reached this *impasse,* I decided to abandon the external evidence entirely, and to be guided solely by what I felt and had ascertained with regard to the characters of the people concerned. We do not in the animal kingdom expect the tiger to behave like the sheep, or the rabbit to comport itself in the manner natural to the wolf. The Scriptures inform us that we cannot look for grapes from thorns or figs from thistles. An overwhelming passion might shock any of us into the commission of a sudden violent act, but a carefully premeditated poisoning cannot be referred to this category. It must, without fail, be an indication of such evil traits of character as selfishness, inflated self-importance, or perhaps its dangerous opposite, a corroding sense of inferiority. There must be a ruthless disregard of others, a ruthless determination to achieve the desired end no matter what may stand in the way. When I began to look for these characteristics I found them all, with the exception of the inferiority complex, in Mrs Latter herself. Everyone to whom I talked about her made some contribution to this view of her character. Even seen through the eyes of a grief-stricken and adoring husband, she appeared quite regardless of him or of anyone else who obstructed her wishes. There had been, therefore, one person at Latter End who was qualified to commit cold-blooded and carefully thought-out murder.'

She coughed, turned Derek's stocking, and continued.

'But that person was herself the victim. I began to consider in what way she might have been taken in her own trap. I went back to the statements, and I noticed two things. Miss Mercer had watched from the doorway and seen Mrs Latter putting what she thought was sugar or some sweetening compound into one of the cups. I considered originally that it might have been glucose, which exactly resembles powdered sugar, but I now began to examine the probability that it was the powdered morphia. The other point I noticed was that Miss Mercer had apparently stated that she did not see what happened to the coffee-cups after she and Mrs Latter returned from the terrace. The form of the narrative certainly gave the impression that Miss Mercer had followed Mrs Latter immediately when she left the drawing-room for the terrace, but it was nowhere actually stated, and I began to think that Miss Mercer had not told all she knew, and that she might have altered the position of the cups. I thought it very improbable that Mrs Latter would have risked leaving both cups together on the tray. When nobody seemed to remember who had placed Mr Latter's cup on the table beside his chair, I thought it more than probable that Mrs Latter had done so herself, in which case Miss Mercer must have seen her do it, since she had her in view from the time she put the powder into the cup until she went out upon the terrace. I became convinced that Miss Mercer had changed the cups. The reason for her silence was obvious. She wished to protect Mr Latter from the knowledge that his wife had attempted to poison him.'

Frank Abbott gazed at her with unfeigned admiration.

'The nonpareil and wonder of her kind!'

'My dear Frank!'

He said hastily, 'Go on—I didn't mean to interrupt you.'

'That night Miss Mercer walked in her sleep. She would, I am sure, have crossed the hall to the drawing-room, but Miss Julia turned her back. When she said in tones of the deepest distress "What have I done!" I was quite sure that I was on the right track. On the following night, as you know, she again walked in her sleep. This time she re-enacted the events of Wednesday night. With what I had already guessed, it was clear to me that she took an imaginary cup from the tray and set it down by Mr Latter's chair. She then came back with her hand still out before her as if it were holding a cup. She came like this as far as the table where the tray had been, and then stretched out her hand again as if she were putting something down. She said, "Oh, God—what have I done!" and I felt quite sure that the mystery was solved. Next morning at breakfast I had a natural opportunity of enquiring whether Mr Latter liked his tea or coffee sweet. When I received the reply that he never took more than one lump in either, I concluded that this would be Miss Mercer's reason for having changed the cups. Meanwhile Polly's evidence had provided proof that Mrs Latter had deliberately prepared the powdered morphia.'

'When do you think she took it? Before the scene between Mr Latter and Miss Mercer on Tuesday evening, when Miss Mercer said she thought the morphia bottle had been moved?'

Miss Silver's needles clicked.

'Oh, yes, she had taken it before then—possibly whilst the family were at breakfast. You will remember that she had hers in her room. The scene in Mr Antony's room had taken place during the night. The idea of getting rid of her husband may not have been a new one, but after that scene I believe she decided to proceed to extremities. Probably all the family knew where Miss Mercer kept the key of her medicine cupboard. Mrs Latter found the morphia, took what she wanted, wiped the bottle carefully, and put it back, not inside the box from which she had taken it, but on the shelf. You see, it was certainly part of her plan that Mr Latter should be supposed to have committed suicide. She therefore left the bottle where it would have been convincingly easy to find. Just before lunch she crushed the tablets and put the powder into that little snuffbox. Then, some time after seven in the evening, Gladys Marsh came to her with her tale of Mr Latter being in Miss Mercer's room asking her for something to make him sleep. When she heard that he had actually handled the morphia bottle, that Miss Mercer had told him it was dangerous and he had replied, "I don't care how dangerous it is so long as it makes me sleep", she must indeed have felt that she had all the cards in her hand. Consider, for instance—if Miss Mercer had not changed those cups and Mr Latter had died of morphia poisoning, would there have been any question of murder? There was Gladys Marsh's evidence that he had said, "I don't care how dangerous it is so long as it makes me sleep"—evidence which Miss Mercer would have been bound to confirm. He had actually handled the morphia bottle. There could have been no suspicion of anything except suicide. A local jury would probably have brought in a verdict of accidental death. They would have taken the line that he was so desperate for sleep as to be reckless of the dose he took, a conclusion warranted by his own words. Mrs Latter must have thought that the way before her was a safe and easy one. And then Miss Mercer changed the cups.'

Frank looked at her with a sparkle in his eyes.

'The Perfect Moral Tract!' Then, rather hastily, 'How much do you suppose Antony had to do with it? Did she go off the deep end about him, or was she just fed up to the teeth with Jimmy Latter?'

Miss Silver coughed.

'You want to know more than I can tell you. I am inclined to think that she was thoroughly disappointed in her marriage and beginning to realise that however much her husband adored her, there were some things she could not make him do. He would not leave Latter End and live in London, and he did not like her friends. At the time she married him she was, I gather, financially embarrassed and very uncertain as to the outcome of the case which was pending over her first husband's will. If she had been certain of the money she would, I feel sure, have preferred Antony Latter. She did not care enough for him to take him as he was, but once she was financially secure she wished to get him back. The fact that he was no longer in love with her, and that he was quite obviously attracted by Miss Julia roused up all the wilful obstinacy of her nature. Everyone to whom I talked had the same thing to say about her. They put it in different ways, but this is what it amounted to—if she wanted a thing she had to have it.'

Frank reached for the last sandwich. After a moment he said,

'Did you ever take Mrs Maniple seriously?'

'Oh, my dear Frank, I took her very seriously indeed. Not, of course, as a principal in the murder. But as a Contributory Circumstance—oh, dear me, yes.'

Mrs Maniple as a Contributory Circumstance was very nearly too much for Sergeant Abbott. He escaped choking by a very narrow margin. He straightened his face with difficulty and contrived to utter the single word,

'Perpend.'

Miss Silver was not unwilling to do so.

'I found it quite impossible to believe that the person responsible for those preliminary attacks had any design on Mrs Latter's life. The effects were much too slight and too transitory. But as soon as I began to suspect Mrs Latter herself I saw how these attacks would bring the idea of poison quite vividly before her mind. They would suggest the method of administering it, and the fact that she was genuinely uneasy on her own account may have had its share in urging her to put an end to the situation. This is, of course, mere speculation. I myself am inclined to wonder whether—' She broke off, leaving the sentence unfinished, a thing so unusual as to arouse Frank Abbott's liveliest curiosity.

'Come—you can't leave it at that! What did you wonder?'

Miss Silver set down her knitting on her knee, looked at him gravely, and said,

'There have been moments when I have wondered whether her first husband died a natural death.'

Frank shook his head at her.

'You know, the Chief really does suspect you of keeping a private broomstick. He was brought up on tales of witches, and you revive them quite uncomfortably.'

Miss Silver smiled.

'A most respectable man. We are on excellent terms. But I think you have something to tell me.'

'Well, not very much, but here it is for whatever it's worth. The Chief sent me down to make a few enquiries. I saw the doctor who attended Doubleday. I could see that he had had some uncomfortable moments. Doubleday was ill, but he wasn't all that ill. He might have died the way he did, but— it was a bit unexpected. The doctor himself was away, and a young partner was called in. It was just the sort of case that would be all right ninety-nine times out of a hundred, but the hundredth time there could be something fishy about it. Well, of course no doctor on earth wants to upset his private practice for a hundred-to-one chance like that. I don't think he thought very much about it until it began to leak out that Doubleday had just signed a new will very much in Mrs Doubleday's interest, and that the relations were going to contest it. I think that's when he had his uncomfortable moments, but he hadn't really anything to go on and he held his tongue. Presently he heard with considerable relief that the case had been settled out of court. He'd have been called as a witness of course, and I imagine he wasn't looking forward to it. Of course you'll understand he didn't tell me any of this, except that Doubleday had died when he was away, and that it was all according to Cocker. I had to read between the lines with a pretty strong microscope, but I came away with quite an idea that Mrs Latter had played the game before. They say the poisoner always perseveres.'

Miss Silver coughed.

'Once you become convinced that your wishes and desires are of more importance than a human life, there will not fail to be further opportunities of carrying that conviction into practice.'

Frank gazed at her with delight.

'"Reason in her most exalted mood!"' he declared, adding rather quickly, 'The poet Wordsworth.'

FORTY-ONE

Julia dropped three pairs of stockings into a drawer and shut them in. She was back in London again, and she felt hot and tired, and quite desperately flat. Unpacking is a slightly less sordid occupation than packing, but there isn't much in it, and whether you are going or coming, you always leave something behind. Julia had left her toothpaste, and that meant she would have to go out and buy some. When you have recently been living through a tragedy in a state of extremely high tension there is something paltry about being depressed about toothpaste.

She had opened all the windows, but the room felt hot and airless. There seemed to be an extraordinary amount of dust. She got out a mop and a duster and began to clean up. By the time she had finished she wondered whether it wouldn't have been better to leave the dust where it was—such a lot of it seemed to have collected on her hands and face.

She had made a start with the hands, because it's no use washing your face if your hands are going to come off on it in damp black patches, when the door-bell rang. She took a hasty look in the glass. The face was dirty, but not so very dirty— more, as it were, submerged in a general murk. Or perhaps it wasn't dirty at all, perhaps that was just the way she looked. Anyhow she decided that it would have to do. She dried the partly washed hands, observed that they left a black mark on the towel, and went to the door.

Antony, beautifully tidy, stepped inside, gazed at her with mild surprise, and enquired why she was spring-cleaning. Of course it would be Antony! If she sat waiting for him in her most becoming dress for ninety-nine days out of a hundred she wouldn't see hair, hide or hoof of him, but on the hundredth day, when she was inked to the elbows and more or less negroid with dust, the flat would draw him like a magnet. She said,

'You always come when I'm filthy—but I was just getting it off.'

'There must have been a great deal to start with.'

'Well, there was. You'll have to wait—unless—I suppose you wouldn't like to go out and get me a tube of toothpaste? I've left mine.'

'I'd hate to, but I will.'

It would give her time to change. She really was perfectly clean and tidy by the time he came back.

He produced the toothpaste with a flourish.

'Bridegroom to bride!'

If he expected Julia to laugh he was disappointed. She took the tube away into the cubbyhole which concealed the bath, and came back with one-and-tenpence-half-penny in a hand still damp and pink from scrubbing.

He said, 'What's this for?'

'The toothpaste. Take it, please.'

'Darling, it was a handsome present—bridegroom to bride—part of the worldly goods with which I'm going to thee endow.'

There was rather a thundery pause. Julia had the sort of temper which can take the bit between its teeth. It was touch and go whether it got away with her now.

The moment passed. She put the coins down on the edge of the writing-table and said,

'Just as you like. You can call it a Christmas present in advance, then you won't have to wander round wondering what you can give me in three months' time.'

Antony hit back rather hard.

'Do I give you a Christmas present?'

She said, 'Not since our Christmas tree days.'

Why had she said that? The words were no sooner out than it came over her with a rush how immeasurably good those days had been, and how immeasurably far removed. It was like looking back at a small bright picture a long way off. She turned very pale, and heard Antony say with an odd note in his voice,

'Are we obliged to talk standing up? You look just about all in.'

She was glad enough to feel the sofa under her and a cushion at her back. For one idiotic moment she hadn't quite known what she was going to do. She might have burst into tears—she might have buckled at the knees. Either alternative simply too humiliating to bear thinking about. She found herself saying,

'It's too hot for housework.'

Antony was frowning. They had not met since that early morning funeral a week ago. Frightful! Why couldn't she think about something else? Nobody who was there would ever want to think about it again. But of course that was just the sort of thing you couldn't get out of your head. She wished Antony hadn't come to see her. She wished that he had come and gone. She wished she could feel quite sure that she wasn't going to cry. There wasn't anything she could do about it.

Antony broke in on a note of sharp exasperation.

'My darling child, the ship isn't a total wreck. There are some survivors—you, for instance, and I. Is it necessary for you to look at me as if we were not only dead but buried? Snap out of it! How did you leave the other survivors?'

He was pleased to observe that a little of her colour came back. She said in a hurry,

'I'm sorry—I don't mean to do it. If my eyes were blue it would be all right.'

'Darling, you'd look foul with blue eyes.'

'I know. But I shouldn't give people the pip when I looked at them. I'm always getting told about it, and it's so difficult to remember.'

Antony laughed.

'I shouldn't worry. It's the clutch-at-the-heart-strings touch that does us in. Nobody really likes having their heartstrings clutched. An occasional smile assists us to bear up. Try it! How's Jimmy?'

She answered with relief.

'Oh, definitely better. He isn't going to keep Lois' money, you know.'

'I didn't think he would.'

'No. He's written to the solicitors and told them to make arrangements for handing it back to the Doubledays as soon as they get probate. That's set him up a lot. And then Minnie's awfully good with him. She keeps flying to him with things which can't possibly be decided without the superior male intelligence—new washers for the bathroom taps, how to word an advertisement for a butler, how much extra on the laundry bill is five per cent, and will he please come at once and remove the largest spider ever from the sink in the house-maid's cupboard, because Mrs Huggins has gone, and she and Ellie just can't cope. It's what she used to do, and it's frightfully good for him. Of course he ought to have married her years ago.'

'I don't suppose he ever thought of it.'

'I'm sure he didn't. But just think what a lot we'd all have been saved if he had. This time, I don't mind telling you, I'm going to make it my business to see that he does think.'

Antony laughed, but he didn't stop frowning.

'You'd better leave them alone.'

'Oh, I shan't do anything yet. They'll be all right as long as Ellie and Ronnie are there, but when it comes to Ronnie going off to his job and Ellie going with him, then someone will have to point out to Jimmy that Minnie can't possibly stop on and keep house for him. Too, too compromising.'

'Rubbish!'

'Oh, no—not in a village. Besides, all that matters is that Jimmy should be induced to think. She'll make him frightfully happy, and he deserves something to make up for all this. So does she.'

'Women haven't any consciences at all. All they think about is getting the wretched man where they want him—in the bag.'

'It's an awfully nice bag,' said Julia, her voice deep and soft.

'Oh, yes—that's the way you get us into it. All the comforts of home and a ring through the nose—a nice strong unbreakable wedding-ring. You've had millions of years of practice, and you're awfully good at it, darling.'

When Antony said 'darling' something took hold of Julia's heart and twisted it. The pain made her sit up straight and say,

'Well, I haven't a bag, and I haven't a ring—your nose is perfectly safe. And the sooner you tell everybody that we're disengaged, the better I shall be pleased.'

Antony put up a finger.

'Temper, darling! Always count up to a hundred before you speak. It may slow conversation down a little, but all the best medical authorities agree that our lives are shortened by the fevered rush of the machine age.'

'In spite of which everyone lives a great deal longer than they used to. Do you know that Mr Pickwick was only forty-three, and they all talk about him as a dear old gentleman?'

'Darling, this is not a Dickens Society. And we are not discussing Mr Pickwick. At the moment you dragged him across the trail I was about to go down gracefully on one knee and ask you to name the day. After which you would of course blush becomingly, swoon gracefully, and recover sufficiently to consult an almanac.'

So far from blushing, Julia was quite monumentally pale. She said,

'I wish you would stop talking nonsense. There is no point in our going on pretending to be engaged.'

Antony agreed cheerfully.

'None whatever. Engagements are damnable anyhow. I don't think you've been attending, darling. I wasn't asking you to go on being engaged, I was asking you to marry me.'

Her eyes were turned on him with a flash of anger.

'And I was telling you that I simply won't go on with this pretence any longer! I wouldn't have done it for anyone but Jimmy!'

He met the flash with rather a searching look.

'Oh, it was for Jimmy, was it?'

'You know it was! And there's no need for it any longer, so will you please let everybody know!'

He leaned forward, his hands clasped about his knee.

'Are you supposed to have jilted me, or am I supposed to have jilted you? I'd better know, hadn't I?'

Julia said in a composed voice,

'Neither. We're breaking it off because I think being married would interfere with my writing. But of course we're going to go on being friends.'

Antony burst out laughing.

'The great Career motif! Darling, it's quite dreadfully out of date. The modern woman can take a husband, several careers, a family, and a staffless home all in her stride, without turning a hair. But I think we'd better have a service flat—I seem to remember Manny being rude about your cooking.'

'I do all the right things, but it turns out like lead,' said Julia gloomily. 'Look here, Antony, it's no good dodging. I won't go on with this sham.'

He was silent for a moment. Then he came nearer and took her hands. She had said that she was hot, but he found them icy cold. He held them rather hard and said,

'What about the real thing, Julia?'

Where Julia got enough breath from, she had no idea, but she said,

'No.'

'Is that for me, or for you?'

She said 'Both.'

Because everything in her was shaking the word shook too. She jerked at her hands to get them away, and he let them go.

'You don't love me? Or I don't love you?'

'We don't—neither of us does—'

'Darling, you lie in your teeth! I love you—very much. Didn't you know?'

'You don't!'

'Don't I? Do you remember, I asked you what you would say if I told you I loved you passionately. All right, I'm telling you now. I love you—passionately—and every other way. If you weren't colossally stupid you'd have known without my telling you. Come here and stop talking!'

It was some time later that she said in a protesting voice,

'You simply haven't bothered to ask me whether I care for you. Perhaps I don't.'

'Then you oughtn't to be letting me kiss you.'

'Don't you want to know?'

Antony kissed her.

'Darling, I'm not colossally stupid.'

ABOUT THE AUTHOR

Patricia Wentworth (1878–1961) was one of the masters of classic English mystery writing. Born in India as Dora Amy Elles, she began writing after the death of her first husband, publishing her first novel in 1910. In the 1920s, she introduced the character who would make her famous: Miss Maud Silver, the former governess whose stout figure, fondness for Tennyson, and passion for knitting served to disguise a keen intellect. Along with Agatha Christie's Miss Marple, Miss Silver is the definitive embodiment of the English style of cozy mysteries.

THE MISS SILVER MYSTERIES

FROM OPEN ROAD MEDIA

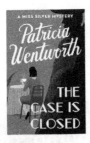
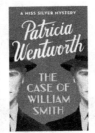

OPEN ROAD

INTEGRATED MEDIA

OPEN ROAD

INTEGRATED MEDIA

Find a full list of our authors and
titles at www.openroadmedia.com

FOLLOW US
@OpenRoadMedia

EARLY BIRD BOOKS
FRESH DEALS, DELIVERED DAILY

Love to read?
Love great sales?

Get fantastic deals on
bestselling ebooks delivered
to your inbox every day!

Sign up today at
earlybirdbooks.com/book

CPSIA information can be obtained
at www.ICGtesting.com
Printed in the USA
JSHW031913260821
18208JS00001B/32